BACK TO
BILLABONG

BILLABONG BOOK SEVEN

MW00973402

BACK TO

BILLABONG BOOK SEVEN

BILLABONG

MARY GRANT BRUCE

Angus&Robertson
An imprint of HarperCollins*Publishers*

AN ANGUS & ROBERTSON BOOK
An imprint of HarperCollinsPublishers

First published in 1921 by Ward Lock, Melb. and Lond.
This revised edition with afterword was prepared by Barbara Ker Wilson
and was published in 1992 by
CollinsAngus&Robertson Publishers Pty Limited (ACN 009 913 517)
A division of HarperCollinsPublishers (Australia) Pty Limited
25 Ryde Road, Pymble NSW 2073, Australia

HarperCollinsPublishers (New Zealand) Limited
31 View Road, Glenfield, Auckland 10, New Zealand

HarperCollinsPublishers Limited
77–85 Fulham Palace Road, London W6 8JB, United Kingdom

National Library of Australia
Cataloguing-in-Publication data:

Bruce, Mary Grant, 1878–1958.
   Back to Billabong.
   ISBN 0 207 17515 2.
   I. Title.

A823'.3

Cover illustration by Lorraine Hannay
Typeset by Docupro
Printed in Australia by Australian Print Group

5 4 3 2 1
95 94 93 92

'Beyond the distant sky-line
  (Now pansy-blue and clear),
We know a land is waiting,
  A brown land, very dear:
A land of open spaces,
  Guant forest, treeless plain:
And if we once have loved it
  We must come back again.'

(DOROTHEA MACKELLAR)

Contents

CHAPTER 1

Lancaster Gate, London

"DO the beastly old map yourself, if you want it. I shan't, anyhow!"

"Wilfred!"

"Aw, Wil-fred!" The boy at the end of the schoolroom table, red-haired, snub-nosed and defiant, mimicked the protesting tone. "I've done it once, and I'm blessed if I do it again."

"No one would dream that it was ever meant for Africa." The young teacher glanced at the scrawled and blotted map before her. "It — it doesn't look like anything earthly. You must do it again, Wilfred."

"Don't you, Wilf." Wilfred's sister leaned back in her chair, tilting it on its hind legs.

"You have nothing to do with Wilfred's work, Avice. Go on with your French."

"Done it, thanks," said Avice. "And I suppose I can speak to my own brother if I like."

"No, you can't — in lesson time," said the teacher.

"Who's going to stop me?"

1

Cecilia Rainham controlled herself with an effort.

"Bring me your work," she said.

She went over the untidy French exercise with a quick eye. When she had finished it resembled a stormy sky — a groundwork of blue-black, blotted writing, lit by innumerable dashes of red. Cecilia put down her red pencil.

"It's hopeless, Avice. You haven't tried a bit. And you know it isn't hard — you did a far more difficult piece of translation without a mistake last Friday."

"Yes, but the pantomime was coming off on Saturday," said Wilfred, with a grin. "Jolly little chance of tickets from Bob if she didn't!"

"You shut up!" said Avice.

"Be quiet, both of you," Cecilia ordered, a spot of red in each pale cheek. "Remember, there will be other Saturdays. Bob will do nothing for you if I can't give him a decent report of you." It was the threat she hated using, but without it she was helpless. And the red-haired pair before her knew to a fraction the extent of her helplessness.

For the moment the threat was effective. Avice went back to her seat, taking with her the excited-looking French exercise, while Wilfred sullenly recommenced a dispirited attack upon the African coastline. Cecilia leaned back in her chair, and took up a half-knitted sock — to drop it hastily, as a long-drawn howl came from a low chair by the window.

"Whatever is the matter, Queenie?"

"I per-ricked my finger," sobbed the youngest

Miss Rainham. She stood up, tears raining down her plump cheeks. No one, Cecilia thought, ever cried so easily, so copiously, and so frequently as Queenie. As she stood holding out a very grubby forefinger, on which appeared a minute spot of blood, great tears fell in splashes on the dark green linoleum, while others ran down her face to join them, and more trembled on her lower eyelids, propelled from some artesian fount within.

"Oh, dry up, Queenie!" said Wilfred irritably. "Anyone 'ud think you'd cut your silly finger off!"

"Well — it'th bleed-in'!" wailed Queenie. She dabbed the injured member with the pillow case she was hemming, adding a scarlet touch in pleasant contrast to its prevailing grime.

"Well — you're too big a girl to cry for a prick," said Cecilia wearily. "People who are nearly seven really don't cry except for something awfully bad."

"There — I'll tell the mater you said 'awfully'!" Avice jeered. "Who bites our heads off for using slang, I'd like to know?"

"You wouldn't have much head left if I bit for every slang word you use," retorted her half-sister. "Do get on with your French, Avice — it's nearly half-past twelve, and you know Eliza will want to lay the table presently. Come here, Queenie." She took the pillow case, and unpicked a few stitches, which clearly indicated that the needle had been taking giant strides. "Just hem that last inch or two again, and see if you can't make it look nice. I believe the needle only stuck into your finger because you were making it sew so badly. Have you got a handkerchief? — but, of course, you haven't." She polished the fat, tear-stained cheek with her own. "Now run and sit down again."

Queenie turned to go obediently enough — she was too young, and possibly too fat, to plan, as yet, the deliberate malice in which her brother and sister took their chief pleasure. Unfortunately, Wilfred arrived at the end of Africa at the wrong moment for her. He pushed the atlas away from him with a jerk that overturned the ink bottle, sending a stream of ink towards Avice — who, shoving her chair backwards to escape the deluge, cannoned into Queenie, and brought her headlong to the floor. Howls broke out anew, mingled with a crisp interchange of abuse between the elder pair, while Cecilia vainly sought to lessen the inky flood with a duster. Upon this pleasant scene the door opened sharply.

"A nice way you keep order at lessons," said Mrs. Mark Rainham acidly. "And the ink all over the cloth. Well, all I can say is, you'll pay for a new one, Cecilia."

"I did not knock it over," said Cecilia, in a low tone.

"It's your business to look after the children, and see that they do not destroy things," said her stepmother.

"The children will not obey me."

"Pouf!" said Mrs. Rainham. "A mere question of management. High-spirited children want tact in dealing with them, that is all. You never trouble to exercise any tact whatever." Her eyes dwelt fondly on her high-spirited son, whose red head was bent attentively over Africa while he traced a mighty mountain range along the course of the Nile. "Wilfred, have you nearly finished your work?"

"Nearly, Mater," said the industrious Wilfred, manufacturing mountains tirelessly. "Just got to stick in a few more things."

"Say 'put', darling, not 'stick'. Cecilia, you might point out those little details — that is, if you took any interest in their English."

"Thethilia thaid 'awfully' jutht now," said Queenie, in a shrill pipe.

"I don't doubt it," said Mrs. Rainham, bitterly. "Of course, anyone brought up in Paris is too grand to trouble about English — but we think a good deal of these things in London." A little smile hovered on her thin lips, as Cecilia flushed, and Avice and her brother grinned broadly. The Mater could always make old Cecilia go as red as a beetroot, but it was fun to watch, especially when the sport beguiled the tedium of lessons.

A clatter of dishes on a tray heralded the approach of Eliza.

"It is time the table was clear," Mrs Rainham said. "Wilfred, darling, I want you to post a letter. Put up your work and get your cap. Cecilia, you had better try to clean the cloth before lunch; it is ruined, of course, but do what you can with it. I will choose another the next time I go shopping. And just make sure that the children's things are all in order for the dancing lesson this afternoon. Avice, did you put out your slippers to be cleaned?"

"Forgot all about it, Mater," said Avice cheerfully.

"Silly child — and it is Jackson's day off. Just brush them up for her, Cecilia. When the children have gone this afternoon, I want you to see to the drawing-room; some people are coming in tonight, and there are fresh flowers from Brown's to arrange."

Cecilia looked up, with a sudden flush of dismay. The children's dancing lesson gave her one free afternoon during the week.

"But — but I am going to meet Bob," she stammered.

"Oh, Bob will wait, no doubt; you need not keep him long, if you hasten yourself. Yes, Eliza, you can have the table." Mrs. Rainham left the room, with the children at her heels.

Cecilia whisked the lesson books hastily away; Eliza was waiting with a lowering brow, and Eliza was by no means a person to be offended. Maids were scarce enough in England in the months after the end of the war; and, even in easier times, there had been a dreary procession of arriving and departing servants in the Rainham household — the high-spirited characteristics of the children being apt to pall quickly upon anyone but their mother. In days when there happened to be no Eliza, it was Cecilia who naturally inherited the vacant place, adding the duties of house-maid to those of nurse, governess, companion and general factotum; all exacting posts, and all of them unpaid. As Mrs. Rainham gracefully remarked, when a girl was not earning her own living, as so many were, but was enjoying the comfort of home, the least she could do was to make herself useful.

"Half a minute, Eliza." She smiled at the slatternly girl. "Sorry to keep you waiting; there's a river of ink gone astray here." She placed the soaked cloth on the waste-paper basket and polished the top of the table vigorously.

"I'll bet it worn't you wot spilt it — but it's you wot 'as the cleanin' up," muttered Eliza. "Lemme rub that up now, Miss." She put down her tray and took the cloth from Cecilia's hand.

"Thanks, ever so, Eliza — but you've got plenty to do yourself."

"Well, if I 'ave, I ain't the on'y one wot 'as," said Eliza darkly. Her wizened little face suddenly flushed. "Lor, Miss," she said confidentially, "you doan't know wot a success that 'at you trimmed for me is. It's a fair scream. I wore it larst night, an' me young man — 'im wot's in the Royal Irish — well, it fair knocked 'im! An' 'e wants me to go out wiv 'im next Bank 'oliday — out to 'ampstead 'eath. 'E never got as far as arstin' me that before. I know it was that 'at wot done it."

"Not it, Eliza," Cecilia laughed. "It was just your hair under the hat. I told you how pretty it would be, if you would only brush it more."

"Well, I never 'ad no brush till you give me your old one," said Eliza practically. "I did brush it, though, a hundred times every night, till Cook reckoned I was fair cracked. But 'air's on'y 'air, an' anyone 'as it — it's not everyone 'as an 'at like that." She clattered plates upon the table violently. "You goin' out this afternoon, Miss?"

"As soon as I can, Eliza." Cecilia's face fell. "I must arrange flowers first."

"I'll 'ave the vases all ready wiv clean water for you," said Eliza. "An' don't you worry about the drorin'-room — I'll see as it's nice."

"Oh, you can't, Eliza — you have no time. I know it's silver-cleaning afternoon."

"Aw, I'll squeeze it in some'ow." Eliza stopped suddenly, at a decided footstep in the passage, and began to rattle spoons and forks with a vigour born of long practice. Cecilia picked up the inky cloth, and went out.

Her stepmother was standing by the hall-stand, apparently intent on examining Wilfred's straw hat. She spoke in a low tone as the girl passed her.

"I wish you did not find so much pleasure in gossiping with servants, Cecilia. It is such a bad example for Avice. I have spoken about it to you before."

Cecilia did not answer. She went upstairs with flaming cheeks, and draped the cloth across the hand basin in the bathroom, turning the tap vengefully. A stream of water flowed through the wide stain.

"There's more real kindness in that poor little Cockney's finger than there is in your whole body!" Cecilia whispered, apparently addressing the unoffending cloth — which, having begun life as a dingy green and black, did not seem greatly the worse for its new decoration. "Hateful old thing!" A smile suddenly twitched the corners of her mouth. "Well, she can't stop the money for a new cloth out of this quarter's allowance, because I've just got it. That's luck, anyhow. I'll give it to Bob

to keep, in case she goes through my desk again."
She poured some ammonia upon the stain, and
rubbed gingerly, surveying the result with a tilted
nose. It was not successful. "Shall I try petrol? But
petrol's an awful price, and I've only got the little
bottle I use for my gloves. Anyhow, the horrible
old cloth is so old and thin that it will fall to pieces
if I rub it. Oh, it's no use bothering about it —
nothing will make it better." She squeezed the
water from the cloth and spread the stained area
over a chair to dry, looking disgustedly at her own
dyed fingernails. "Now for Avice's shoes before I
scrub my hands."

Avice's shoes proved a lengthy task, since the
younger Miss Rainham had apparently discovered
some clay to walk through in Regent's Park on her
way home from the last dancing lesson; and
well-hardened clay resists ordinary cleaning
methods, and demands edged tools. The luncheon
bell rang loudly before Cecilia had finished. She
gave the shoes a final hurried rub, and then fell
to cleaning her hands; arriving in the dining-room
pink and breathless some minutes later, to find a
dreary piece of tepid mutton rapidly congealing on
her plate.

"I think you might manage to be down in time
for meals, Cecilia," was Mrs. Rainham's chilly
greeting.

Cecilia said nothing. She had long realised the
uselessness of any excuses. To be answered merely
gave her stepmother occasion for further
fault-finding — you might, as Cecilia told Bob,
have a flawless defence for the sin of the moment,

but in that case Mrs. Rainham merely changed her ground, and waxed eloquent about the sin of yesterday, or of last Friday week, for which there might happen to be no defence at all. It was so difficult to avoid being a criminal in Mrs. Rainham's eyes that Cecilia had almost given up the attempt. She attacked her greasy mutton and sloppy cabbage in silence, unpleasantly conscious of her stepmother's freezing glance.

Mrs. Rainham was a short, stout woman, with colourless, rather pinched features, and a wealth of glorious red hair. Someone had once told her that her profile was classic, and she still rejoiced in believing it, was always photographed from a side view, and wore in the house loose and flowing garments of strange tints, calculated to bring out the colour of her glowing tresses. Cecilia, who worshipped colour with every bit of her artist soul, adored her stepmother's hair as thoroughly as she detested her dresses. Bob, who was blunt and inartistic, merely detested her from every point of view. "Don't see what you find to rave about in it," he said. "All the warmth of her disposition has simply gone to her head."

There was certainly little warmth in Mrs. Rainham's heart, where her stepdaughter was concerned. She disapproved very thoroughly of Cecilia in every detail — of her pretty face and delicate colouring, of the fair hair that rippled and curled and gleamed in a manner so light-hearted as to seem distinctly out of place in the dingy room, of the slender grace that was in vivid contrast to her own stoutness. She resented the very way Cecilia put on her clothes — simple clothes, but worn with an air that made her own elaborate dresses cheap and common by comparison. It was so easy for her to look well turned out; and it would never be easy to dress Avice, who bade fair to resemble her mother in build, and had already a passion for frills and trimmings, and a contempt for plain things. Mrs. Rainham had an uneasy conviction that the girl who bore all her scathing comments in silence actually dared to criticise her in her own mind — perhaps openly to Bob, whose blue eyes held many unspoken things as he looked at her. Once she had overheard him say to Cecilia: "She looks like an over-ornamented pie!" Cecilia had laughed, and Mrs. Rainham had passed on, unsuspected, her mind full of a wild surmise. They would never dare to mean her — and yet — that new dress of hers was plastered with queer little bits of purposeless trimmings. She never again wore it without that terrible sentence creeping into her mind. And she had been so pleased with it, too! An over-ornamented pie. If she could only have been sure they meant her!

She thought of it again as she sat looking at Cecilia. The new dress was lying on her bed, ready to be worn that afternoon; and Cecilia was going to meet Bob — Bob, who had uttered the horrible remark. Well, at least there should be no haste about the meeting. It would do Bob no harm to cool his heels for a little. She set her thin lips tightly together, as she helped the rice pudding.

The meal ended, amidst loud grumbles from

Wilfred that the pudding was rice; and Cecilia
hurried off to find the flowers and arrange them.
The florist's box was near the vases left ready by
the faithful Eliza; she cut the string with a happy
exclamation of "Daffodils!" as she lifted the lid.
Daffodils were always a joy; this afternoon they
were doubly welcome, because easy to arrange.
She sorted them into long-necked vases swiftly,
carrying each vase, when filled, to the
drawing-room — a painful apartment, crowded
with knick-knacks until it resembled a bazaar
stall, with knobby and unsteady bamboo furniture
and much drapery of a would-be artistic nature.
It was stuffy and airless. Cecilia wrinkled her
pretty nose as she entered. Mrs. Rainham held
pronounced views on the subject of what she
termed the "fresh-air fad", and declined to let
London air — a smoky commodity at best —
attack her cherished carpets; with the result that
Cecilia breathed freely only in her little attic,
which had no carpet at all.

The lady of the house rustled in, in her flowing
robe, as Cecilia put the last vase into position on
the piano — finding room for it with difficulty
amid a collection of photograph frames and china
ornaments. She carried some music, and cast a
critical eye round the room.

"This place looks as if it had not been properly
dusted for a week," she remarked. "See to it before
you go, Cecilia." She opened the piano. "Just come
and try the accompaniment to this song — it's
rather difficult, and I want to sing it tonight."

Cecilia sat down before the piano, with woe in

her heart. Her stepmother's delusion that she could sing was one of the minor trials of her life. She had been thoroughly trained in Paris, under a master who had prophesied great things for her; now her hours at the Rainhams' tinkly piano, playing dreary accompaniments to sentimental songs with Mrs. Rainham's weak soprano wobbling and flattening on the high notes, were hours of real distress, from which she would escape feeling her teeth on edge. Her stepmother, however, had thoroughly enjoyed herself since the discovery that no accompaniment presented any difficulty to Cecilia. It saved her a world of trouble in practising; moreover, when standing, it was far easier to let herself go in the affecting passages, which always suffered from scantiness of breath when she was sitting down. Therefore she would stand beside Cecilia, pouring forth song after song, with her head slightly on one side, and one hand resting lightly on the piano — an attitude which, after experiment with a mirror, she had decided upon as especially becoming.

The song of the moment did not make demands upon her attention. It had a disconcerting way of changing from sharps to flats; trouble being caused by the singer failing to change also. Cecilia took her through it patiently, going over and over again the tricky passages, and devoutly wishing that Providence in supplying her stepmother with boundless energy, a tireless voice and an enormous stock of songs had also equipped her with an ear for music. At length the lady desisted from her efforts.

"That's quite all right," she said, with satisfaction. "I'll sing it tonight. The Simons will be here, and they do like to hear what's new. Go on with your dusting; I'll just run through a few pieces, and you can tell me if I go wrong."

Cecilia hesitated, glancing at the clock.

"It is getting very late," she said. "Eliza told me she could dust the room."

"Eliza!" said Mrs. Rainham. "Why, it's her silver day; she had no business to tell you anything of the sort — and neither had you, to ask her to do it. Goodness knows it's hard enough to make the lazy thing do her own work. Just get your duster, and make sure as you come down that the children are properly dressed for the dancing class." She broke into a waltz.

Cecilia ran. Sounds of woe greeted her as she neared Avice's room, and she entered, to find that damsel plunged in despair over a missing button.

"It was on all right last time I wore the beastly dress," wailed she. "If you'd look after my clothes like Mater said you had to, I wouldn't be late. Whatever am I to do? I can't make the old dress shut with a safety pin."

"No, you certainly can't," said her half-sister. "Never mind; there are spare buttons for that frock, and I can sew one on." She accomplished the task with difficulty, since Avice appeared quite unable to stand still.

"Now, are you ready, Avice? Shoes, hat, gloves — where are your gloves? How do you ever manage to find anything in that drawer?" She rooted swiftly in a wild chaos, and finally unearthed the gloves. "Yes, you'll do. Now, where's Wilfred?" Search revealed Wilfred, who hated dancing, reading a "penny dreadful" in his room — ready to start, save for the trifling detail of having neglected to wash an extremely dirty face. Cecilia managed to make him repair the omission, after a struggle, and saw them off with a thankful heart — which sank anew as she heard a neighbouring clock strike three. Three — and already she should be meeting Bob in Hyde Park. She fled for a duster, and hurried to the drawing-room. Eliza encountered her on the way.

"Now, wotcher goin' to do wiv that duster, Miss?" she inquired. "I told yer I'd do it for yer."

"Mrs. Rainham is waiting for me to do it, Eliza. I'm sorry."

"Ow!" Eliza's expression and her tilted nose spoke volumes. "Suppose she finks I wouldn't clean 'er old silver proper. Silver, indeed! — 'lectrer-plyte, an' common at that. Just you cut and run as soon as she's out of the 'ouse, Miss; I know she's goin', 'cause 'er green and yaller dress is a-airin' on 'er bed."

"It's not much good, Eliza. I ought to be in the Park now." Cecilia knew she should not allow the girl to speak of her mistress so contemptuously. But she was disheartened enough at the moment not to care.

"Lor!" said Eliza. "A bloomin' shyme, I calls it!"

Cecilia found her stepmother happily engaged upon a succession of wrong notes that made her wince. She dusted the room swiftly, aware all the time of a watchful eye. Occasionally came a crisp

comment: "You didn't dust that windowsill."
"Cecilia, that table has four legs — did you only
notice two?" — the effort to speak while playing
generally bringing the performer with vigour upon
a wrong chord. The so-called music became almost
a physical torment to the over-strained girl.

"If she would only stop — if she would only go
away!" she found herself murmuring, over and
over. Even the thought of Bob waiting in Hyde
Park in the chill east wind became dim beside that
horrible piano, banging and tinkling in her ear.
She dusted mechanically, picking up one cheap
ornament after another — leaving the collection
upon the piano until the last, in the hope that by
the time she reached it the thirst for music would
have departed from the performer. But Mrs.
Rainham's tea appointment was not yet; she was
thoroughly enjoying herself, the charm of her own
execution added to the knowledge that Cecilia was
miserable, and Bob waiting somewhere, with what
patience he might. She held on to the bitter end,
while the girl dusted the piano's burden with a
set face. Then she finished a long and painful run,
and shut the piano with a bang.

"There — I've had quite a nice practice, and it
isn't often the drawing-room gets really decently
dusted," she remarked. "Nothing like the eye of
the mistress; I think I must practise every day
while you are dusting, Cecilia. Oh, and, Cecilia,
give the legs of the piano a good rubbing. Dear
me, I must go and dress."

Cecilia dragged herself upstairs a few minutes
later. All the spring was gone out of her; it really

did not seem to matter much now whether she met Bob or not; she was too tired to care. This was only a sample of many days; so it had been for two years — so it would be for two more, until she was twenty-one, and her own mistress. But it did not seem possible that she could endure through another two years.

She reached her own room, and was about to shut the door, when the harsh voice rasped upwards.

"Cecilia! Cecilia! Come here a minute."

The girl went down slowly. Mrs. Rainham was standing before her mirror.

"Just come and hook my dress, Cecilia. This new dressmaker has a knack of making everything hard to fasten. There — see that you start with the right hook and eye."

At the moment, physical contact with her stepmother was almost the last straw for the girl. She obeyed in silence, shrinking back as far as she could from the stout, over-scented body and the powdered face with the thin lips. Mrs. Rainham watched her with a little smile.

"Yes, that's all right," she said. "Now, my hat, Cecilia — it's in the bandbox under the bed. I can't stoop in this dress, that's the worst of it. And my gloves are in that box on the chest of drawers — the white pair. Hurry, Cecilia, my appointment is for four o'clock."

"Mine was for three o'clock," said the girl in a low voice.

"Oh, well, you should manage your work better. I always tell you that. Nothing like method in

getting through every day. However, Bob is only
your brother — it would be more serious if it was
a young man you were meeting. Brothers don't
matter much."

Cecilia flamed round upon her.

"Bob is more to me than anyone in the world,"
she cried. "And I would rather keep any other man
waiting."

"Really? But I shouldn't think it very likely that
you'll ever have to trouble about other young men,
Cecilia; you're not the sort. Too thin and scraggy."
Mrs. Rainham surveyed her own generous
proportions in the glass, and gathered up her
gloves with a pleased air. For the moment she
could not possibly believe that anyone could have
referred to her as "an over-ornamented pie".
"Goodbye, Cecilia; don't be late for tea." She sailed
down the stairs.

Even the bang of the hall door failed to convey
any relief to Cecilia. For the second time she toiled
upstairs, to the bare freshness of her little room.
Generally, it had a tonic effect upon her; today it
seemed that nothing could help her. She leaned
her head against the window, a wave of homesick
loneliness flooding all her soul. So deep were its
waters that she did not hear the hall door open
and close again, and presently swift feet pounding
up the stairs. Someone battered on her door.

"Cecilia! Are you there?"

She ran to open the door. Bob stood there, a
short, muscular fellow, in Air Force blue, with
twinkling eyes. She put out her hands to him with
a little pitiful gesture.

"Don't say that horrible name again," she whispered. "If anyone else calls me Cecilia I'll just go mad."

Bob came in, and flung a brotherly arm round her shoulders.

"Has it been so beastly?" he said. "Poor little Tommy. Oh, Tommy, I saw the over-ornamented pie sailing down the street, and I dived into a side alley until she'd gone out of range. I guessed from her proud and happy face that you'd been scarified."

"Scarified!" murmured Cecilia. But Bob was not listening. His face was radiant.

"I couldn't wait in the park any longer," he said. "I had to come and tell you. Tommy, old thing — I'm demobilised!"

CHAPTER 2

The Rainhams

IT was one of Mrs. Mark Rainham's grievances that, comparatively late in her married life, she should suddenly find herself brought into association with the children of her husband's first marriage. They were problems that Fate had previously removed from her path; she found it extremely annoying — at first — that Fate should cease to be so tactful, casting upon her a burden long borne by other shoulders. It was not until she had accepted Mark Rainham, eleven years before, that she found out the very existence of Bob and Cecilia; she resented the manner of the discovery, even as she resented the children themselves. Not that she ever dreamed of breaking off her engagement on their account. She was a milliner in a Kensington shop, and to marry Mark Rainham, who was vaguely "something in the city", and belonged to a good club, and dressed well, was a distinct step in the social scale, and two unknown children were not going to make her draw back. But to mother them was quite another question.

Luckily, Fate had a compassionate eye upon the young Rainhams, and was quite willing to second their stepmother's resolve that they should come

into her life as little as possible. Their father had
never concerned himself greatly about them. A
lazy and selfish man, he had always been willing
to shelve the care of his small son and daughter
— babies were not in his line, and the aunt who
had brought up their mother was only too anxious
to take Bob and Cecilia when that girl-mother had
slipped away from life, leaving a week-old Cecilia
and a sturdy, solemn Bob of three.

The arrangement suited Mark Rainham very
well. Aunt Margaret's house at Twickenham was
big enough for half a dozen babies; the children
went there, with their nurse, and he was free to
slip back into bachelor ways, living in comfortable
chambers within easy reach of his club and not
too far, with a good train service, from a golf links.
The regular weekend visits to the babies suffered
occasional interruptions, and gradually grew fewer
and fewer, until he became to the children a vague
and mysterious person named Papa, who dropped
from the skies now and then, asked them a
number of silly questions, talked with great
politeness to Aunt Margaret — who, they
instinctively felt, liked him no better than they
did — and then disappeared, whereupon everyone
was immensely relieved. Even the fact that he
generally brought them a packet of expensive
sweets was as nothing beside the harrowing
knowledge that they must kiss him, thereby
having their faces brushed with a large and
scrubby moustache. Aunt Margaret and Nurse did
not have to endure this infliction — which seemed
to Bob and Cecilia obviously unfair. But the visits

did not often happen — not enough to disturb
seriously an existence crammed with interesting
things like puppies and kittens, the pony cart,
boats on the river that ran just beyond the lawn,
occasional trips to London and the Zoo, and
delirious fortnights at the seaside or on
Devonshire moors. Cecilia had never known even
Bobby's shadowy memories of their own mother.
Aunt Margaret was everything that mattered, and
the person called Papa was merely an unpleasant
incident. Other little boys and girls whom they
knew owned, in their houses, delightful people
named Daddy and Mother; but Cecilia and Bob
quite understood that everyone could not have the
same things, for possibly those fortunate children
had no puppies or pony carts. Nurse had pointed
out this, so that it was perfectly clear.

It was when Cecilia was eight and Bob eleven
that their father married again. To the children it
meant nothing; to Aunt Margaret it was a bomb.
If Mark Rainham had happened to die, or go to
the North Pole, she would have borne the
occurrence calmly; but that he should take step
which might mean separating her from her
beloved babies shook her to her foundations. Even
when she was assured that the new Mrs. Rainham
disliked children, and had not the slightest
intention of adding Bob and Cecilia to her
household, Aunt Margaret remained uneasy. The
red-haired person, as she mentally labelled her,
might change her mind. Mark Rainham was wax
in her hands, and would always do as he was told.
Aunt Margaret, goaded by fear, became heroic.

She let the beloved house at Twickenham while Mr. and Mrs. Rainham were still on their honeymoon, packed up the children, her maids, Nurse, the parrot and most of the puppies, and kept all her plans a profound secret until she was safely established in Paris.

To the average Londoner, Paris is very far off. There are, of course, very many people who run across the Channel as easily as a Melbourne man may weekend in Gippsland or Bendigo, but the suburban section of London is not fond of voyaging across a strip of water with unpleasant possibilities in the way of choppiness, to a strange country where most of the inhabitants have the bad taste not to speak English. Neither Mark Rainham nor his new wife had ever been in France, and to them it seemed, as Aunt Margaret had shrewdly hoped it would, almost as though the Twickenham household had gone to the North Pole. A great relief fell upon them, since there could now be no question of assuming duties when those duties were suddenly beyond their reach. And Aunt Margaret's letter was convincing — such a good offer, suddenly, for the Twickenham house; such excellent educational opportunities for the children, in the shape of semi-English schools, where Bob and Cecilia might mix with English children and retain their nationality while acquiring Parisian French. If Mark Rainham felt any inward resentment at the summary disposal of his son and daughter, he did not show it; as of old, it was easier to let things slide. Aunt Margaret was given a free hand, save that at fourteen Bob

returned to school in England; an arrangement
that mattered little, since all his holidays were
spent at the new home at Fontainebleau — a
house which, even to the parrot, was highly
reminiscent of Twickenham.

Bob and Cecilia found life extremely interesting.
They were cheery, happy-go-lucky youngsters,
with an immense capacity for enjoyment; and
Aunt Margaret, while much too shrewd an old lady
to spoil children, delighted in giving them a good
time. They found plenty of friends in the little
English community in Paris, as well as among
their French neighbours. Paris itself was full of
fascination; then there were wonderful excursions
far afield — holidays in Brussels, in the South of
France, even winter sporting in Switzerland. Aunt
Margaret was determined that her nurselings
should miss nothing that she could give them. The
duty letters which she insisted on their writing,
once a month, to their father told of happenings
that seemed strangely remote from the humdrum
life of London. "By Jove, the old lady gives those
youngsters a good time!" Mark Rainham would
comment, tossing them across the table to his wife.
He did not guess at the dull rage that filled her
as she read them — the unreasoning jealousy that
these children should have opportunities so far
beyond any that were likely to occur for her own,
who squabbled angrily over their breakfast while
she read.

"She seems to have any amount of money to
spend on gadding about," she would say
unpleasantly.

"Oh, pots of money. Wish to goodness I had some of it," her husband would answer. Money was always scarce in the Rainham household.

When the thunderbolt of war fell upon the world, Aunt Margaret, after the first pangs of panic, stiffened her back, and declined to leave France. England, she declared, was not much safer than anywhere else; and was it likely that she and Cecilia would run away when Bob was coming back? Bob, just eighteen, captain of his school training corps, stroke of its racing boat, and a mighty man of valour at football, slid naturally into khaki within a month of the outbreak of war, putting aside toys, with all the glad company of boys of the Empire, until such time as the Hun should be taught that he had no place among white men. Aunt Margaret and Cecilia, knitting frantically at socks and muffers and Balaclava helmets, were desperately proud of him, and compared his photograph, in uniform, with all the pictures of Etienne and Henri and Armand, and other French boys who had played with him under the trees at Fontainebleau, and had not marched away to join him at the greater game. It was difficult to realise that they were not still little boys in blouses and knickerbockers — difficult even when they swooped down from time to time on short leave, filling the quiet houses with pranks and laughter that were wholly boyish. Even when Bob had two stars on his cuff, and wore the ribbon of the Military Cross, it would have astonished Aunt Margaret and Cecilia very much had anyone suggested that he was grown up.

Indeed, Aunt Margaret was never to think of him as anything but "one of the children". Illness, sudden and fierce, fell upon her after a long spell of duty at the hospital where she worked from the first few months of the war — working as cook, since she had no nursing experience, and was, she remarked, too old to learn a new trade. Brave as she was, there was no battling for her against the new foe; she faded out of life after a few days, holding Cecilia's hand very tightly until the end.

Bob, obtaining leave with much difficulty, arrived a few days later to find a piteous Cecilia, white-faced, stunned and bewildered. She pleaded desperately against leaving France; amidst all the horror and chaos that had fallen upon her, it seemed unthinkable that she should put the sea between herself and Bob. But to remain was impossible. Aunt Margaret's English maids wanted to go back to their friends, and a girl of seventeen could scarcely stay alone in a country torn by two years of war. Besides, Aunt Margaret's affairs were queerly indefinite; there seemed very little money where there had formerly been plenty. There was no alternative for Cecilia but England — and England meant the Rainham household, and such welcome as it might choose to give her.

She was still bewildered when they made the brief journey across the Channel — a new Channel, peopled only with warships of every kind, from grim Dreadnoughts to submarines; with aircraft, bearing the red, white and blue circles of Britain, floating and circling overhead. Last time Cecilia had crossed, it had been with

Aunt Margaret on a big turbine mail boat; they had reached Calais just as an excursion steamer from Margate came up, gay with flags and light dresses, with a band playing ragtime on the well-deck, and people dancing to a concertina at the stern. Now they zigzagged across, sometimes at full speed, sometimes stopping dead or altering their course in obedience to the destroyer nosing ahead of them through the Channel mist; and she could see the face of the captain on the bridge, strained and anxious. There were so few civilians on board that Cecilia and the two old servants were greeted with curious stares; nearly all the passengers were in uniform, their boots caked with the mud of the trenches, their khaki soiled with the grime of war. It was all rather dream-like to Cecilia; and London itself was a very bad dream; darkened and silent, with the great beams of searchlights playing back and forth over the black skies in search of marauding Zeppelins. And then came her father's stiff greeting, and the silent drive to the tall, narrow house in Lancaster Gate, where Mrs. Rainham met her coldly. In after years Cecilia never could think without a shudder of that first meal in her father's house — the struggle to eat, the lagging talk round the table, with Avice and Wilfred, frankly hostile, staring at her in silence, and her stepmother's pale eyes appraising every detail of her dress. It was almost like happiness again to find herself alone, later, in a dingy little attic bedroom that smelt as though it had never known an open window — a sorry little hole, but still, out of the reach of those unblinking eyes.

For the first year Cecilia had struggled to get away to earn her own living. But a very few weeks served to show Mrs. Rainham that chance had sent her, in the person of the girl whose coming she had sullenly resented, a very useful buffer against any period of domestic stress. Aunt Margaret had trained Cecilia thoroughly in all housewifely virtues, and her half-French education had given her much that was lacking in the stodgy damsels of Mrs. Rainham's acquaintance. She was quick and courteous and willing; responding, moreover, to the lash of the tongue — after her first wide-eyed stare of utter amazement — exactly as a well-bred colt responds to a deftly used whip. "I'll keep her," was Mrs. Rainham's inward resolve. "And she'll earn her keep too!"

There was no doubt that Cecilia did that. Wilfred and Avice saw to it, even had not their mother been fully capable of exacting the last ounce from the only helper she had ever had who had not the power to give her a week's notice. Cecilia's first requests to be allowed to take up work outside had been shelved vaguely. "We'll find some nice war-work for you presently" ... and meanwhile, the household was short-handed, Mrs. Rainham was overstrained — Cecilia found later that her stepmother was always "over-strained" whenever she spoke of leaving home — and duties multiplied about her and hemmed her in. Mrs. Rainham was clever; the net closed round the girl so gradually that she scarcely realised its meshes until they were drawn tightly. Even Bob helped. "You're awfully young to start work on your own account," he wrote. "Can't you stick it for a bit, if they are decent to you?" And, rather than cause him any extra worry, Cecilia decided that she must "stick it".

Of her father she saw little. He was, just as she remembered him in her far-back childhood at Twickenham, vague and colourless. Rather to her horror, she found that the ordeal of being kissed by his large and scrubby moustache was just as unpleasant as ever. Cecilia had no idea of how he earned his living — he ate his breakfast hurriedly, concealed behind the *Daily Mail*, and then disappeared, bound for some mysterious place in the city — the part of London that was always full of mystery to Cecilia. Golf was the one thing that roused him to any enthusiasm, and golf was even more of a mystery than the city. Cecilia knew that it was played with assorted weapons, kept in a bag, and used for smiting a small ball over great expanses of country, but beyond these facts her knowledge stopped. Mrs. Rainham had set her to clean the clubs one day, but her father, appearing unexpectedly, had taken them from her hands with something like roughness. "No, by Jove!" he said. "You do a good many odd jobs in this house, but I'm hanged if you shall clean my golf sticks." Cecilia did not realise that the assumed roughness covered something very like shame.

Money matters were rather confusing. A lawyer — also in the city — paid her a small sum quarterly — enough to dress on, and for minor expenses. Bob wrote that Aunt Margaret's affairs were in a beastly tangle. An annuity had died with her, and many of her investments had been hit by the war, and had ceased to pay dividends — had even, it seemed, ceased to be valuable at all. There was a small allowance for Bob also, and some day, if luck should turn, there might be a little more. Bob did not say that his own allowance was being hoarded for Cecilia, in case he "went west". He lived on his pay, and even managed to save something out of that, being a youth of simple tastes. His battalion had been practically wiped out of existence in the third year of the war, and after a peaceful month in a north country hospital, near an aerodrome, the call of the air was too much for him — he joined the cheerful band of flying men, and soon filled his letters to Cecilia with a bewildering mixture of technicalities and aviation slang that left her gasping. But he got his wings in a very short time, and she was prouder of him than ever — and more than ever desperately afraid for him.

The children's daily governess, a downtrodden person, left after Cecilia had been in England for a few months, and the girl stepped naturally into the vacant position until someone else should be found. She had no idea that Mrs. Rainham made no effort at all to discover any other successor to Miss Simpkins. Where, indeed, Mrs. Rainham demanded of herself, would she be likely to find anyone with such qualifications — young, docile, with every advantage of a modern education, speaking French like a native, and above and beyond all else, requiring no pay? It would be flying in the face of Providence to ignore such a chance. Wherefore Cecilia continued to lead her step-sisters and brother in the paths of learning, and life became a thing of utter weariness. For Mrs. Rainham, though shrewd enough to get what she wanted, in the main was not a far-sighted woman; and in her unreasoning dislike and jealousy of Cecilia she failed to see that she defeated her own ends by making her a drudge. Whatever benefit the girl might have given the children was lost in their contempt for her. She had no authority, no power to enforce a command, or to give a punishment, and the children quickly discovered that, so long as they gave her the merest show of obedience in their mother's presence, any shortcomings in education would be laid at Cecilia's door. Lesson time became a period of rare sport for the young Rainhams; it was so easy to bait the new sister with cheap taunts, to watch the quick blood mount to the very roots of her fair hair, to do just as little as possible, and then to see her blamed for the result. Mrs. Rainham's bitter tongue grew more and more uncontrolled as time went on and she felt the girl more fully in her power. And Cecilia lived through each day with tight-shut lips, conscious of one clear thing in her mist of unhappy bewilderment — that Bob must not know: Bob, who would probably leave his job of skimming through the air of her beloved France after the Hun, and snatch an hour to fly to England and annihilate

the entire Rainham household, returning with
Cecilia tucked away somewhere in his aeroplane.
It was a pleasant dream, and served to carry her
through more than one hard moment. But it did
not always serve; and there were nights when
Cecilia mounted to her attic with dragging
footsteps, to sit by her window in the darkness,
gripping her courage with both hands, afraid to
let herself think of the dear, happy past; of Aunt
Margaret, whose very voice was love; least of all
of Bob, perhaps even now flying in the dark over
the German lines. There was but one thing that
she could hold to: she voiced it to herself, over and
over with clenched hands: "It can't last forever! It
can't last forever!"

And then, after the long years of clutching
anxiety, came the Armistice, and Cecilia forgot all
her troubles in its overwhelming relief. No one
would shoot at Bob any longer; there were no more
hideous, squat guns, with muzzles yawning
skywards, ready to shell him as he skimmed high
overhead, like a swallow in the blue. Therefore she
sang as she went about her work, undismayed by
the laboured witticisms of Avice and Wilfred, or
by Mrs. Rainham's venom, which increased with
the realisation that her victims might possibly slip
from her grasp, since Bob would come home, and
Bob was a person to be reckoned with. Certainly
Bob had scarcely any money; moreover, Cecilia
was not of age, and, therefore, still under her
father's control. But Mrs. Rainham felt vaguely
uneasy, and visions floated before her of the old
days when governesses and maids had departed

with unpleasant frequency, laving her to face all sorts of disagreeable consequences. She set her thin lips, vowing inwardly that Cecilia should remain.

Nevertheless it was a relief to her that early demobilisation did not come for Bob. At the time of the Armistice he was attached to an Australian flying squadron, and for some months remained abroad; then he was sent back to England, and employed in training younger fliers at a Surrey aerodrome. This had its drawbacks in Mrs. Rainham's eyes, since he was often able to run up to London, and, to Bob, London merely meant Cecilia. It was only a question of time before he discovered something of what life at Lancaster Gate meant — his enlightenment beginning upon an afternoon when, arriving unexpectedly, and being left by Eliza to find Cecilia for himself, he had the good fortune to overhear Mrs. Rainham in one of her best efforts — a "wigging" to which Avice and Wilfred were listening delightedly, and which included not only Cecilia's sin of the moment, but her upbringing, her French education, her "foreign fashion of speaking", and her sinful extravagance in shoes. These, and other matters, were furnishing Mrs. Rainham with ample material for a bitter discourse when she became aware of another presence in the room, and her eloquence faltered at the sight of Bob's astonished anger.

Mrs. Rainham did not recall with any enjoyment the interview which followed — Cecilia and the children having been brushed out of the

way by the indignant soldier. Things which had
been puzzling to Bob were suddenly made clear —
traces of distress which Cecilia had often
explained away vaguely, the children's
half-contemptuous manner towards her, even
Eliza's tone in speaking of her — a queer blend
of anger and pity. Mrs. Rainham held her ground
to some extent, but the brother's questions were
hard to parry, and some of his comments stung.

"Well, I'll take her away," he stormed at length.
"It's evident that she does not give you
satisfaction, and she certainly isn't happy. She had
better come away with me today."

"Ah," said his stepmother freezingly, "and where
will you take her?"

Bob hesitated.

"There are plenty of places —" he began.

"Not for a young girl alone. Cecilia is very
ignorant of England; you could not be with her.
Your father would not hear of it. You must
remember that Cecilia is under his control until
she is twenty-one."

"My father has never bothered about either of
us," Bob said bitterly. "He surely won't object if I
take her off your hands."

"He will certainly not permit any such thing.
Whatever arrangement he made during your
aunt's lifetime was quite a different matter. If you
attempt to take Cecilia from his control you
commit an illegal action," said Mrs. Rainham —
hoping she was on safe ground. To her relief Bob
did not contradict her. English law and its
mysteries were beyond him.

"I don't see that that matters," he began
doubtfully. His stepmother cut him short.

"You would very soon find that it matters a good
deal," she said coldly. "It would be quite simple
for your father to get some kind of legal injunction,
forbidding you to interfere with your sister. Home
training is what she needs, and we are determined
that she shall get it. You will only unsettle and
inure her by trying to induce her to disobey us."

The hard voice fell like lead on the boy's ears.
He felt very helpless; if he did indeed snatch his
sister away from this extremely unpleasant home,
and their father had only to stretch out a long,
legal tentacle and claw her back, it was clear that
her position would be harder than ever. He could
only give in, at any rate, for the present, and in
his anxiety for the little sister whom Aunt
Margaret had always trained him to protect, he
humbled himself to beg for better treatment for
her. "No one ever was angry with her," he said.
"She'll do anything for you if you're decent to her."

"She might give less cause for annoyance if she
had had a little more severity," said Mrs. Rainham
with an unspoken sneer at poor Aunt Margaret.
"You had better advise her to do her best in return
for the very comfortable home we give her." With
which Bob had to endeavour to be content, for the
present. He went off to find Cecilia, with a
lowering brow, leaving his stepmother not nearly
so easy in her mind as she seemed. For Bob had
a square jaw, and was apt to talk little and do a
good deal; and his affection for Cecilia was, in Mrs.
Rainham's eyes, little short of ridiculous.

Thereafter, the brother and sister took counsel together and made great plans for the future, when once the Air Force should decide that it had no further wish to keep Captain Robert Rainham from earning his living on terra firma. What that future was to be for Bob was very difficult to plan. Aunt Margaret had intended him for a profession; but the time for that had gone by, even had the money been still available. "I'm half glad that it isn't," Bob said. "I don't see how a fellow could go back to swotting over books after being really alive for nearly five years." There seemed nothing but "the land" in some shape or form; they were not very clear about it, but Bob was strenuously "keeping his ears open" — like so many lads of his rank in the early months of 1919, when the future that had seemed so indefinite during the years of war suddenly loomed up, very large and menacing. Cecilia had less anxiety; she had a cheerful faith that Bob would manage something — a three-roomed cottage somewhere in the country, where he could look after sheep, or crops, or something of the kind, while she cooked and mended for him, and grew such flowers as had bloomed in the dear garden at Fontainebleau. Sheep and crops, she was convinced, grew themselves, in the main; a person of Bob's ability would surely find little difficulty in superintending the process. And, whatever happened, nothing could be worse than life in Lancaster Gate.

Neither of them ever thought of appealing to their father, either for advice or for help. He remained, as he had always been to them, utterly colourless; a kind of well-bred shadow of his wife, taking no part in her hard treatment of Cecilia, but lifting not a finger to save her. He did not look happy; indeed, he seldom spoke — it was not necessary, when Mrs. Rainham held the floor. He had a tiny den which he used as a smoking-room, and there he spent most of his time when at home, being blessed in the fact that his wife disliked the smell of smoke, and refused to allow it in her drawing-room. Nobody took much notice of him. The younger children treated him with cool indifference; Bob met him with a kind of strained and uncomfortable civility.

Curiously enough, it was only Eliza who divined in him a secret hankering after his eldest daughter — Cecilia, who would have been very much astonished had anyone hinted at such a thing to her. The sharp eyes of the little Cockney were not to be deceived in any matter concerning the only person in the house who treated her as if she were a human being and not a grate-cleaning automaton.

"You see 'im foller 'er wiv 'is eyes, that's all," said Eliza to Cook, in the privacy of their joint bedroom. "Fair 'ungry he looks, sometimes."

"No need for 'im to be 'ungry, if 'e 'ad the sperrit of a man," said Cook practically. "Ain't she 'is daughter?"

"Well, yes, in a manner of speakin'," said Eliza doubtfully. "But there ain't much of father an' daughter about them two. I'd rather 'ave my ole man, down W'itechapel way; 'e can belt yer a fair terror, w'en 'e's drunk, but 'e'll allers take yer out

an' buy yer a kipper afterwards. Thet's on'y
decent, fatherly feelin'."

"Well, Master don't belt 'er, does 'e?"

"No, but 'e don't buy 'er the kipper, neither. An'
I'd rather 'ave the beltin' from my ole man, even
wivout no kipper, than 'ave us allers lookin' at
each other as if we was wooden images. Even a
beltin' shows as 'ow a man 'as some regard for 'is
daughter."

"It do," said Cook. "Pity is, you ain't 'ad more
of it, that's the only thing!"

CHAPTER 3

Playing Truant

"DEMOBILISED! Oh, Bob — truly?"

"Truly and really," said Bob. "At least, I shall be in twenty-seven days. Got my orders. Show up for the last time on the fifteenth of next month. Get patted on the head, and told to run away and play. That's the programme, I believe, Tommy. The question is — What shall we play at?"

Cecilia brushed the hair from her brow.

"I don't know," she said vaguely. "It's too big to think of; and I can't think in this awful house, anyhow. Take me out, quick, please, Bobby."

"Sure," said Bob, regarding her with an understanding eye. "But you want to change or something, don't you, old girl?"

"Why, yes, I suppose I do," said Cecilia, with a watery smile, looking at her schoolroom overall. "I forgot clothes. I've had a somewhat packed morning."

"You look as if this had been your busy day," remarked Bob. "Right-oh, old girl; jump into your things, and I'll wait on the mat. Any chance of the she-dragon coming back?"

"No; she's gone out to tea."

"More power to her," said Bob cheerfully. "And the dragon puppies?"

"Oh, they're safely out of the way. I won't be five minutes, Bob. Don't shut the door tight — you might disappear before I opened it."

"Not much," said Bob, through the crack of the door. "I'm a fixture. Want any shoes cleaned?"

"No, thanks, Bobby dear. I have everything ready."

"From what the other fellows say about their sisters, I'm inclined to believe that you're an ornament to your sex," remarked Bob. "When you say five minutes, it really does mean not more than five and a half, as a rule; other girls seem to mean three-quarters of an hour."

"I get all my things ready the night before when I'm going to meet you," said Cecilia. "Catch me losing any time on my one day out. You can come back again — my coat's on the hanger there, Bobby." He put her into it deftly, and she leaned back against him. "If you knew how good it is to see you again — and you smell of clean fresh air and good tobacco and Russia leather, and all sorts of nice things."

"Good gracious, I'll excite attention in the street!" grinned Bob. "I didn't imagine I was a walking scent factory!"

"Neither you are — but everything in this house smells of coal smoke and cabbage water and general fustiness, and you're a nice change, that's all," said Cecilia. They ran downstairs together light-heartedly, and let themselves out into the street.

"Do we catch a train or a bus?"

"Oh, can't we walk?" Cecilia said. "I think if I walked hard I might forget Mrs. Rainham."

"I'd hate you to remember her," Bob said. "Tell me what she has been doing anyhow, and then we won't think of her any more."

"It doesn't sound much," Cecilia said. "There never is anything very much. Only it goes on all the time." She told him the story of her day, and managed to make herself laugh now and then over it. But Bob did not laugh. His good-humoured young face was set and angry.

"There isn't a whole lot in it, is there?" Cecilia finished. "And no one would think I was badly off — especially when the thing that hit me hardest of all was just dusting that awful drawing-room while she plays her awful tunes. Yes, I know I shouldn't say awful, and that no lady says it — that must be true because Mrs. Rainham frequently tells me so — but it's such a relief to say whatever I feel like."

"You can say what you jolly well please," said Bob wrathfully. "Who's she, I'd like to know, to tell us what to say? And she kept you there all the afternoon, when she knew you were due to meet me! My hat, she is a venomous old bird! And now it's half-past four, and what time does she expect you back?"

"Oh — the usual thing; the children's tea-time at six. She told me not to be late."

Bob set his jaw.

"Well, you won't be late, because you won't be there," he said. "No going back to tea for you. We'll have dinner at the Petit Riche in Soho, and then

we'll do a theatre, and then I'll take you home and
we'll face the music. Are you game?"

Cecilia laughed.

"Game? Why, of course — but there will be
awful scenes, Bobby."

"Well, what can she do to you?" asked Bob
practically. "You're too big to beat, or she'd
certainly do it; she can't stop your pay, because
you don't get any; and as you have your meals
with the youngsters, she can't dock your rations.
That doesn't leave her much beside her tongue. Of
course, she can do a good deal with that; do you
think you can stand it?"

"Oh, yes," said Cecilia. "You see, I generally
have it, so it really doesn't matter much. But if
she forbids me to go out with you again, Bobby?"

Bob pondered.

"Well — you're nineteen," he said. "And the very
first minute I can, I'm going to take you away from
her altogether. If you were a kid I wouldn't let you
defy her. But, hang it all, Tommy, I'm not going
to let her punish you as though you were ten. If
she forbids you to meet me — well, you must just
take French leave, that's all."

"Oh, Bob, you are a satisfying person!" said
Cecilia, with a sigh.

"Well, I don't know — it's you who will have to
stand the racket," said Bob. "I only wish I could
take my share, old girl. But, please goodness, it
won't be for long."

"Bob," said Cecilia, and paused. "What about
that statement of hers — that it would be illegal
for you to take me away? Do you think it's true?"

"I've asked our Major, and he's a bit doubtful," said Bob. "All the other fellows say it's utter non-sense. But I'm going to ask the old lawyer chap who has charge of Aunt Margaret's money — he'll tell me. We won't bother about it, Tommy; if I can't get you politely, I'll steal you. Just forget the she-dragon and all her works."

"But have you thought about what you are going to do?"

"I don't think of much else, and that's the truth, Tommy," said her brother ruefully. "You see, there's mighty little in sight. I could get a clerkship, I suppose. I could certainly get work as a day labourer. But I don't see much in either of those possibilities towards a little home with you, which is what I want. I'm going to answer every advertisement I can find for fellows wanted on farms." He straightened his square shoulders. "Tommy, there must be plenty of work for any chap as strong as an ox, as I am."

"I'm sure there's work," said Cecilia. "But the men who want jobs don't generally advertise themselves as 'complete with sister'. I'm what's technically known as an encumbrance, Bob."

"You!" said Bob. "You're just part of the firm, so don't you forget it. Didn't we always arrange that we should stick together?"

"We did — but it may not be easy to manage," Cecilia said, doubtfully. "Perhaps we could get some job together; I could do inside work, or teach, or sew."

"No!" said Bob explosively. "If I can't earn

enough for us both, I ought to be shot. Aunt Margaret didn't bring you up to work."

"But the world has turned upside down since Aunt Margaret died," said Cecilia. "And I have worked pretty hard for the last two years, Bob; and it hasn't hurt me."

"It has made you older — and you ought to be only a kid yet," said Bob wistfully. "You haven't had any of the fun girls naturally ought to have. I don't want you to slave all your time, Tommy."

"Bless you!" said his sister. "But I wouldn't care a bit, as long as it was near you — and not in Lancaster Gate."

They had turned across Hyde Park, where a big company of girl guides was drilling, watched by a crowd of curious onlookers. Across a belt of grass some boy scouts were performing similar evolutions, marching with all the extra polish and swagger they could command, just to show the guides that girls were all very well in their way, but that no one with skirts could really hope to do credit to a uniform. Cecilia paused to watch them.

"Thank goodness, the children can come and drill in the park again!" she said. "I hated to come here before the armistice — soldiers, soldiers, drilling everywhere, and guns and searchlight fixings. Whenever I saw a squad drilling it made me think of you, and of course I felt sure you'd be killed!"

"I do like people who look on the bright side of life!" said Bob laughing. "And whenever you saw an aeroplane I suppose you made sure I was crashing somewhere?"

"Certainly I did," said his sister with dignity.

"Women are queer things," Bob remarked. "If you had these unpleasant beliefs, how did you manage to write as cheerfully as you did? Your letters were a scream — I used to read bits of 'em out to the fellows."

"You had no business to do any such thing," said Cecilia, blushing.

"Well, I did, anyhow. They used to make 'em yell. How did you manage them?"

"Well, it was no good assuring you you'd be killed," said Cecilia practically. "I thought it was more sensible to try to make you laugh."

"You certainly did that," said Bob. "I fancied from your letters that life with the she-dragon was one huge joke, and that Papa was nice and companionable, and the kids sweet little darlings who ate from your hand. And all the time you were just the poor old toad under the harrow!"

"I'm not a toad!" rejoined his sister indignantly. "Don't you think you could find pleasanter things to compare me to?"

"Toads aren't bad," said Bob, laughing. "Ever seen the nice old fellow in the Zoo who shoots out a tongue a yard long and picks up a grub every time? He's quite interesting."

"I certainly never had any inclination to do any such thing," Cecilia laughed.

They had turned into Piccadilly and were walking down, watching the crowded motor traffic racing north and south. Suddenly Bob straightened up and saluted smartly, as a tall staff officer, wearing a general's badges, ran down the steps of a big club, and nearly cannoned into Cecilia.

"I beg your pardon!" he said — and then, noticing Bob — "How are you, Rainham?" He dived into a waiting taxi, and was whisked away.

"Did he bump you?" inquired Bob.

"No — though it would be almost a privilege to be bumped by anyone as splendid as that!" Cecilia answered. "He knows you too! Who is he, Bobby?"

"That's General Harran, the Australian," said Bob proudly. "He's a great man. I've run into him occasionally since I've been with the Australians in France."

"He looks nice."

"He is nice," replied Bob. "Awful martinet about duty, but he treats everyone under him jolly well. Never forgets a face or a name, and he's always got a decent word for everybody. He's had some quite long talks to me, when we were waiting for some plane or other to come back."

"Why wouldn't he?" asked Cecilia, who considered it a privilege for anyone to talk to her brother.

Bob regarded her in amazement.

"Good gracious!" he ejaculated. "Why, he's a major-general; I can tell you, most men of his rank haven't any use for small fry like me — to talk to, that is."

Cecilia had a flash of memory.

"Isn't he the general who was close by when you

brought that German aeroplane down behind our lines? Didn't he say nice things to you about it?"

"Oh that was only in the way of business," said Bob somewhat confused. "The whole thing was only a bit of luck — and, of course, it was luck, too, that he was there. But he is just as nice to fellows who haven't had a chance like that."

Out the crowd two more figures in Air Force uniform came, charging at Bob with outstretched hands.

"By Jove, old chap! What luck to meet you!"

They shook hands tumultuously, and Bob made them known to Cecilia — comrades he had not seen for months, but with whom he had shared many strange experiences in the years of war. They fell into quick talk, full of the queer jargon of the air. The newcomers, it appeared, had been with the army of occupation in Germany; there seemed a thousand things they urgently desired to tell Bob within the next few minutes. One turned to Cecilia, presently, with a laughing interpretation of some highly technical bit of slang.

"Oh you needn't bother to translate to Tommy," Bob said. "She knows all about it."

The other boys suddenly gave her all their attention.

"Are you Tommy? But we know you awfully well."

"Me?" Cecilia turned pink.

"Rather. We used to hear your letters."

The pink deepened into a fine scarlet.

"Bob!" said his sister reproachfully. "You really shouldn't."

"Oh, don't say that," said the taller boy, by name Harrison. "They were a godsend — there used to be jolly little to laugh about, pretty often, and your letters made us all yell. Didn't they, Billy?"

"They did," said Billy, who was small and curly-haired — and incidentally a captain, with a little row of medal ribbons. "Jolliest letters ever. We passed a vote of thanks to you in the mess, Miss Tommy, after old Bob here had gone. Someone was to write and tell him about it, but I don't believe anyone ever did. I say, you must have had a cheery time — all the funny things that ever happened seemed to come your way."

Cecilia stammered something, her scarlet confusion deepening. A rather grim vision of the war years swept across her mind — of the ceaseless quest in papers and journals, and wherever people talked, for "funny things" to tell Bob; and of how, when fact and rumour gave out, she used to sit by her attic window at night, deliberately inventing merry jests. It had closely resembled a job of hard work at the time; but apparently it had served its purpose well. She had made them laugh; and someone had told her that no greater service could be rendered to the boys who risked death, and worse than death, during every hour of the day and night. But it was extremely difficult to talk about it afterwards.

Bob took pity on her.

"I'll tell you just what sort of a cheery time she

had, some time or other," he remarked. "What are you fellows doing this evening?"

"We were just going to ask you the same thing," declared Billy. "Can't we all go and play about somewhere? We've just landed, and we want to be looked after. Any theatres in this little town still?"

"Cheer-oh!" ejaculated Billy. "Let's all go and find out."

So they went, and managed very successfully to forget war and even stepmothers. They were all little more than children in enjoyment of simple pleasures still, since war had fallen upon them at the very threshold of life, cutting them off from all the cheery happenings that are the natural inheritance of all young things. The years that would ordinarily have seen them growing tired of play had been spent in grim tasks; now they were children again, clamouring for the playtime they had lost. They found enormous pleasure in the funny little French restaurant, where Madame, a lady whose sympathies were as boundless as her waist, welcomed them with wide smiles, delighting in the broken French of Billy and Harrison, and deftly tempting them to fresh excursions in her language. She put a question in infantile French to Bob presently, whereupon that guileless youth, with a childlike smile, answered her with a flood of idiomatic phrases, in an accent purer than her own — collapsing with helpless laughter at her amazed face. After which, Madame neglected her other patrons to hover about their table like a stout, presiding goddess, guiding them gently to the best dishes on the menu, and occasionally putting aside their own selection with a hasty, "Mais non; you vill not like that one today." She patted Cecilia in a motherly fashion at parting, and their bill was only about half what it should have been.

They found a musical comedy, and laughed their way through it — Billy and Harrison had apparently no cares in the world, and Bob and Cecilia were caught up in the whirl of their high spirits, so that anything became a huge joke. The evening flew by on airy wings, when Billy insisted on taking them to supper after the theatre. Cecilia allowed herself a fleeting vision of Mrs. Rainham, and then, deciding that she might as well be hanged for a sheep as a lamb, followed gaily. And supper was so cheery a meal that she forgot all about time — until, just at the end, she caught sight of the restaurant clock.

"Half-past eleven! Oh, Bobby!"

"Well, if it is — you poor little old Cinderella," said Bob.

But he hurried her away, for all that, amid a chorus of farewells and efforts, on the part of Billy and Harrison, to arrange further meetings. They ran to the nearest tube station, and dived into its depths; and, after being whisked underground for a few minutes, emerged into the cool night. Cecilia slipped her arm through her brother's as they hurried along the empty street.

"Now, you keep your nose in the air," Bobby told her. "You aren't exactly a kid now, and she can't really do anything to you. Oh, by Jove — I was thinking, in the theatre, she might interfere with our letters."

"She's quite equal to it," said Cecilia.

"Just what she'd revel in doing. Well, you can easily find out. I'll write to you tomorrow, and again the next day — just ordinary letters, with nothing particular in them except an arrangement to meet next Saturday. If you don't get them you'll know she's getting at the mail first."

"What shall I do, then?"

"Drop me a line — or, better still, wire to me," said Bob. "Just say, 'Address elsewhere'. Then I'll write to you at Mr. M'Clinton's; the old solicitor chap in Lincoln's Inn; and you'll have to go there and get the letters. You know his address, don't you?"

"Oh, yes. I have to write to him every quarter when he sends me my allowance. You'll explain to him, then, Bob, or he'll simply redirect your letters here."

"Oh, of course. I want to go and see the old chap, anyhow, to talk over Aunt Margaret's affairs. I might as well know a little more about them. Tommy, the she-dragon can't actually lock you up, can she?"

"No — it couldn't be done," said Cecilia. "Modern houses aren't built with dungeons and things. Moreover, if she tried to keep me in the house she would have to take the children out for their walks herself; and she simply hates walking."

"Then you can certainly post to me, and get my

letters, and I'll be up again as soon as ever I can.
Buck up, old girl — it can't be for long now."

They turned in at the Rainhams' front gate, and
Cecilia glanced up apprehensively. All the
windows were in darkness; the grey front of the
house loomed forbiddingly in the faint moonlight.

"You're coming in, aren't you?" she asked, her
hand tightening on his arm.

"Rather — we'll take the edge off her tongue
together." Bob rang the bell. "Wonder if they have
all gone to bed. The place looks pretty dark."

"She's probably in the little room at the back —
the one she calls her boudoir."

"Horrible little den, full of bamboo and
draperies and pampas grass — I know," nodded
Bob. "Well, either she's asleep or she thinks it's
fun to keep us on the mat. I'll try her again." He
pressed the bell, and the sound of its whirring
echoed through the silent house.

CHAPTER 4

Coming Home

THE bolt grated, as if grudgingly, and slowly the door opened as far as the limits of its chain would permit, and Mrs. Rainham's face appeared in the aperture. She glared at them for a minute without speaking.

"So you have come home?" she said at last. The chain fell, and the door opened. "I wonder you trouble to come home at all. May I ask where you have been?"

"She has been with me, Mrs. Rainham," Bob said cheerfully. "May I come in?"

Mrs. Rainham did not move. She held the door half open, blocking the way.

"It is far too late for me to ask you in," she answered frigidly. "Cecilia can explain her conduct, I presume."

"Oh, there's really nothing to explain," Bob answered. "It was so late when she got out this afternoon that I kept her — why, it was after half-past four before she was dressed."

"I told her to be in for tea."

"Yes, but I felt sure you couldn't realise how late she was in getting out," said Bob in a voice of honey.

"That was entirely her own mismanagement —"
began the hard tones.

"Oh, no, Mrs. Rainham, really it wasn't," said
Cecilia mildly. "Your accompaniments, you
remember — your dress — your music," she
stopped, in amazement at herself. It was rarely
indeed that she answered any accusation of her
stepmother's. But to be on the mat at midnight,
with Bob in support, seemed to give her
extraordinary courage.

"You see, Mrs. Rainham, there seems to have
been quite a number of little details that Cecilia
couldn't mismanage," said Bob following up the
advantage. It was happily evident that his
stepmother's rage was preventing her from
speaking, and, as he remarked later, there was no
knowing when he would ever get such a chance
again. "She really needed rest. I'm sure you'll
agree that every one is entitled to some free time.
Of course, you couldn't possibly have realised that
it was a week since she had been off duty."

"It's her business to do what I tell her," said
Mrs. Rainham, finding her voice, in an explosive
fashion that made a passing policeman glance up
curiously. "She knew I had company, and expected
her help. I had to see to the children's tea myself.
And how do I know where she's been? —
gallivanting round to all sorts of places! I tell you,
young lady, you needn't think you're going to walk
in here at midnight as if nothing was the matter."

"I never expected to," said Cecilia cheerfully.
"But it was worth it."

Bob regarded her in solemn admiration.

"I don't think we gallivanted at all reprehensibly," he said. "Just dinner and a theatre. I haven't made much claim to her time during the last four years, Mrs. Rainham; surely I'm entitled to a little of it now."

"You!" Mrs. Rainham's tone was vicious. "You don't give her a home, do you? And as long as I do, she'll do what I tell her."

"No; I don't give her a home — yet," said Bob very quietly. "But I very soon will, I assure you; and meanwhile, she earns a good deal more than her keep in her father's house. You can't treat her worse than your servants —"

Cecilia suddenly turned to him.

"Ah, don't, Bob darling. It doesn't matter — truly — not a bit." With the end of the long penance before her, it seemed beyond the power of the angry woman in the doorway to hurt her much. What she could not bear was that their happy evening should be spoiled by hard and cruel words at its close. Bob's face, that had been so merry, was sterner than she had ever seen it, all its boyishness gone. She put up her own face, and kissed him.

"Goodnight — you mustn't stay any longer. I'll be all right." She whispered a few quick words of French, begging him to go, and Bob, though unwillingly, gave in.

"All right," he said. "Go to bed, little 'un. I'll do as I promised about writing." He saluted Mrs. Rainham stiffly. "You'll remember, Mrs. Rainham, that she stayed out solely at my wish — I take full responsibility, and I'll be ready to tell my father so." The door close behind Cecilia, and he strode away down the street, biting his lip. He felt abominably as though he had deserted the little sister — and yet, what else could he do? One could not remain forever, brawling on a doorstep at midnight — and Tommy had begged him to go. Still —

"Hang it!" he said viciously. "If she were only a decent Hun to fight!"

In the grim house in Lancaster Gate Cecilia was facing the music alone. She listened unmoved, as she had listened many times before, to the catalogue of her sins and misdeeds — only she had never seen her stepmother quite so angry. Finally, a door above opened, and Mark Rainham looked out, his dull, colourless face weakly irritable.

"I wish you'd stop that noise, and let the girl go to bed," he said. "Come here, Cecilia."

She went to him hesitating, and he looked at her with a spark of compassion. Then he kissed her.

"Goodnight," he said, as though he had called her to him simply to say it, and not to separate her from the furious woman who stood looking at them. "Run off to bed, now — no more talking." Cecilia ran upstairs obediently. Behind her, as she neared her attic, she heard her stepmother's voice break out anew.

"Just fancy Papa!" she muttered. Any other sensations were lost in wonder at her father's actually having intervened. The incredible thing had happened. For a moment she felt a wave of pity for him, left alone to face the shrill voice. Then she shrugged her shoulders.

"Ah, well — he married her," she said. "I suppose he has had it many a time. Perhaps he knows how to stop it — I don't!" She laughed, turning the key in the lock, and sitting down beside the open window. The glamour of her happy evening was still upon her; even the scene with her stepmother had not had power to chase it away. The scene was only to be expected; the laughter of the evening was worth so everyday a penalty. And the end of Mrs. Rainham's rule was nearly in sight. Not even to herself for a moment would she admit that there was any possibility of Bob failing to "make good" and take her away.

She went downstairs next morning to an atmosphere of sullen resentment. Her father gave her a brief, abstracted nod in response to her greeting, and went on with his bacon and his *Daily Mail*; her stepmother's forbidding expression checked any attempt at conversation. The children stared at her with a kind of malevolent curiosity; they knew that a storm had been brewing for her the night before, and longed to know just how thoroughly she had "caught it". Eliza, bringing in singed and belated toast, looked at her with pity, tinged with admiration. Cook and she had been awakened at midnight by what was evidently, in the words of Cook, "a perfickly 'orrible bust-up", and knowing Cecilia to have been its object, Eliza looked at her as one may look who expects to see the scars of battle. Finding none, but receiving instead a cheerful smile, she returned to the kitchen, and reported to Cook that Miss Cecilia was "nuffink less than a neroine".

But as that day and the next wore on, Cecilia found it difficult to be cheerful. That she was in disgrace was very evident, Mrs. Rainham said no more about her sins of the night before; instead, she showed her displeasure by a kind of cold rudeness that gave a subtle insult to her smallest remark. The children were manifestly delighted. Cecilia was more or less in the position of a beetle on a pin, and theirs was the precious opportunity of seeing her wriggle. Wherefore they adopted their mother's tone, openly defied her, and turned school hours into a pandemonium.

Cecilia at last gave up the attempt to keep order. She opened her desk and took out her knitting.

"Well, this is all very pleasant," she said, calmly. "You seem determined to do no work at all, so I can only hope that in time you will get tired of being idle. I can't attempt to teach you any more. I am quite ready, however, if you bring your lessons to me."

"You'll get into a nice row from the Mater," jeered Wilfred.

"Very possibly. She may even punish me by finding another governess," said Cecilia, with a twinkle. "However that may be, I do not feel compelled to talk to such rude little children as you any more. When you are able to speak politely you may come to me for anything you want; until then, I shall not answer you." She bent her attention to the mysteries of heel-turning.

The children were taken aback. To pinprick with rudeness a victim who answered back was entertaining; but there was small fun in baiting anybody who sat silently knitting with a half-smile of contempt at the corners of her mouth. They gave it up after a time, and considered the question of going out; a pleasant thing to do, only that their mother had laid upon them a special injunction not to leave Cecilia, and she was in a mood that made disobedience extremely dangerous. Cecilia quite understood that she was being watched. No letters had yet come from Bob, and she knew that her stepmother had been hovering near the letter-box whenever the postman had called. Mrs. Rainham had accompanied them on their walk the day before; a remark of Avice's revealed that she meant to do so again today.

"It's all so silly," the girl said to herself. "If I chose to dive into a tube station or board a motor bus she couldn't stop me; and she can't go on watching me and intercepting my letters indefinitely. I suppose she will get tired of it after a while." But meanwhile she found the spying rather amusing. Avice popped up unexpectedly if she went near the front door; Wilfred's bullet head peeped in through the window whenever she fancied herself alone in the schoolroom. Only her attic was safe — since to spy upon it would have required an aeroplane.

The third day brought no letter from Bob. Cecilia asked for her mail when she went down to breakfast, and was met by a blank stare from her stepmother. "I suppose if there had been any letters for you they would be on your plate." She flushed a little under the girl's direct gaze, and turned her attention to Queenie's table manners, which were at all times peculiar; and Cecilia sat down with a faint smile. It was time to obey orders and telegraph to Bob.

She planned how to do it, during a long morning when the children actually did some work — since to be rude or idle meant that their teacher immediately retired into her shell of silence, and knitted, and life became too dull. To employ Eliza was her first thought — rejected, since it seemed unlikely that Eliza would be able to get time off to go out. If Mrs. Rainham's well-known dislike for walking proved too strong for her desire to watch her stepdaughter, it would be easy enough to do it during the afternoon; but this hope proved vain, for when she appeared in the hall with her charges at three o'clock the lady of the house sailed from the drawing-room, ready for the march. They moved off in procession; Mrs. Rainham leading the way, with Avice and Wilfred, while Cecilia brought up the rear, holding Queenie's podgy hand.

She had telegraph forms in her desk, and the message, already written, and even stamped, was in the pocket of her coat. There was nothing for it but to act boldly, and accordingly, when they entered a street in which there was a post office, she let Queenie lag until they were a little distance behind the others. Then, as they reached the post office, she turned sharply in.

"Wait a minute, Queenie."

She thrust her message across the counter hurriedly. The clerk on duty was provokingly slow; he finished checking a document, and then lounged across to the window and took the form, running over it leisurely.

"Oh, you've got the stamps on. All right," he said, and turned away just as quick steps were heard, and Mrs. Rainham bustled in, panting.

"What are you doing?"

Cecilia met her with steady eyes.

"Nothing wrong, I assure you." She had had visions of covering her real purpose by buying stamps — but rejected it with a shrug.

"Thethilia gave the man a pieth of paper!" said Queenie shrilly.

"What was it? I demand to know!" cried Mrs. Rainham. She turned to the clerk, who stood open-mouthed, holding the telegraph in his hand. "Show me that telegram. I am this young lady's guardian."

The clerk grinned broadly. The stout and angry lady made no appeal to him, and Cecilia was a pretty girl, and moreover her telegraph was for a flying captain. The clerk wore a returned soldier's badge himself. He fell back on Regulations.

"Can't be done, ma'am. The message is all in order."

"Let me see it."

"Much as my billet's worth, if I did," said the clerk. "Property of the Postmaster-General now, ma'am. Couldn't even give it back to the young lady."

"I'll report you!" Mrs. Rainham fumed.

"Do, ma'am. I'll get patted on the head for doin' me duty." The clerk's grin widened. Cecilia wished him good afternoon gravely, and slipped out of the office, pursued by her stepmother.

"What was in that telegram?"

"It was to my brother."

"What was in it?"

"It was to Bob, and that is guarantee that there was nothing wrong in it." Cecilia said steadily. "It was on private business."

"You have no right to have any business that I do not know about."

Cecilia found her temper rising.

"My father may have the power to say that — I do not know," she said. "But you have none, Mrs. Rainham."

"I'll let you see whether I have the right!" her stepmother blazed. "For two pins, young lady, I'd lock you up."

Cecilia laughed outright.

"Ah, that's not done now," she said. "You really couldn't, Mrs. Rainham — especially as I have done nothing wrong." She dropped her voice — passers-by were looking with interest at the elder woman's face. "Why not let me go? You do not approve of me — let me find another position."

"You'll stay in your father's house," Mrs. Rainham said. "We'll see what the law has to say to your leaving with your precious Bob. Your father's your legal guardian, and in his control you stay until you're twenty-one, and be very thankful to make yourself useful. The law will deal with Bob if he tries to take you away — you're a minor, and it'd be abduction." The word had a pleasantly legal flavour; she repeated it with emphasis. "Abduction; that's what it is, and there's a nice penalty for it. Now you know, and if you don't want to get Bob into trouble, you'd best be careful."

Cecilia had grown rather white. The law was a great and terrible instrument, of which she knew nothing. It seemed to have swallowed up Aunt Margaret's money; it might very well have left her defenceless. Her stepmother seemed familiar with its powers, and able to evoke them at will; and though she did not trust her, there was something in her glib utterance that struck fear into the girl's heart. She did not answer, and Mrs. Rainham followed up her advantage.

"We'll go home," she said. "And you make up your mind to tell me what was in that telegram, and not to have any secrets from me. One thing I can tell you — until you decide to behave yourself — Bob shan't show his nose in my house, and you shan't go out to meet him, either. He only leads you into mischief; I don't consider he has at all a good influence over you. The sooner he's away somewhere, earning his own living in a proper manner, the better for everyone; and it'll be many a long day before he can give you as good a home as you've got now." She paused for breath. "Anyhow, he's not going to have the chance," she finished grimly.

CHAPTER 5

The Turn of Fortune's Wheel

"IS Mr. M'Clinton in?"

The clerk, in a species of rabbit hutch, glanced out curiously at the young flying officer.

"Yes; but he's very busy. Have you an appointment?"

"No — I got leave unexpectedly. Just take him my card, will you?"

The clerk handed the card to another clerk, who passed it to an office boy, who disappeared with it behind a heavy oaken door. He came back presently.

"Mr. M'Clinton will see you in ten minutes, if you can wait, sir."

"I'll wait," said Bob, sitting down upon a high stool. "Got a paper?"

"Today's *Times* is here, sir." He whisked off, to return in a moment with the paper, neatly folded.

"You'll find a more comfortable seat behind the screen, sir."

"Thanks," said Bob, regarding him with interest — he was so dapper, so alert, so all that an

office-boy in a staid lawyer's establishment ought
to be. "How old might you be?"

"Fourteen, sir."

"And are you going to grow into a lawyer?"

"I'm afraid I'll never do that sir," said the
office-boy gravely. "I may be head clerk, perhaps.
But —" he stopped, confused.

"But what?"

"I'd rather fly, sir, than anything in the world!"
He looked worshippingly at Bob's uniform. "If the
war had only not stopped before I was old enough,
I might have had a chance!"

"Oh, you'll have plenty of chances," Bob told him
consolingly. "In five years' time you'll be taking
Mr. M'Clinton's confidential papers across to Paris
in an aeroplane — and bringing him back a reply
before lunch!"

"Do you think so, sir?" The office-boy's eyes
danced. Suddenly he resumed his professional
gravity.

"I must get back to my work, sir." He
disappeared behind another partition; the office
seemed to Bob to be divided into water-tight
compartments, in each of which he imagined that
a budding lawyer or head clerk was being brought
up by hand. It was all rather grim and solid and
forbidding. To Bob the law had always been full
of mystery; this grey, silent office, in the heart of
the city, was a fitting place for it. He felt a little
chill at his heart, a foreboding that no comfort
could come of his mission there.

The inner door opened, after a little while, and
a woman in black came out. She passed hurriedly

through the outer office, pulling down her veil over a face that showed traces of tears. Bob looked after her compassionately.

"Poor soul!" he thought. "She's had her gruel, evidently. Now I suppose I'll get mine."

A bell whirred sharply. The alert office-boy sprang to the summons, returning immediately.

"Mr. M'Clinton can see you now, sir."

Bob followed him through the oaken door, and along a narrow passage to a room where a spare, grizzled man sat at a huge roll-top desk. He rose as the boy shut the door behind his visitor.

"Well, Captain Rainham. How do you do?"

Bob gripped the lean hand offered him — it felt like a claw in his great palm. Then he sat down and looked uncomfortably at the lawyer.

"I had thought to have seen you here before, Captain."

"I suppose I should have shown up," said Bob — concealing the fact that the idea had never occurred to him. "But I've been very busy since I've been back to England."

"And what brings you now?"

"I'm all but demobilised," Bob told him, "and I'm trying to get employment."

"What — in this office?"

"Heavens, no!" ejaculated Bob, and at once turned a fine red. "That is — I beg your pardon, sir; but I'm afraid I'm not cut out for an office. I want to get something to do in the country, where I can support my sister."

"Your sister? But does not your father support her? She is an inmate of his house, is she not?"

"Very much so," said Bob bitterly. "She's governess, and lady help, and a good many other things. You couldn't call it a home. Besides, we have always been together. I want to take her away."

"And what does your father say?"

"He says she mustn't go. At least, that's what my stepmother says, so my father will certainly say it too."

"Your sister is under age, I think?"

"She's just nineteen — I'm over twenty-two. Can my father prevent her going with me, sir?"

"Mph," said the lawyer, pondering. "Do I gather that the young lady is unhappy?"

"If she isn't, it's because she has pluck enough for six people, and because she always hopes to get away."

"And do you consider that you could support her?"

"I don't know," said Bob unhappily. "I would certainly have thought I could, but there seems mighty little chance for a fellow whose only qualification is that he's been fighting Huns for nearly five years. I've answered advertisements and interviewed people until my brain reels; but there's nothing in it, and I can't leave Tommy there."

"Tommy?" queried the lawyer blankly.

Bob laughed.

"My sister, I mean, sir. Her name's Cecilia, but, of course, we've never called her that. Even Aunt Margaret called her Tommy."

Mr. M'Clinton made no reply. He thought deeply

for a few moments. Then he looked up, and there
was a glint of kindness in his hard grey eyes.

"I think you had better tell me all about it,
Captain Rainham. Would it assist you to smoke?"

"Thanks awfully, sir," said Bob, accepting the
proffered cigarette. He plunged into his story; and
if at times it was a trifle incoherent, principally
from honest wrath, yet on the whole Cecilia's case
lost nothing in the telling. The lawyer nodded from
time to time, comprehendingly.

"Aye," he said at last, when Bob paused. "Just
so, just so. And why did you come to me, Captain?"

"I want your advice, sir," Bob answered. "And I
should like to know something about my aunt's
property — if I can hope for any help from that
source. I should have more chance of success if I
had a little capital to start with. But I understand
that most of it was lost. My father seemed very
disappointed over the small amount she left." He
hesitated. "But apart from money, I should like to
know if I am within the law in taking my sister
away."

Mr M'Clinton thought deeply before replying.

"I had better speak frankly to you, Captain
Rainham," he said. "Your aunt, as you probably
know, did not like your father. I am not sure that
she actually distrusted him. But she considered
him weak and indolent, and she recognised that
he was completely under the thumb of his second
wife. Your late aunt, my old friend, had an
abhorrence for that lady that was quaint,
considering that she had scarcely ever seen her."
He permitted himself the ghost of a smile. "She

was deeply afraid of any of her property coming under the control of your father — and through him, of his wife. And so she tied up her money very carefully. She left direct to you and your sister certain assets. The rest of her property she left, in trust, to me."

"To you, sir?"

"Aye. Very carefully tied up, too," said Mr. M'Clinton, with a twinkle. "I can't make ducks and drakes of it, no matter how much I may wish to. It is tied up until your sister comes of age. Then my trust ceases."

"By Jove!" Bob stared at him. "Then — do we get something?"

"Certainly. Unfortunately, many of your aunt's investments were very hard hit through the war. Certain stocks which paid large dividends ceased to pay altogether; others fell to very little. The sum left to you and your sister for immediate use should have been very much larger, but all that is left of it is the small allowance paid to you both. I imagine that a smart young officer like yourself found it scarcely sufficient for tobacco."

"I've saved it all," said Bob simply. "A bit more, too."

"Saved it!" said the lawyer in blank amazement. "Do you tell me, now? You lived on your pay?"

"Flying pay's pretty good," said Bob. "And there was always Tommy to think of, you know, sir. I had to put something away for her, in case I crashed."

"Dear me," said Mr. M'Clinton. "Your aunt had great confidence in you as a boy, and it seems she was justified. I'm very glad to hear this, Captain, for it enables me to do with a clear conscience something which I have the power to do. There is a discretionary clause in your aunt's will, which gives me power to realise a certain sum of money, should you need it. I could hand you over about three thousand pounds."

"Three thousand!" Bob stared at him blankly.

"Aye. And I see no reason why I should not do it — provided I am satisfied as to the use you will make of it. As a matter of form I should like a letter from your commanding officer, testifying to your general character."

"That's easy enough," said Bob. "But — three thousand! My hat, what a difference it will make to Tommy and me! Poor old Aunt Margaret — I might have known she'd look after us."

"She loved you very dearly. And now, Captain, about your sister."

"She's the big thing," said Bob. "Can I kidnap her?"

"It's rather difficult to say just how your father might act. Left to himself, I do not believe he would do anything. But urged by your stepmother, he might make trouble. And the good lady is more likely to make trouble if she suspects that there is any money coming to your sister."

"That's very certain," Bob remarked. "I wish to goodness I could get her right out of England, sir. How about Canada?"

The lawyer pondered.

"Do you know anyone there?"

"Not a soul. But I suppose one could get

introductions. And one can always get Government expert advice there, I believe, to prevent one chucking away one's money foolishly."

Mr. M'Clinton nodded approvingly.

"I don't know, but you might do worse," he said. "I believe in these new countries for young people; the old ones are getting overcrowded and worn out. And your relations are likely to give trouble if you are within their reach. A terrible woman, that stepmother of yours; a terrible woman. She came to see me with your father; he said nothing, but she talked like a mill-race. Miss Tommy has my full sympathy. A brawling woman in a wide house, as the Scripture says. I reproach myself, Captain, that I did not inquire personally into Miss Tommy's well-being. She told you nothing of her trials, you say, during the war?"

"Not a word. Wrote as if life were a howling joke always. I only found out for myself by accident a few months ago."

"A brave lassie. Well, I'll do what I can to help you, Captain. I'll keep a lookout for a likely land investment for your money, and endeavour to prepare a good legal statement to frighten Mrs. Rainham if she objects to your taking your sister away. Much may be done by bluffing, especially if you do it very solemnly and quietly. So keep a good heart, and come and see me next time you're in London. Miss Tommy will be in any day, I presume, after the telegram you told me about?"

"Sure to be," said Bob. "She'll be anxious for her letters. I'm leaving one for her, if you don't mind, and I'll write to her again tonight." He got up, holding out his hand. "Goodbye — and I don't know how to thank you, sir."

"Bless the boy — you've nothing to thank me for," said the lawyer. "Just send me that letter from your commanding officer, and remember that there's no wild hurry about plans — Miss Tommy can stand for a few weeks longer what she has borne for two years."

"I suppose she can — but I don't want her to," Bob said.

The brisk office-boy showed him out, and he marched down the grey streets near Lincoln's Inn with his chin well up. Life had taken a sudden and magical turn for the better. Three thousand pounds! — surely that meant no roughing it for Tommy, but a comfortable home and a chance of success in life. It seemed a sum of enormous possibilities. Everything was very vague still, but at least the money was certain — it seemed like fairy gold. He felt a sudden desire to get away somewhere, with Tommy, away from crowded England to a country where a man could breathe; his heart rejoiced at the idea, just as he had often exulted when his aeroplane had lifted him away from the crowded, buzzing camp, into the wide, free places of the air. Canada called to him temptingly. His brain was seething with plans to go there when, waiting for a chance to cross a crowded thoroughfare, he heard his own name.

"Asleep, Rainham?"

Bob looked up with a start. General Harran, the Australian, was beside him, also waiting for a break in the crawling string of motor buses and taxi cabs. He was smiling under his close-clipped moustache.

"I beg your pardon, sir," stammered the boy, coming to the salute stiffly. "I was in a brown study, I believe."

"You looked it. I spoke to you twice before you heard me. What is it? — demobilisation problems?"

"Just that, sir," said Bob, grinning. "Most of us have got them, I suppose — fellows of my age, anyhow. It's a bit difficult to come down to earth again, after years spent in the air."

"Very difficult," Harran agreed gravely. He glanced down with interest at the alert face and square-built figure of the boy beside him. There were so many of them, these boys who had played with Death for years. They had saved their country from horror and ruin, and now it seemed very doubtful if their country wanted them. They were in every town in England, looking for work; their pitiful, plucky advertisements greeted the eye in every newspaper. The problem of their future interested General Harran keenly. He liked his boys; their freshness and pluck and unspoiled enthusiasm had been a tonic to him during the long years of war. Now it hurt him that they should be looking for the right to live.

"I'm just going to lunch, Rainham," he said. "Would you care to come with me?"

Bob lifted a quaintly astonished face.

"Thanks, awfully, sir," he stammered.

"Then jump on this bus, and we'll go to my club," said the General, swinging his lean, athletic body up the stairs of a passing motor bus as he spoke. Bob followed, and they sped, rocking, through the packed traffic until the General, who had sat in silence, jumped up, threaded his way downstairs, and dropped to the ground again from the footboard of the hurrying bus — with a brief shake of the head to the conductor, who was prepared to check the speed of his craft to accommodate a passenger with such distinguished badges of rank. Bob was on the ground almost as quickly, and they turned out of the crowded street into a quieter one that presently led them into a silent square, where dignified grey houses looked out upon green trees, and the only traffic was that of gliding motors. General Harran led the way into one of the grey houses, up the steps of which officers were constantly coming and going. A grizzled porter in uniform, with the Crimean medal on his tunic, swung the door open and came smartly to attention as they passed through. The General greeted him kindly.

"How are you, O'Shea? The rheumatism better?"

"It is, sir, thank you." They passed on, through a great hall lined with oil paintings of famous soldiers, and trophies of big game from all over the world; for this was a Service club, bearing a proud record of soldier and sailor members for a hundred years. Presently they were in the dining-room, already crowded. The waiter found them a little table in a quiet corner.

There was a sprinkling of men whom Bob already knew; he caught several friendly nods of recognition as he glanced round. Then General

Harran pointed out others to him — Generals, whose names were household words in England — a notable Admiral, and a Captain with the VC ribbon earned at Zeebrugge. He seemed to know everyone, and once or twice he left his seat to speak to a friend — during which absence Bob's friends shot him amazed glances, with eyebrows raised in astonishment that he should be lunching with a real Major-General. Bob was somewhat tongue-tied with bewilderment over the fact himself. But when their cold beef came, General Harran soon put him at his ease, leading him to talk of himself and his plans with quiet tact. Before Bob fairly realised it he had unfolded all his little story — even to Tommy and her hardships. The General listened with interest.

"And was it Tommy I saw you with on Saturday?"

"Yes, sir. She was awfully interested because it was you," blurted Bob. "You see, she and I have always been pals. I'm jolly keen to get some place to take her to."

"And you think of Canada. Why?"

"Well — I really don't know, except that it would be out of reach of England and unpleasantness," Bob answered. "And my money would go a lot further there than here, wouldn't it, sir? Three thousand won't buy much of a place in England — not to make one's living by, I mean."

"That's true. I advise every youngster to get out to one of the new countries, and, of course, a man with a little capital has a far greater chance. But why Canada? Why not Australia?"

"There's no reason why not," said Bob laughing. "Only it seems further away. I don't know more of one country than the other — except the sort of vague idea we all have that Canada is all cold and Australia all heat!"

General Harran laughed.

"Yes — the average Englishman's ideas about the new countries are pretty sketchy," he said. "People always talk to me about the fearfully hot climate of Australia, and seem mildly surprised if I remark that we have about a dozen different climates, and that we have snow and ice, and very decent winter sports, in Victoria. I don't think they believe me, either. But seriously, Rainham, if you have no more leaning towards one country than the other, why not think of Australia? I could help you there, if you like."

"You, sir!" Bob stammered.

"Well, I can pull strings. I dare say I could manage a passage out for you and your sister — you see, you were serving with the Australians, and you're both desirable immigrants — young and energetic people with a little capital. That would be all right, I think, especially now that the first rush is over. And I could give you plenty of introductions in Australia to the right sort of people. You ought to see something of the country, and what the life and work are, before investing your money. It would be easy enough to get you on to a station or big farm — you to learn the business, and your sister to teach or help in the house. She wouldn't mind that for about a year, with nice people, would she?"

"Not she!" said Bob. "It was her own idea, in fact; only I didn't want to let her work. But I can see that it might be best. Only I don't know how to thank you, sir — I never imagined —"

General Harran cut him short.

"Don't worry about that. If I can help you, or any of the flying boys, out of a difficulty, and at the same time get the right type of settlers for Australia — she needs them badly — then I'm doing a double-barrelled job that I like. But see here — do I understand that what you really want to do is to take your sister without giving your father warning? To kidnap her, in short?"

"I don't see anything else to do, sir. I spoke to him a while ago about taking her away, and he only hummed and hawed and said he'd consult Mrs. Rainham. And my stepmother will never let her go as long as she can keep her as a drudge. We owe them nothing — he's never been a father to us, and as for my stepmother — well, she should owe Tommy for two years' hard work. But honestly, to all intents and purposes, they are strangers to us — it seems absolutely ridiculous that we should be controlled by them."

"You say your aunt's family lawyer approves?"

"Yes, or he wouldn't let me have the money. I could get him to see you, sir, if you like; though I don't see why you should be bothered about us," said Bob flushing.

"Give me his address — I'll look in on him next time I'm in Lincoln's Inn," said the General. "Your own, too, Now, if I get you and your sister passages on a troopship, can you start at short notice — say forty-eight hours?"

Bob gasped, but recovered himself. After all, his training in the air had taught him to make swift decisions.

"Any time after the fifteenth, sir. I'll be demobilised then, and a free agent. I'll get my kit beforehand."

"Don't get much," counselled the General. "You can travel in uniform — take flannels for the tropics; everything you need in Australia you can get just as well, or better, out there. Most fellows who go out take tons of unnecessary stuff. Come into the smoking-room and give me a few more details."

They came out upon the steps of the club a little later. Bob's head was whirling. He tried to stammer out more thanks and was cut short, kindly but decisively.

"That's all right, my boy. I'll send you letters of introduction to various people who will help you, and a bit of advice about where to go when you land. Tell your sister not to be nervous — she isn't going to a wild country, and the people there are much the same as anywhere else. Now, goodbye, and good luck," and Bob found himself walking across the Square in a kind of solemn amazement.

"This morning I was thinking of getting taken on as a farm hand in Devonshire, with Tommy somewhere handy in a labourer's cottage," he pondered. "And now I'm a bloated capitalist, and Tommy and I are going across the world to Australia as calmly as if we were off to Margate for the day! Well, I suppose it's only a dream, and I'll wake up soon. I guess I'd better go back and tell Mr. M'Clinton; and I've got to see Tommy somehow." He bent his brows over the problem as he turned towards Lincoln's Inn.

CHAPTER 6

Sailing Orders

"ARE you there, miss?"
The sepulchral whisper came faintly to
Cecilia's ears as she sat in her little room, sewing
a frock of Queenie's. The children were out in the
garden at the back of the house. Mrs. Rainham
was practising in the drawing-room. The sound of
a high trill floated upwards as she opened the
door.

"What is it, Eliza?"

"It's a letter, miss. A kid brought it to the
kitchen door — a bit of a boy. Asked for me as if
'e'd known me all 'is life — called me Elizer! 'e's
waitin' for an answer. I'll wait in me room, miss,
till you calls me." The little Cockney girl slipped
away, revelling in furthering any scheme to defeat
Mrs. Rainham and help Cecilia.

Cecilia opened the letter hurriedly. It contained
only one line.

"Can you come at once to Lincoln's Inn?
Important. — BOB."

Cecilia knitted her brows. It was nearly a month
since the memorable evening when she and Bob
had revolted; and though she was still made to
feel herself in disgrace, and she knew her letters
were watched, the close spying upon her

movements had somewhat relaxed. It had been too uncomfortable for Mrs. Rainham to keep it up, since it made heavy demands upon her own time, and interfered with too many plans; moreover, in spite of it, Cecilia had slipped away from the house two or three times, going and coming openly, and replying to any questions by the simple answer that she had been to meet Bob. Angry outbreaks on the part of her stepmother she received in utter silence, against which the waves of Mrs. Rainham's wrath spent themselves in vain.

Indeed, the girl lived in a kind of waking dream of happy anticipation, beside which none of the trials of life in Lancaster Gate had power to trouble her. For on her first stolen visit to Mr. M'Clinton's office the wonderful plan of flight to Australia had been revealed to her, and the joy of the prospect blotted out everything else. Mr. M'Clinton, watching her face, had been amazed by the wave of delight that had swept over it.

"You like it, then?" he had said. "You are not afraid to go so far?"

"Afraid — with Bob? Oh, the farther I can get from England the better," she had answered. "I have no friends here; nothing to leave, except the memory of two bad years. And out there I should feel safe — she could not get a policeman to bring me back." There was no need to ask who "she" was.

Cecilia had made her preparations secretly. She had not much to do — Aunt Margaret had always kept her well dressed, and the simple and pretty things she had worn two years before, and which had never been unpacked since she put on mourning for her aunt, still fitted her, and were perfectly good. It had never seemed worthwhile to leave off wearing mourning in Lancaster Gate — only when Bob had come home had she unpacked some of her old wardrobe. Much was packed still, and in store under Mr. M'Clinton's direction, together with many of Aunt Margaret's personal possessions. It was as well that it was so, since Mrs. Rainham had managed to annex a proportion of Cecilia's things for Avice. To Lancaster Gate she had only taken a couple of trunks, not dreaming of staying there more than a short time. So packing and flitting would be easy, given ordinary luck and the certain co-operation of Eliza. Her few necessary purchases had been made on one of her hurried excursions with Bob; she had not dared to have the things sent home, and they had been consigned in a tin uniform case to Bob's care.

She pondered over his note now, knitting her brows. It would be easy enough to act defiantly and go at once; but if this meant that the final flight was near at hand she did not wish to excite anew her stepmother's anger and suspicion. Then, as she hesitated, she heard a heavy step on the stairs, and she crushed the note hurriedly into her pocket.

Mrs. Rainham came into the room without the formality of knocking — a formality she had never observed where Cecilia was concerned. The afternoon post had just come, and she carried some letters in her hand.

"Cecilia, I want you to put on your things and

go to Balding's for me," she said, her voice more civil than it had been for a month. "I'm asked up to Liverpool for a few days; my sister there is giving a big At Home — an awfully big thing, with the Lady Mayoress and all the Best People at it — and she wants me to go up. I suppose she'll want me to sing."

"That is nice," said Cecilia, speaking with more truth than Mrs. Rainham guessed. "What will you wear?"

"That's just it," said her stepmother eagerly. "My new evening dress isn't quite finished — we ran short of trimming. I can't go out, because the Simons are coming in to afternoon tea; so you just hurry and go over to Balding's to match it. I got it there, and they had plenty. Here's a bit." She held out a fragment of gaudy sequin trimming. "I think you could finish the dress without me getting in the dressmaker again — she's that run after she makes a regular favour of coming."

"Very well," said Cecilia — who would, at the moment, have agreed to sew anything or everything that might hasten her stepmother's journey. "When do you go?"

"The day after tomorrow. I'll stay there a few days, I suppose; not worth going so far for only one evening. Mind, Cecilia, you're not to have Bob here while I'm away. When I come back, if I'm satisfied with you, I'll see about asking him again."

"That is very good of you," said the girl slowly.

"Well, that's all right — you hurry and get ready; there's always a chance they may have sold out, because it was a bargain line, and if they have you'll have to try other places. I don't know what on earth I'll do if you can't match it." She turned to go and then hesitated. "I was thinking you might take Avice with you — but you'll get about quicker alone, and she isn't ready. The tubes and buses are that crowded it's no catch to take a child about with you." In moments of excitement Mrs. Rainham's English was apt to slip from her. At other times she cultivated it carefully, assisted by a dramatic class, which an enthusiastic maiden lady, with leanings towards the stage, conducted each winter among neighbouring kindred souls.

Cecilia had caught her breath in alarm, but she breathed a sigh of relief as the stout, over-dressed figure went down the narrow stairs, with a final injunction to hurry. There was, indeed, no need to give Cecilia that particular command. She scribbled one word, "Coming," on Bob's note, thrust it into an envelope and addressed it hastily, and then tapped on the wall between the servants' room and her own.

Eliza appeared with the swiftness of a Jack-in-the-box, full of suppressed excitement.

"Lor! I fought she was never goin'," she breathed. "Got it ready, Miss? The boy'll fink I've gorn an' eloped wiv it." She took the envelope and pattered swiftly downstairs.

A very few moments saw Cecilia flying in her wake — to Balding's first, as quickly as tube and motor bus could combine to take her, since she dared not breathe freely until Mrs. Rainham's commission had been settled. Balding's had never seemed so huge and so complicated, and when she at length made her way to the right department the suave assistant regretted that the trimming was sold out. It was Cecilia's face of blank dismay that made him suddenly remember that there was possibly an odd length somewhere, and a search revealed it, put away in a box of odds and ends. Cecilia's thanks were so heartfelt that the assistant was mildly surprised.

"For she don't seem the sort to wear ghastly stuff like that," he pondered, glancing after the pretty figure in the well-cut coat and skirt.

Outside the great shop Cecilia glanced up and caught the eye of a taxi driver who had just set down a fare.

"I'll be extravagant for once," she thought. She beckoned to the man, and in a moment was whirring through the streets in the peculiar comfort a motor gives to anyone in a hurry in London — since it can take direct routes instead of following the roundabout methods of buses and underground railways. She leaned back, closing her eyes. If this summons to Bob indeed meant that their sailing orders had come, she would need all her wits and her coolness. For the first time she realised what her stepmother's absence from home might mean — a thousandfold less plotting and planning, and no risk of a horrible scene at the end. Cecilia loathed scenes; they had not existed in Aunt Margaret's scheme of existence. Since Bob's plans had become at all definite, she had looked forward with dread to a final collision with Mrs. Rainham — it was untold relief to know that it might not come.

She hurried up the steps of Mr. M'Clinton's office. The alert office boy — who had been Bob's messenger to Lancaster Gate — met her.

"You're to go straight in, miss. The Captain's there."

Bob was in the inner sanctum with Mr. M'Clinton. They rose to meet her.

"Well — are you ready, young lady?" the old man asked.

"Is it — are we to sail soon?"

"Next Saturday — and this is Monday. Can you manage it, Tommy?" Bob's eyes were dancing with excitement.

"Oh, Bobby — truly?" She caught at his coat sleeve. "When did you hear?"

"I had a wire from General Harran this morning. A jolly good ship, too, Tommy; one of the big Australian liners — the *Nauru* sails from Liverpool."

"Bobby!" Cecilia's face fell. "I thought we went from Gravesend or Tilbury, or somewhere."

"So did I. But the General's wire says Liverpool, so it seems we don't," said Bob. "And that she-dragon is going there too!"

"I don't think you need really worry," Mr. M'Clinton said drily. "Liverpool is not exactly a village. The chances are that if you went there, trying to meet someone, you would hunt for him for a week in vain. And you'll probably go straight from the train to the docks, so that you won't be in the least likely to encounter Mrs. Rainham."

"Why, of course, we'd never run into her in a huge place like Liverpool," Bob said, laughing.

"Don't be afraid, Tommy — you'll have seen the last of her when you say goodbye on Wednesday."

"It seems too good to be true," said Cecilia solemnly. "I remember how I felt once before, when she went away to visit her sister in Liverpool; the beautiful relief when one woke, to think that not all through the day would one even have to look at her. It's really very terrible to look at her often; her white face and hard eyes seem to fascinate one. Oh, I don't suppose I ought to talk like that, especially here." She looked shamefacedly at Mr. M'Clinton, and blushed scarlet.

Both men laughed.

"The good lady had something of the same effect on me," Mr. M'Clinton admitted. "I found her a very terrible person. Cheer up, Miss Tommy, you've nearly finished with her. And, now, what about getting you away?"

Cecilia turned to her brother.

"What am I to do, Bob?"

"We'll have to go to Liverpool on Friday," Bob replied promptly. "I can't find out the *Nauru*'s sailing time, and it isn't safe to leave it until Saturday. There's a train somewhere about two o'clock that gets up somewhere about seven or eight that evening. Mr. M'Clinton and I don't want to leave it to the last moment to get your luggage away from Lancaster Gate. Can you have it ready the night before?"

"It would really be safer to take it in the afternoon," Cecilia said after a moment's thought. "Mrs. Rainham's absence will make that quite

easy, for I know I can depend upon Eliza and
Cook. I can get my trunks ready, leave them in
my room, and tell Eliza you will be there to call
for them, say, at four o'clock. Then I take the three
children out for a walk, and when we return
everything is gone. Will that do?"

"Perfectly," said Bob, laughing. "And four o'clock
suits me all right. Then you'll saunter out on
Friday morning with an inoffensive brown paper
parcel containing the rest of your worldly effects,
and meet me for lunch at the Euston Hotel. Is
that clear?"

"Quite. I suppose I had better put no address
on my trunks?"

"Not a line — I'll see to that. And don't even
mention the word 'Australia' this week, just in
case your eye dances unconsciously, and sets
people thinking! I think you'd better cultivate a
downtrodden look, at any rate until Mrs. Rainham
is out of the house; at present you look far too
cheerful to be natural — doesn't she, sir?"

"You have to see to it that she does not look
downtrodden again, after this week," said Mr.
M'Clinton. "Remember that, Captain — she's
going a long way, and she'll have no one but you."

"I know, sir. But, bless you, it's me that will
look downtrodden," said Bob with a grin. "She
bullies me horribly — always did." He slipped his
hand through her arm, and they looked up at him
with such radiant faces that the old man smiled
involuntarily.

"Ah, I think you'll be all right," he said.
"Remember, Miss Tommy, I'll expect to hear from

you — fairly often, too. I shall not say goodbye now — you'll see me on Friday at luncheon."

They found themselves down in the grey precincts of Lincoln's Inn, which, it may be, had rarely seen two young things prancing along so dementedly. In the street they had to sober down, to outward seeming; but there was still something about them, as they hurried off to find a teashop to discuss final details, that made people turn to look at them. Even the waitress beamed on them, and supplied them with her best cakes — and London waitresses are a bored race. But at the moment, neither Cecilia nor Bob could have told you whether they were eating cakes or sausages.

"The money is all right," Bob said. "It'll be available at a Melbourne bank when we get there; and meanwhile, there's plenty of ready money, with what I've saved and my war gratuity. So if you want anything, Tommy, you just say so, and don't go without any pretties just because you think we'll be in the workhouse."

"Bless you — but I don't really need anything," she told him gratefully. "It would be nice to have a little money to spend at the ports, but I think we ought to keep the rest for Australia, don't you, Bob?"

"Oh, yes, of course; but you're not to go without a few pounds if you want 'em," said Bob. "And, Tommy, don't leave meeting me on Friday until lunch time. I'll be worrying if you do, just in case things may have gone wrong. Make it eleven o'clock at the Bond Street tube exit, and if you're

not there in half an hour I'll jolly well go and fetch
you."

"I'll be there," Cecilia nodded. "You had better
give me the half-hour's grace, though, in case
might be held up at the last moment. One never
knows — and Avice and Wilfred are excellent little
watchdogs."

"Anyhow, you won't have the she-dragon to
reckon with, and that's a big thing," Bob said. "I
don't see how you can have any trouble — Papa
certainly will not give you any."

"No, he won't bother," said Cecilia slowly. "It's
queer to think how little he counts — our own
father."

"A pretty shoddy apology for one, I think," Bob
said bitterly. "What has he ever done for us? But
I'd forgive him that when I can't forgive him
something else — the way he has let you be
treated these two years."

"He hasn't known everything, Bobby."

"He has known quite enough. And if he had the
spirit of a man he'd have saved you from it. No,
we don't owe him any consideration, Tommy, and
he saw to it years ago that we should never owe
him any affection. So we really needn't worry our
heads about him. By the way, there are to be some
Australians on the *Nauru* who General Harran
says may be of use to us — I don't remember their
names, but he's going to give me a letter to them.
And probably there will be some other flying
people whom I may know. I think the voyage
ought to be rather good fun."

"I think so, too. It will be exciting to be on a

troopship," Cecilia said. "But, then, anything will be heavenly after Lancaster Gate!"

She hurried home, as soon as the little meal was over, knowing that Mrs. Rainham would be impatiently awaiting her. Luckily, her success in matching the trimming made her stepmother forget how long she had been away; and from that moment until a welcome four-wheeler removed the mistress of the house on Wednesday, she sewed and packed for her unceasingly. Her journey excited Mrs. Rainham greatly. She talked almost affably of her sister's grandeur, and of the certainty of meeting wealthy and gorgeously dressed people at her party.

"Not that I'll be at all ashamed of my dress," she added, looking at the billowy waves on which Cecilia was plastering yet more trimming. "Unusual and artistic, that's what it is; and it'll show off my hair. Don't forget the darning when I'm gone, Cecilia. There's a tablecoth to mend, as well as the stockings. I'll be home on Saturday night, unless they persuade me to stay over the week-end."

Cecilia nodded, sewing busily.

"And just see if you can't get on a bit better with the children. You've got to make allowances for their high spirits, and treat them tactfully. Of course you can't expect them to be as obedient to you as they would be to a regular governess, you being their own half-sister, and not so much older than Avice, after all. But tact does wonders, especially with children."

"Yes," said Cecilia, and said no more.

"Well, just bear it in mind. I don't suppose you'll see much of your father, so you needn't worry about him. But don't let Eliza gossip and idle; she never does any work if she's not kept up to it, and you know you're much too familiar with her. Always keep girls like her at a distance, and they'll work all the better, that's what I say. Treat her as an equal, and the next thing you know she'll be trying on your hats!"

"I haven't caught Eliza at that yet," said Cecilia with the ghost of a smile.

"It'll come, though, if you're not more stand-offish with her — you mark my words. Keep them in their place — that's what I always do with my servants and governesses," said Mrs. Rainham without the slightest idea that she was saying anything peculiar. "Now, I'll go and put my things out on my bed, and as soon as you've finished that you can come up and pack for me."

Cecilia stood at the hall door that afternoon to watch her go — bustling into the cab, with loud directions to the cabman, her hard face full of self-importance and satisfaction. The plump hand waved a highly scented handkerchief as the clumsy four-wheeler moved off.

"To think I'll never see you again!" breathed the girl. "It seems too good to be true!"

A kind of wave of relief seemed to have descended upon the house. The children were openly exulting in having no one to obey; an attitude which, in the circumstances, failed to trouble their half-sister. Eliza went about her work with a cheery face; even Cook, down in the basement, manifested lightness of heart by singing love songs in a cracked soprano and by making scones for afternoon tea. Mark Rainham did not come home until late — he had announced his intention of dining at his club. Late in the evening he sauntered into the dining-room, where Cecilia sat sewing.

"Still at it?" he asked. He sat down and poked the fire. "What are you sewing?"

"Just darning," Cecilia told him.

He sat looking at her for a while — at the pretty face and the well-tended hair, and who shall say what thoughts stirred in his dull brain?

"You look a bit pale," he said at last. "Do you go out enough?"

"Oh, yes, I think so," Cecilia answered in astonishment. Not in two years had he shown so much interest in her; and it braced her to a sudden resolve. She had never been quite satisfied to leave him without a word; whatever he was, he was still her father. She put her darning on her knee, and looked at him gravely.

"You know Bob is demobilised, don't you, Papa?"

"Yes — he told me so," Mark Rainham answered.

"And you know he wants to take me away?"

Her father's eyes wavered and fell before her.

"Oh, yes — but the idea's ridiculous, I'm afraid. You're under age, and your stepmother won't hear of it." He poked the fire savagely.

"But if Bob could make a home for me! We have always been together, you know, Papa."

"Oh, well — wait and see. Time enough when

you're twenty-one, and your own mistress; Bob will
have had a chance to make good by then. I — I
can't oppose my wife in the matter — she says
she's not strong enough to do without your help."

"But she never seems satisfied with me."

Mark Rainham rose with an irritably nervous
movement.

"Oh, no one is ever perfect. I suspect, if each of
you went a little way to meet the other, things
would be better. Your stepmother says her nerves
are all wrong, and I'm sure you do take a great
deal of trouble off her shoulders."

"Then you won't let me go?" The girl's low voice
was relentless, and her father wriggled as though
he were a beetle and she were pinning him down.

"I — I'm afraid it's out of the question, Cecilia.
I should have to be very satisfied first that Bob
could offer you a home — and by that time he'll
probably be thinking of getting married, and won't
want you. Why can't you settle down comfortably
to living at home?"

"There isn't any home for me apart from Bob,"
said the girl.

"Well, I can't help it." Mark Rainham's voice
had a hopeless tone. He walked to the door, and
then half turned. "If you can make my wife agree
to your going, I won't forbid it. Goodnight."

"Goodnight," said Cecilia. The slow footsteps
went up the stairs, and she turned to her darning
with a lip that curled in scorn.

"Well, that lets me out. I don't owe you anything
— not even a goodbye note on my pincushion," she
said presently, and laughed a little. She folded a

finished pair of socks deliberately, and, rising, stretched her arms luxuriously above her head. "Two more days," she whispered. She switched off the light, and crept noiselessly upstairs.

CHAPTER 7

The Watchdogs

"WELL, if you ask me, she's up to something," said Avice with conviction.

"How d'you mean?" Wilfred looked up curiously.

"Lots of things. She looks all different. First of all — look how red she is all the time, and the excited look in her eyes."

"That's all look — look!" jeered her brother. "Girls always have those rotten ideas about nothing at all. Just because Cecilia's got a bit sunburnt, and because she's havin' an easy time 'cause Mater's away —"

"Oh, you think because you're a boy, you know everything," retorted his sister hotly. "You just listen, and see if I've got rotten ideas. Did you know, she's kept her room locked for days?"

"Well — if she has? That's nothing."

"You shut up and let me go on. Yesterday she forgot, and left it open while she was down talking to Cook, and I slipped in. And there was one of her great big trunks, that she always keeps in the box room, half-packed with her things. I nicked this necklace out of it, too," said Avice with triumph, producing a quaint string of Italian beads.

"Good business," said Wilfred with an appreciative grin. "Did she catch you?"

"Not she — I can tell you I didn't wait long, 'cause she always comes upstairs as quick as lightning. She did come, too, in an awful hurry, and locked up the room — I only got out of the way just in time. And every minute she could, yesterday, she was up there."

"Well, I don't see much in that."

"No, but look here, I got another chance of looking into her room this morning, and that trunk was gone!"

"Gone back to the box-room," said Wilfred with superiority.

"No, it wasn't — I went up and looked. And her other trunk's not there, either."

"Oh, you're dreaming! I bet she'd just pushed it under her bed."

"Pooh!" said Avice. "That great big trunk wouldn't go under her bed — you know she's only got a little stretcher bed. And I tell you they're both gone. I bet you anything she's going to run away."

"Where'd she run to?"

"Oh, somewhere with Bob."

"Well, let her go."

"Yes, and Mater'd have to spend ever so much on a new governess; and most likely she'd be a worse beast than Cecilia. And no governess we ever had did half the things Mater makes Cecilia do to help in the house. Why, she's like an extra servant, as well as a governess. Mater told me all

about it. I tell you what, Wilfred, it's our business
to see she doesn't run away."

"All right," said Wilfred. "I suppose we'd better
watch out. When do you reckon she'd go? People
generally run away at night, don't they?"

"Well, anyone can see she's just taking
advantage of Mater being away. Yes, of course
she'd go at night. She might have sent her boxes
away yesterday by a carrier — I bet that horrid
little Eliza would help her. Ten to one she means
to sneak out tonight — she knows Mater will be
home tomorrow."

"What a sell it will be for her if we catch her!"
said Wilfred with glee. "I say, what about telling
Pater?"

Avice looked sour.

"I did tell him something yesterday, and he only
growled at me. At least, I said, 'Do you think
Cecilia would ever be likely to run away?' And he
just stared at me, and then he said, 'Not your
business if she does.' So I'm not going to speak to
him again."

"Well, we'd better take it in turns to watch her,"
Wilfred said. "After dark's the most likely time, I
suppose, but we'd better be on the lookout all the
time. Where's she now, by the way?"

"Why, I don't know. I say, she's been away a
long time — I never noticed," said Avice, in sudden
alarm. "She said we were to go on with our French
exercises — and that's ages ago."

"Come on and see," said Wilfred jumping up.

Outside the room he caught Avice by the arm.

"Kick off your shoes," he said. "We'll sneak up to her room."

They crept up silently. The door of Cecilia's room was ajar. Peeping in, they saw her standing before her tiny looking-glass, pinning on her hat. A small parcel lay upon her bed, with her gloves and parasol. The children were very silent — but something struck upon the girl's tightly strung nerves. She turned swiftly and saw them.

"What are you doing?" she demanded. "How dare you come into my room?"

"Why, we thought you were lost," said Avice.

"We finished our French ages ago. Where are you going?"

"I am going out," said Cecilia. "I'll set you more work to do while I'm away."

"But where are you going?"

"That has nothing to do with you. Come down to the schoolroom."

Avice held her brother firmly by the arm. Together they blocked the way.

"Mater wouldn't let you go out in lesson time. I believe you're going to run away!"

A red spot flamed in each of Cecilia's white cheeks.

"Stand out of my way, you little horrors!" she said angrily. She caught up her things and advanced upon them.

"I'm hanged if you're going," said Wilfred doggedly. He pushed her back violently, and slammed the door.

The attic doors in Lancaster Gate, like those of many London houses, were fitted with heavy iron

bolts on the outside — a precaution against
burglars who might enter the house by rooms
ordinarily little used. It was not the first time that
Cecilia had been bolted into her room by her
step-brother. When first she came, it had been a
favourite pastime to make her a prisoner — until
their mother had made it an offence carrying a
heavy penalty, since it had often occurred that
Cecilia was locked up when she happened to need
her.

But this time Cecilia heard the heavy bolt shoot
home with feelings of despair. It was already time
for her to leave the house. Bob would be waiting
for her in Bond Street, impatiently scanning each
crowd of passengers that the lift shot up from
underground. She battered at the door wildly.

"Let me out! How dare you, Wilfred! Let me out
at once!"

Wilfred laughed disagreeably.

"Not if we know it — eh, Avice?"

"Rather not," said Avice. "What d'you think
Mater'd say to us if we let you run away?"

"Nonsense!" said Cecilia, controlling her voice
with difficulty. "I was going to meet Bob."

There was silence, and a whispered
consultation. Then Avice spoke.

"Will you give us your word of honour you
weren't going to run away?"

Words of honour meant little to the young
Rainhams. But they knew that Cecilia held it as
a commonplace of decent behaviour that people did
not tell lies. They had, indeed, often marvelled
that she preferred to "take her gruel" rather than

use any ready untruth that would have shielded
her from their mother's wrath. Avice and Wilfred
had no such scruples on their own account: but
they knew that they could depend upon Cecilia's
word. They were, indeed, just a little afraid of
their own action in locking her up; their mother
might have condoned it as "high spirits", but their
father was not unlikely to take a different view.
So they awaited her reply with some anxiety.

Cecilia hesitated. Never in her life had she been
so tempted. Perhaps because the temptation was
so strong she answered swiftly.

"No — I won't tell you anything of the kind. But
look here — if you will let me out I'll give you
each ten shillings."

Ten shillings! It was wealth, and the children
gasped. Wilfred, indeed, would have shot back the
bolt instantly. It was Avice who caught at his arm.

"Don't you!" she whispered. "It'll cost heaps
more than that to get a new governess — and we'll
make Mater give us each ten shillings for keeping
her. I say, we'll have to get the Pater home."

"How?" Wilfred looked at her blankly.

"Easy. You go to the post office and telephone
to him at his office. Tell him to come at once. I'll
watch here, in case Eliza lets her out. Run — hard
as you can. Mater'll never forgive us if she gets
away."

Wilfred clattered off obediently, awed by his
sister's urgency. Avice sat down on the head of the
stairs, close to the bolted door; and when Cecilia
spoke again, repeating her offer, she answered her
in a voice unpleasantly like her mother's.

"No, you don't, my fine lady. Wilfred's gone for the Pater — he'll be here presently. You just stay there quietly till he comes."

"Avice!" The word was a wail. "Oh, you don't know how important it is — let me out. I'll give you anything in the world."

"So'll Mater if I stop your little game," said Avice. "You just keep quiet."

Eliza's sharp little face appeared at the foot of the flight of stairs.

"Wot's up, Miss Avice? Anything wrong with Miss 'Cilia?"

"Nothing to do with you," said Avice rudely. "I'm looking after her." But Cecilia's sharp ears had caught the new voice.

"Eliza! Eliza!' she called.

The girl came up the stairs uncertainly. Avice rose to confront her.

"Now, you just keep off," she said. "You're not coming past here. The master'll be home directly, and till he comes, no one's going up these stairs." She raised her voice, to drown that of Cecilia, who was speaking again.

Eliza looked at her doubtfully. She was an undersized, wizened little Cockney, and Avice was a big, stoutly built girl — who held, moreover, the advantage of a commanding position on the top step. In an encounter of strength there was little doubt as to who would win. She turned in silence, cowed, and went down to the kitchen, while Avice sang a triumphant song, partly as a chant of victory, and partly to make sure that no one would hear the remarks that Cecilia was steadily

making. She herself had caught one phrase —
"Tell my brother" — and her sharp little mind was
busy. Did that mean that Bob would be coming,
against its mistress's orders, to Lancaster Gate?

In the kitchen Eliza poured out a frantic appeal
to Cook.

"She's got Miss 'Cilia locked up — the little
red-'eaded cat! An' Master Wilfred gorn to fetch
the Master! Oh, come on, Cookie darlin', an' we'll
let 'er out."

Cook shook her head slowly.

"Not good enough," she said. "I got a pretty good
place. I ain't goin' to risk it by 'avin' a
rough-an'-tumble with the daughter of the 'ouse
on the hattic stairs. You better leave well alone,
Liza. You done your bit, 'elpin' 'er git them trunks
orf yes'day."

"Wot's the good of 'avin the trunks off if she
can't go, too?" demanded Eliza.

"Oh, she'll git another chance. Don't worry your
'ead so much over other people's business. If the
Master comes 'ome an' finds us scruffin' 'is
daughter, 'e'll 'and us both over to the police for
assault — an' then you'll 'ave cause for worry. Now
you git along like a good gel — I got to mike
pastry." Cook turned away decisively.

Wilfred had come home and had raced up the
stairs.

"Did you get him?" Avice cried.

"No — he was out. So I left a message that he
was to come home at once, 'cause something was
wrong."

"That'll bring him," said Avice with satisfaction.

"Now, look here, Wilf — I believe Bob may come.
You go and be near the front door, to block Eliza,
if he does. Answer any ring."

"What'll I say if he comes?"

"Say she's gone out to meet him — if he thinks
that, he'll hurry back to wherever they were to
meet. Don't give him a chance to get in. Hurry!"

"Right," said Wilfred, obeying. He sat down in
a hall chair, and took up a paper, with an eye
wary for Eliza. Half an hour passed tediously,
while upstairs Cecilia begged and bribed in vain.
Then he sprang to his feet as a ring came.

Bob was at the door, and suddenly Wilfred
realised that he had always been afraid of Bob.
He quailed inwardly, for never had he seen his
half-brother look as he did now — with a kind of
still, terrible anger in his eyes.

"Where's Cecilia?"

"Gone out," said the boy.

"Where?"

"Gone to meet you."

"Did she tell you so?"

"Yes, of course — how'd I know if she didn't?"

"Then that's a lie, for she wouldn't tell you. Let
me in."

"I tell you, she's gone out," said Wilfred, whose
only spark of remaining courage was due to the
fact that he had prudently kept the door on the
chain. "And Mater said you weren't to come in
here."

From the area below a shrill voice floated
upwards.

"Mr. Bob! Mr. Bob! Don't you believe 'im. They got Miss 'Cilia locked up in 'er room."

"By Jove!" said Bob between his teeth. "Bless you, Eliza! Open that door, Wilfred, or I'll make it hot for you." He thrust a foot into the opening, with a face so threatening that Wilfred shrank back.

"I shan't," he said. "You're not going to get her."

"Am I not?" said Bob. He leaned back, and then suddenly flung all his weight against the door. The chain was old and the links eaten with rust — it snapped like a carrot, and the door flew open. Bob brushed Wilfred out of his way, and went upstairs, three at a time.

Avice blocked his path.

"You aren't coming up."

"Oh, yes, I think so," Bob said. He stooped, with a quick movement, and picked her up, holding her across his shoulder, while she beat and clawed unavailingly at his back. So holding her, he thrust back the bolt of Cecilia's door and flung it open.

"Did you think they had got you, Tommy?"

She could only cling to his free arm for a moment, speechless. Then she lifted her face, her voice shaking, still in fear.

"We must hurry, Bob. They've sent for Papa."

"Have they?" said Bob, with interest. "Well, not a regiment of papas should stop you now, old girl. Got everything?"

Cecilia gathered up her things, nodding.

"Then we'll leave this young lady here," said Bob. He placed Avice carefully on Cecilia's bed, and made for the door, having the pleasure, as he shot the bolt, of hearing precisely what the younger Miss Rainham thought of him and all his attributes, including his personal appearance.

"A nice gift of language, hasn't she?" he said. "Inherits it from her mamma, I should think." He put his arm round Cecilia and held her closely as they went downstairs, his face full of the joy of battle. Wilfred was nowhere to be seen, but by the door Eliza waited. Bob slipped something into her hand.

"I expect you'll lose your place over this, Eliza," he said. "Well, you'll get a better — I'll tell my lawyer to see to that. He'll write to you — by the way, what's your surname? Oh, Smithers — I'll remember. And thank you very much."

They shook hands with her, and passed out into the street. Cecilia was still too shaken to speak — but as Bob pulled her hand through his arm and hurried her along, her self-control returned, and the face that looked up at his presently was absolutely content. Bob returned the look with a little smile.

"Didn't you know I'd come?" he asked. "You dear old stupid."

"I knew you'd come — but I thought Papa would get there first," Cecilia answered. "Somehow, it seemed the end of everything."

"It isn't — it's only the beginning," Bob answered.

There was a narrow side street that made a short cut from the tube station to the Rainhams' home; and as they passed it Mark Rainham came hurrying up it. Bob and Cecilia did not see him.

He looked at them for a moment, as if reading the meaning of the two happy faces — and then shrank back into an alley and remained hidden until his son and daughter had passed out of sight. They went on their way, without dreaming that the man they dreaded was within a stone's throw of them.

"So it was that," said Mark Rainham slowly, looking after them. "Out of gaol, are you — poor little prisoner! Well, good luck to you both!" He turned on his heel, and went back to his office.

CHAPTER 8

How Tommy Boarded a Strange Taxi

"WE'RE nearly in, Tommy."
Cecilia looked up from her corner with a start, and the book she had been trying to read slipped to the floor of the carriage.

"I believe you were asleep," said Bob laughing. "Poor old Tommy, are you very tired?"

"Oh, nothing, really. Only I was getting a bit sleepy," his sister answered. "Are we late, Bob?"

"Very, the conductor says. This train generally makes a point of being late. I wish it had made a struggle to be on time tonight; it would have been jolly to get to the ship in daylight." Bob was strapping up rugs briskly as he talked.

"How do we get down to the ship, Bob?"

"Oh, no doubt there'll be taxis," Bob answered. "But it may be no end of a drive — the conductor tells me there are miles and miles of docks, and the *Nauru* may be lying anywhere. But he says there's always a military official on duty at the station — a transport officer, and he'll be able to tell me everything." He did not think it worthwhile to tell the tired little sister what another man had told him that it was very doubtful whether they would be allowed to board any transport at night, and that Liverpool was so crowded that to find beds in it might be an impossibility. Bob refused to be depressed by the prospect. "If the worst came to the worst, there'd be a YWCA that would take in Tommy," he mused. "And it wouldn't be the first time I've spent a night in the open." Nothing seemed to matter now that they had escaped. But, all the same, there seemed no point in telling Tommy, who was extremely cheerful, but also very white-faced.

They drew into an enormous station, where there seemed a dense crowd of people, but no porters at all. Bob piled their hand luggage on the platform, and left Cecilia to guard it while he went on a tour of discovery. He hurried back to her presently.

"Come on," he said, gathering up their possessions. "There's a big station hotel opening on to the platforms. I can leave you sitting in the vestibule while I gather up the heavy luggage and find the transport officer. I'm afraid it's going to take some time, so don't get worried if I don't turn up very soon. There seem to be about fifty thousand people struggling round the luggage vans, and I'll have to wait my turn. But I'll be as quick as I can."

"Don't you worry on my account," Cecilia said. "This is ever so comfortable. I don't mind how long you're away!" She laughed up at him, sinking into a big chair in the vestibule of the hotel. There were heavy glass doors on either side that were constantly swinging to let people in or out; through them could be seen the hurrying throng of people on the station, rushing to and fro under the great electric lights, gathered round the bookstall, struggling along under luggage, or — very occasionally — moving in the wake of a porter with a barrow heaped with trunks. There were soldiers everywhere, British and Australian, and officers in every variety of Allied uniform.

An officer came in with a lady and two tiny boys — Cecilia recognised them as having been passengers on their train. With them came an old Irish priest, who had met them, and the officer left them in his care while he also went off on the luggage quest. The small boys were apparently untired by their journey; they immediately began to use the swinging glass doors as playthings to the imminent risk of their own necks, since they were too little to be noticed by anyone coming in or out, and were nearly knocked flat a dozen times by the swing of the doors. The weary mother spent a busy time in rescuing them, and was not always entirely successful — bumps and howls testified to the doors being occasionally quicker than the boys. Finally, the old priest gathered up the elder, a curly-haired, slender mite, into his arms and told him stories, while his plump and solemn brother curled upon his mother's knee and dozed. It was clearly long after their bed-time.

The procession of people came and went

unceasingly, the glass doors always aswing. In and
out, in and out, men and women hurried, and just
beyond the kaleidoscope of the platforms moved
and changed restlessly under the glaring arc
lights. Cecilia's bewildered mind grew weary of it
all, and she closed her eyes. It was sometime later
that she woke with a start, to find Bob beside her.

"Sleepy old thing," he said. "Oh, I've had such
a wild time, Tommy. To get information of any
kind is as hard as to get one's luggage. However,
I've got both. And the first thing is we can't go on
board tonight."

"Bob! What shall we do?"

"I was rather anxious about that same thing
myself," said Bob, "since everyone tells me that
Liverpool is more jammed with people than even
London — which is saying something. However,
we've had luck. I went to ask in here, never
imagining I had the ghost of a chance, and they'd
just had telegrams giving up two rooms. So we're
quite all right; and so is the luggage. I've had all
the heavy stuff handed over to a carrier to be put
on the *Nauru* tomorrow morning."

"You're the great manager," said Cecilia
comfortably. "Where is the *Nauru*, by the way?"

"Sitting out in the river, the transport officer
says. She doesn't come alongside until the
morning; and we haven't to be on board until three
o'clock. She's supposed to pull out about six. So
we really needn't have left London today — but I
think it's as well we did."

"Yes, indeed," said Cecilia, with a shiver. "I
don't think I could have stood another night in

Lancaster Gate. I've been awake for three nights
wondering what we should do if any hitch came
in our plans."

"Just like a woman!" said Bob, laughing. "You
always jump over your hedges before you come to
them." He pulled her gently out of her chair.
"Come along. I'll have these things sent up to our
rooms, and then we'll get some dinner — after
which you'll go to bed." It was a plan which
sounded supremely attractive to his sister.

Not even the roar and rattle of the trains under
the station hotel kept Cecilia awake that night.
She slept, dreamlessly at first; then she had a
dream that she was just about to embark in a
great ship for Australia; that she was going up
the gangway, when suddenly behind her came her
father and her stepmother, with Avice, Wilfred
and Queenie, who all seized her, and began to drag
her back. She fought and struggled with them, and
from the top of the gangway came Mr. M'Clinton
and Eliza, who tugged her upwards. Between the
two parties she was beginning to think she would
be torn to pieces, when suddenly came swooping
from the clouds an aeroplane, curiously like a
wheelbarrow, and in it Bob, who leaned out as he
dived, grasped her by the hair, and swung her
aboard with him. They whirred away over the sea;
where, she did not know, but it did not seem
greatly to matter. They were still flying between
sea and sky when she woke, to find the sunlight
streaming into her room, and someone knocking
at her door.

"Are you awake, Tommy?" It was Bob's voice. "Lie still, and I'll send you up a cup of tea."

That was very pleasant, and a happy contrast to awakening in Lancaster Gate; and breakfast a little later was delightful, in a big sunny room, with interesting people coming and going all the time. Bob and Cecilia smiled at each other like two happy children. It was almost unbelievable that they were free; away from tyranny and coldness, with no more plotting and planning, and no more prying eyes.

Bob went off to interview the transport officer after breakfast, and Cecilia found the officer's wife with the two little boys struggling to attend to her luggage, while the children ran away and lost themselves in the corridors or endeavoured to commit suicide by means of the lift. So Cecilia took command of them and played with them until the harassed mother had finished, and came to reclaim her offspring — this time with the worry lines smoothed out of her face. She sat down by Cecilia and talked, and presently it appeared that she also was sailing in the *Nauru*.

"Indeed, I thought it was only wives who were going," she said. "I didn't know sisters were permitted."

"I believe General Harran managed our passages," Cecilia said. "He has been very kind to my brother."

"Well, you should have a merry voyage, for there will be scarcely any young girls on board," said Mrs. Burton, her new friend. "Most of the women

on the transports are brides, of course. Ever so
many of our men have married over here."

"You are an Australian?" Cecilia asked.

"Oh, yes. My husband isn't. He was an old
regular officer, and returned to his regiment as
soon as war broke out. I don't think there will be
many women on board: the *Nauru* isn't a family
ship, you know."

"What is that?" Cecilia queried.

"Oh, a ship with hundreds of women and
children — privates' wives and families, as well
as officers'. I believe they are rather awful to
travel on — they must be terrible in rough
weather. The non-family ships carry only a few
officers' wives, as a rule: a much more comfortable
arrangement for the lucky few."

"And we are among the lucky few."

"Yes. I only hope my small boys won't be a
nuisance. I've never been without a nurse for them
until last night. However, I suppose I'll soon get
into their ways."

"You must let me help you," Cecilia said. "I love
babies." She stroked Tim's curly head as she
spoke: Dickie, his little brother, had suddenly
fallen asleep on his mother's knee.

Mrs. Burton smiled her thanks.

"Well, it is pleasant to think we shan't go on
board knowing no one," she said. "I hope our
cabins are not far apart. Oh, here is my husband.
I hope that means all our luggage is safely on
board."

Colonel Burton came up — a pleasant soldierly
man, bearing the unmistakable stamp of the

regular officer. They were still chatting when Bob arrived, to be introduced — a ceremony which appeared hardly necessary in the case of the Colonel and himself.

"We've met at intervals since last night in various places where they hide luggage," said the Colonel. "I'm beginning to turn faint at the sight of a trunk!"

"It's the trunks I can't get sight of that make me tremble," grinned Bob. "One of mine disappeared mysteriously this morning, and finally, after a breathless hunt, turned up in a lamp room — your biggest Saratoga, Tommy! Why anyone should have put it in a lamp room seems to be a conundrum that is going to excite the station for ever. But there it was."

"And have they really started for the ship?" asked Cecilia.

"Well — I saw them all on a lorry, checked over my list with the driver's, and found everything right, and saw him start," said Bob, laughing. "More than that no man may say."

"It would simplify matters if we knew our cabin numbers," said Colonel Burton. "But we don't; neither does anyone, as far as I can gather, since cabins appear to be allotted just as you go on board — a peculiar system. Can you imagine the ghastly heap of miscellaneous luggage that will be dumped on the *Nauru*, with frenzied owners wildly trying to sort it out!"

"It doesn't bear thinking of," said Bob, laughing. "Come along, Tommy, and we'll explore Liverpool."

They wandered about the crowded streets of the

great port, where may, perhaps, be seen a queerer mixture of races than anywhere in England, since ships from all over the world ceaselessly come and go up and down the Mersey. Then they boarded a train and journeyed out of the city, among miles of beautiful houses, and, getting down at the terminus, walked briskly for an hour, since it would be long before there would be any land for them to walk on again. They got back to the hotel rather late for lunch, and very hungry; and afterwards it was time to pack up their light luggage and get down to the docks. General Harran had warned them to take enough hand-baggage to last them several nights, since it was quite possible that their cabin trunks would be swept into the baggage room, and fail to turn up for a week after sailing.

A taxi whisked them through streets that became more and more crowded. The journey was not a long one; they turned down a slope presently, and drew up before a great gate across the end of a pier where two policemen were on duty to prevent the entrance of anyone without a pass. Porters were there in singular numbers — England had grown quite used to being without them; and Bob had just transferred their luggage to the care of a cheerful lad with a barrow when Cecilia gave a little start of dismay.

"Bob, I've left my watch!"

"Whew!" whistled her brother. "Where?"

"I washed my hands just before I left my room," said the shamefaced Cecilia. "I remember slipping it off my wrist beside the basin."

"Well, there's no need to worry," said Bob cheerfully. "Ten to one it's there still. You'll have to take the taxi and go back for it, Tommy: I can't leave the luggage, and I may be wanted to show our papers, besides; but you won't have any difficulty. Come along, and I'll see that the policeman lets you through when you come back."

The constable was sympathetic. He examined Cecilia's passport, declared that he would know her anywhere again, and that she had no cause for anxiety.

"Is it time? Sure, you'll be tired of waitin' on the old pier hours after ye get back," he said cheerfully. "I know them transports. Why, there's not one of the troops marched in yet. There comes the furrst lot."

A band swung round the turn of the street playing a quickstep: behind it, a long line of Australian soldiers, marching at ease, each man with his pack on his shoulder. A gate with a military sentry swung wide to admit them, and they passed on to where a high overhead bridge carried them aboard a great liner moored to the pier.

" 'Tis the soldiers have better treatment than the officers whin it comes to boardin' transports," said the friendly policeman. "They get marched straight on board. The officers and their belongin's has to wait till they've gone through hivin knows what formalities. So you needn't worry, miss, an' take your time. The old ship'll be there hours yet."

The taxi driver appeared only too glad of further employment, and Cecilia, much cheered, though still considerably ashamed of herself, leaned back comfortably in the cab as they whisked through the streets. At the hotel good fortune awaited her, for a chambermaid had just found her watch and had brought it to the office for safekeeping. Cecilia left her thanks, with something more substantial for the girl, and hurried back to the cab.

The streets seemed more thronged than ever, and presently traffic was blocked by a line of marching men — more "diggers" on their way to the transport. Cecilia's chauffeur turned back into a side street, evidently a short cut. Halfway along it the taxi jarred once or twice and came to a standstill.

The chauffeur got out and poked his head into the bonnet, performing mysterious rites, while Cecilia watched him, a little anxiously. Presently he came round to the door.

"I'm awful sorry, miss," he said respectfully. "The old bus has broke down. I'm afraid I can't get another move out of 'er — I'll 'ave to get 'er towed to a garage."

"Oh!" said Cecilia, jumping out. "Do you think I can find another near here?"

"You oughter pick one up easy in the street up there," said the chauffeur. "Plenty of 'em about 'ere. Even if you shouldn't miss, you can get a tram down to the docks — any policeman'll direct you. You could walk it, if you liked — you've loads of time." He touched his cap as she paid him. "Very sorry to let you down like this, miss — it ain't my fault. All the taxis in England are just about droppin' to pieces — it'll be a mercy when repair shops get goin' again."

"It doesn't matter," Cecilia said cheerfully. She decided that she would walk; it would be more interesting, and the long wait on the pier would be shortened. She set off happily towards the main street where the tram lines ran, feeling that short cuts were not for strangers in a big city.

Even in the side street the shops were interesting. She came upon a fascinating curio shop, and stopped a moment to look at the queer medley in its window; such a medley as may be seen in any port where sailormen bring home strange things from far countries. She was so engrossed that she failed to notice a woman who passed her, and then, with an astonished stare, turned back. A heavy hand fell on her wrist.

"Cecilia!"

She turned, with little cry. Mrs. Rainham's face, inflamed with sudden anger, looked into her own. The hard grasp tightened on her wrist.

"What are you doing here, you wicked girl? You've run away."

At the moment no speech was possible to Cecilia. She twisted her arm away fiercely, freeing herself with difficulty, and turning, ran, with her stepmother at her heels. Once, Mrs. Rainham gasped "Police!" after which she required all her breath to keep near the flying girl. The street was quiet; only one or two interested passers-by turned to look at the race, and a street urchin shouted: "Go it, red 'ead — she's beatin' yer!"

It follows naturally, when one person pursues

another through city streets, that the pursued falls
under public suspicion and is liable to be caught
and held by any officious person. Cecilia felt this,
and her anxiety was keen as she darted round the
corner into the next street, looking about wildly
for a means of escape. A big van, crawling across
the road, held Mrs. Rainham back for a moment,
giving her a brief respite.

Just in front of her, a block in the traffic was
beginning to move. A taxi was near her. She held
up her hand desperately, trying to catch the
driver's eyes. He shook his head, and she realised
that he was already engaged — there was a pile
of luggage beside him with big labels, and a
familiar name struck her — "HMT *Nauru*". A girl,
leaning from the window of the taxi, met her
glance, and Cecilia took a sudden resolve. She
sprang forward, her hand on the door.

"I am a passenger by the *Nauru*. Could you take
me in your car?" she gasped.

"Why, of course," said the other girl. "Plenty of
room, isn't there, Dad?"

"Yes, certainly," said the other occupant of the
cab — a big, grizzled man, who looked at the
new-comer in blank amazement. He had half
risen, but there was no time for him to assist his
self-invited guest; she had opened the door and
jumped in before his daughter had finished
speaking. Leaning forward, Cecilia saw her
stepmother emerge from the traffic, crimson-faced,
casting wild and wrathful glances about her. Then
her wandering eye fell upon Cecilia, and she began
to run forward. Even as she did the chauffeur

quickened his pace, and the taxi slid away, until the running, shouting figure was lost to view.

Cecilia sat back with a gasp, and began to laugh helplessly. The others watched her with faces that clearly showed that they began to suspect having entertained a lunatic unawares.

"I do beg your pardon," said Cecilia, recovering. "It was inexcusable. But I was running away."

"So it seemed," said the big man, in a slow, pleasant voice. "I hope it wasn't from the police?"

"Oh no!" Cecilia flushed. "Only from my stepmother. My own taxi had just broken down, and she found me, and she would have made a scene in the street — and scenes are so vulgar, are they not? When I saw *Nauru* on your luggage, you seemed to me to have dropped from heaven."

She looked at them, her pretty face pink, her eyes dancing with excitement. There was something appealing about her, in the big childish eyes, and in the well-bred voice with its faint hint of a French accent. The girl she looked at could hardly have been called pretty — she was slender and long-limbed, with honest grey eyes and a sensitive mouth that seemed always ready to break into smiles. A little smile hovered at its corners now, but her voice held a note of protection.

"I don't think we need bother you to tell us," she said. "In our country it's a very ordinary thing to give anyone a lift, if you have a seat to spare. Isn't it, Daddy?"

"Of course," said her father. "And we are to be

fellow passengers, so it was very lucky that we were there in the nick of time."

Cecilia looked at them gratefully. It might have been so different, she thought; she might have flung herself on the mercy of people who would have been suspicious and frigid, or of others who would have treated her with familiarity and curious questioning. These people were pleasantly matter-of-fact; glad to help, but plainly anxious to show her that they considered her affairs none of their business. There was a little catch in her throat as she answered.

"It is very good of you to take me on trust — I know I did an unwarrantable thing. But my brother, Captain Rainham, will explain everything, and he will be as grateful to you as I am. He is at the ship now."

"Then we can hand you over to his care," said her host. "By the way, is there any need to guard against the — er — lady you spoke of? Is she likely to follow you to the docks?"

"She doesn't know I'm going," said Cecilia, dimpling. "Of course, if it were in a novel she would leap into a swift motor and bid the driver follow up, and be even now on our heels —"

"Goodness!" said the other girl. She twisted so that she could look out of the tiny window at the rear, turning back with a relieved face.

"Nothing near us but a carrier's van and a pony cart," she said. "I shouldn't think you need worry."

"No. I really don't think I need. My stepmother did see me in the taxi, but her brain doesn't move very swiftly, nor does she, for that matter — and

I'm sure she wouldn't try to follow me. She knows, too, that if she found me she couldn't drag me away as if I were two years old. Oh, I'm sure I'm safe from her now," finished Cecilia, with a sigh of relief.

"At any rate, if she comes to the docks she will have your brother to deal with," said the big man. "And here we are."

They got out at the big gate where the Irish policeman greeted Cecilia with a friendly "Did ye find it now, miss?" and beamed upon her when she held up her wrist, with her watch safely in its place. He examined her companions' passports, but let her through with an airy "Sure, this young lady's all right," which made Cecilia feel that no further proof could be needed of her respectability. Then Bob came hurrying to meet her.

"I was just beginning to get uneasy about you," he said. "Did you have any trouble?"

"My taxi broke down," Cecilia answered. "But this lady and gentleman most kindly gave me a seat, and saved me ever so much trouble. I'll tell you my story presently."

Bob turned, saluting.

"Thanks, awfully," he said. "I wasn't too happy at letting my little sister run about alone in a strange city, but it couldn't be helped."

"I'm very glad we were there," said the big man. "Now, can you tell me where luggage should go? My son and a friend are somewhere on the pier, I suppose, but it doesn't seem as though finding them would be an easy matter."

The pier, indeed, resembled a hive in which the

bees have broken loose. Beside it lay the huge bulk of the transport, towering high above all the dock buildings near. Already she swarmed with Australian soldiers, and a steady stream was still passing aboard by the overhead gangway to the blare and crash of a regimental march. The pier itself was crowded with officers, with a sprinkling of women and children — most of them looking impatient enough at being kept ashore instead of being allowed to seek their quarters on the ship. Great heaps of trunks were stacked here and there, and a crane was steadily at work swinging them aboard.

"We can't go aboard yet, nobody seems to know why," Bob said. "An individual called an embarkation officer, or something of the kind, has to check our passports; he was supposed to be here before three o'clock, but there's no sign of him yet, and everyone has to wait his convenience. It's hard on the women with little children — the poor mites are getting tired and cross. Luggage can be left in the care of the ship's hands, to be loaded; I'll show you where, sir, if you like. Is this yours?" His eye fell on a truck-load of trunks, wheeled up by a porter, and lit up suddenly as he noticed the name of their labels.

"Oh — are you Mr. Linton?" he exclaimed. "I believe I've got a letter for you, from General Harran."

"Now I was wondering where I'd heard your name before, when your sister happened to say you were Captain Rainham," said the big man. "How stupid of me — of course, I met Harran at my club this week, and he told me about you." He held out his hand, and took Bob's warmly; then he turned to his daughter. "Norah, it's lucky that we have made friends with Miss Rainham already, because you know she's in our care, after a fashion."

Norah Linton turned with a quick smile.

"I'm so glad," she said. "I've been wondering what you would be like, because we didn't know of anyone else on board."

"General Harran told my brother that you would befriend us, but I did not think you would begin so early," Cecilia said. "Just fancy, Bob, they rescued me almost from the clutches of the she-dragon!"

Bob jumped.

"You don't mean to say you met her?"

"I did — as soon as my cab broke down. And I lost my head and ran from her like a hare, and jumped into Mr. Linton's car!"

Bob regarded her with solemn amazement.

"So this is what happens when I let you go about alone!" he ejaculated. "Why, you might have got yourself into an awful mess — it might have been anybody's car —"

"Yes, but it wasn't," said his sister serenely. "You see, I looked at Miss Linton first, and I knew it would be all right."

The Lintons laughed unrestrainedly.

"That's your look of benevolent old age, Norah," said her father. "I've often noticed it coming."

"I wish you'd mention it to Wally," Norah said. "He might treat me with more respect if you did."

"I doubt it; it isn't in Wally," said her father. "Now, Rainham, shall we see about this luggage?"

They handed it over to the care of deck hands, and watched it loaded, with many other trunks, into a huge net, which the crane seized, swung to an enormous height and then lowered gently upon the deck of the *Nauru*. Just as the operation was finished two figures threaded their way through the crowd towards them; immensely tall young officers, with the badge of a British regiment on their caps.

"Hullo, Dad," said the taller — a good-looking grave-faced fellow, with a strong resemblance to Norah. "We hardly expected you down so early."

"Well, Norah and I had nothing to do, so we thought we might as well come; though it appears that we would have been wiser not to hurry," said Mr. Linton. "Jim, I want to introduce you to two courageous emigrants — Miss Rainham, Captain Rainham — my son."

Jim Linton shook hands, and introduced his companion, Captain Meadows, who was dark and well built, with an exceedingly merry eye.

"We've been trying to get round the powers that be, to make our way on board," he said. "The chief difficulty is that the powers that be aren't there; everything is hung up waiting for this blessed official. I suppose the honest man is sleeping off the effects of a heavy lunch."

"If he knew what hearty remarks are being made about him by over two hundred angry people, it might disturb his rest," said Wally

Meadows. "Come along and see them — you're only on the fringe of the crowd here."

"Wally's been acting as nursemaid for the last half hour," Jim said, as they made their way along the pier. "He rescued a curly-haired kid from a watery grave — at least, it would have been if he hadn't caught it by the hind leg — and after that the kid refused to let him go."

"He was quite a jolly kid," said Wally. "Only he seems to have quicksilver in him, instead of blood. I'm sorry for his mother — she'll have a packed time for the next five weeks." He sighed. "Hide me, Norah — there he is now!"

The curly-haired one proved to be little Tim Burton, who detached himself from his mother on catching sight of Wally, and trotted across to him with a shrill cry of "There's mine officer!" — whereat Wally swung him up on his shoulder, to his infinite delight. Mrs. Burton hurried up to claim her offspring, and was made known to everyone by Cecilia.

"It's such an awful wait," she said wearily. "We came here soon after two o'clock, thinking we would get the children on board early for their afternoon sleep; now it's after four, and we have stood here ever since. It's too tantalising with the ship looking at us, and the poor babies are so tired. Still, I'm not the worst off. Look at that poor girl."

She pointed out a white-faced girl who was sitting in a drooping attitude on a very dirty wooden case. She was dainty and refined in appearance; and looking at her, one felt that the filthy case was the most welcome thing she had

found that afternoon. Her husband, an officer
scarcely more than a boy, stood beside, trying
vainly to hush the cries of a tiny baby. She put
up her arms wearily as they looked at her.

"Oh, give her to me, Harry." She took the little
bundle and crooned over it; and the baby wailed
on unceasingly.

"Oh!" said Norah Linton. She took a quick stride
forward. They watched her accost the young
mother — saw the polite, yet stiff, refusal on the
English girl's face; saw Norah, with a swift decided
movement stoop down and take the baby from the
reluctant arms, putting any protest aside with a
laugh. A laugh went round the Linton party also.

"I knew she'd get it," said Jim.

"Rather!" his friend echoed. "But she hasn't
arms enough for all the babies who want
mothering here."

There were indeed plenty of them. Tired young
mothers stood about everywhere, with children
ranging from a few months to three or four years,
all weary by this time, and most of them cross.
Harassed young husbands, unused to travelling
with children — unused, indeed, to anything but
War — went hither and thither trying to hasten
the business of getting on board — coming back,
after each useless journey, to try and soothe a
screaming baby or restrain a tiny boy anxious to
look over the edge of the pier. It was only a few
minutes before Cecilia had found a mother
exhausted enough to yield up her baby without
much protest; and Jim and Wally Meadows and
Bob "adopted" some of the older children, and took

them off to see the band; which diversions helped
to pass the time. But it was after five o'clock before
a stir went round the pier, and a rush of officers
towards a little wooden room at the foot of the
gangway told that the long-waited-for official had
arrived.

"Well, we won't hurry," said Mr. Linton. "Let
the married men get on first."

There were not many who did not hurry. A few
of the older officers kept back; the majority, who
were chiefly subalterns, made a dense crowd about
the little room, their long-pent impatience
bursting out at last. Passports examined, a
procession began up the gangway, each man
compelled to halt at a barrier on top, where two
officers sat allotting cabins. It was difficult to see
why both these preliminaries could not have been
managed before, instead of being left until the
moment of boarding; the final block strained
everyone's patience to breaking point.

The Lintons and the Rainhams were almost the
last to board the ship, having, not without
thankfulness, relinquished their adopted babies.
The officers allotting berths nodded
comprehendingly on hearing the names of the two
girls.

"Oh yes — you're together." He gave them their
number.

"Together — how curious!" said Cecilia.

"Not a bit; you're the only unmarried ladies on
board. And they're packed like sardines — not a
vacant berth on the ship. Over two thousand men
and two hundred officers, to say nothing of wives

and children." He leaned back, thankful that his rush of work was over. "Well, when I make a long voyage I hope it won't be on a trooper!"

"Well, that's a bad remark to begin one's journey on," said Jim Linton, following the girls up the gangway. "Doesn't it scare you, Miss Rainham?"

"No," she said, with a little laugh. "Nothing would scare me except not going."

"Why, that's all right," he said. His hand fell on his sister's shoulder. "And what about you, Nor?"

The face she turned to him was so happy that words were hardly needed.

"Why — I'm going back to Billabong!" she said.

CHAPTER 9

The Welcome of Australia

A PATH of moonlight lay across the sea. Into it drifted a great ship, her engines almost stopped, so that only a dull, slow throb came up from below, instead of the swift thud-thud of the screw that had pounded for many weeks. It was late; so late that most of the ship's lights were extinguished. But all through her was a feeling of pulsating life, of unrest, of a kind of tense excitement, of long-pent expectation. There were low voices everywhere; feet paced the decks; along the port railings on each deck soldiers were clustered thickly, looking out across the grey, tossing sea to a winking light that flashed and twinkled out of the darkness like a voice that cried, "Greeting!" For it was the Point Lonsdale light, at the sea gate of Victoria; and the men of the *Nauru* were nearly home.

There was little sleep for anyone on board on that last night. Most of the *Nauru*'s great company were to disembark in Melbourne; the last two days had seen a general smartening up, a mighty polishing of leather and brass, a "rounding-up" of scattered possessions. The barber's shop had been besieged by shaggy crowds; and since the barber, being but human, could not cope with more than a small proportion of his would-be customers, amateur clipping parties had been in full swing forward, frequently with terrifying results. Nobody minded. "Git it orf, that's all that matters!" was the motto of the long-haired.

No one knew quite when the *Nauru* would berth; it was wrapped in mystery, like all movements of troopships. So everyone was ready the night before — kit bags packed, gear stowed away, nothing left save absolute necessaries. Then, with the coming of dusk, unrest settled down upon the ship, and the men marched restlessly up and down or, gripping pipe stems between their teeth, stared from the railings northwards. And then, like a star at first, the Point Lonsdale light twinkled out of the darkness, and a low murmur ran round the decks — a murmur without words, since it came from men whose only fashion of meeting any emotion is with a joke; and even for a "digger" there is no joke ready on the lips, but only a catch at the heart, at the first glimpse of home.

Norah Linton had tucked herself away behind a boat on the hurricane deck, and there Cecilia Rainham found her just after dusk. The two girls had become sworn friends during the long voyage out, in the close companionship of sharing a cabin — which is a kind of acid test that generally brings out the best — and worst — of travellers. There was something protective in Norah's nature that responded instantly to the lonely position of the girl who was going across the world to a strange country. Both were motherless, but in Norah's case the blank was softened by a father who had striven throughout his children's lives to be father and mother alike to them, while Cecilia had only the bitter memory of the man who had shirked his duty until he had become less than a stranger to her. If any pang smote her heart at the sight of Norah's worshipping love for the tall grey "Dad" for whom she was the very centre of existence, Cecilia did not show it. The Lintons had taken them into their little circle at once — more, perhaps, by reason of Cecilia's extraordinary introduction to them than through General Harran's letter — and Bob and his sister were already grateful for their friendship. They were a quiet quartet, devoted to each other in their undemonstrative fashion; Norah was on a kind of boyish footing with Jim, the huge silent brother who was a major with three medal ribbons to his credit, and with Wally Meadows, his inseparable chum, who had been almost brought up with the brother and sister.

"They were always such bricks to me, even when I was a little scrap of a thing," she had told Cecilia. "They never said I was 'only a girl', and kept me out of things. So I grew up more than three parts a boy. It was so much easier for Dad to manage three boys, you see!"

"You don't look much like a boy," Cecilia had said, looking at the tall, slender figure and the mass of curly brown hair. They were getting ready for bed, and Norah was wielding a hair brush vigorously.

"No, but I really believe I feel like one — at least, I do whenever I am with Jim and Wally," Norah had answered. "And when we get back to Billabong it will be just as it always was — we'll be three boys together. You know, it's the most ridiculous thing to think of Jim and Wally as grown-ups. Dad and I can't get accustomed to it at all. And as for Jim being a major! A major sounds so dignified and respectable, and Jim isn't a bit like that!"

"And what about Captain Meadows?"

"Oh — Wally will simply never grow up." Norah laughed softly. "He's like Peter Pan. Once he nearly managed it — in that bad time when Jim was a prisoner, and we thought he was killed. But Jim got back just in time to save him from anything so awful. One of the lovely parts of getting Jim again was to see the twinkle come back into Wally's eyes. You see, Wally is practically all twinkle!"

"And when you get back to Australia, what will you all do?"

Norah had looked puzzled.

"Why, I don't know that we've ever thought of it," she said. "We'll just all go to Billabong — we don't seem to think further than that. Anyway, you and Bob are coming too — so we can plan it all out then."

Looking at her, on this last night of the voyage, Cecilia wondered whether the unknown "Billabong" would indeed be enough, after the long

years of war. They had been children when they
left; now the boys were seasoned soldiers, with
scars and honours, and such memories as only
they themselves could know; and Norah and her
father had for years conducted what they termed
a "Home for Tired People", where broken and
weary men from the front had come to be healed
and tended, and sent back refitted in mind and
body. This girl, who leaned over the rail and
looked at the Point Lonsdale light, had seen
suffering and sorrow; the mourning of those who
had given up dear ones, the sick despair of young
and strong men crippled in the very dawn of life,
and had helped them all. Beside her, in
experience, Cecilia felt a child. And yet the old
bush home, with its simple life and the pleasures
that had been everything to her in childhood,
seemed everything to her now.

Cecilia went softly to her side, and Norah
turned with a start.

"Hallo, Tommy!" she said, slipping her arm
through the newcomer's — Cecilia had become
"Tommy" to them all in a very short time, and her
hated, if elegant, name left as a legacy to England.
"I didn't hear you come. Oh, Tommy, it's lovely to
see home again!"

"You can't see much," said Tommy, laughing.

"No, but it's there. I can feel it, and that old
winking eye on Point Lonsdale is saying fifty nice
things a minute. And I can smell the gum leaves
— don't you tell me I can't, Tommy, just because
your nose isn't tuned up to gum leaves yet!"

"Does it take long to tune a nose?" asked Tommy, laughing.

"Not a nice nose like yours." Norah gave a happy little sigh. "Do you see that glow in the sky? That's the lights of Melbourne. I went to school near Melbourne, but I never loved it much; but somehow, it seems different now. It's all just shouting welcomes. And back of beyond that light is Billabong."

"I want to see Billabong," said the other girl. "I never had a home that meant anything like that — I want to see yours."

"And I suppose you'll just think it's an ordinary, untidy old place — not a bit like the trim English places, where the woods look as though they were swept and dusted before breakfast every morning. I suppose it is all ordinary. But it has meant just everything I wanted, all my life, and I can't imagine its meaning anything less now."

"And what about Homewood — the Home for Tired People?"

"Oh, Homewood certainly is lovely," Norah said. "I like it better than any place in the world that isn't Billabong — and it was just wonderful to be able to carry it on for the Tired People: Dad and I will always be thankful we had the chance. But it never was home, and now it's going to run itself happily without us, as a place for partly disabled men, with Colonel Hunt and Captain Hardress to manage it. It was just a single chapter in our lives, and now it is closed. But we're — all of us — parts of Billabong."

Someone came quietly along the deck and to the vacant place on her other side.

"Who's talking Billabong again, old kiddie?" Jim Linton's deep voice was always gentle. Norah gave his shoulder a funny little rub with her head.

"Ah, you're just as bad as I am, so you needn't laugh at me, Jimmy."

"I wasn't laughing at you," Jim defended himself. "I expected to find you ever so much worse. I thought you'd sing anthems on the very word Billabong all through the voyage, especially in your bath. Of course I don't know what Tommy has suffered!"

"Tommy doesn't need your sympathy," said that lady. "However, she wants to look her best for Melbourne, so she's going to bed. Don't hurry, Norah; I know you want to exchange greetings with that light for hours yet!"

She slipped away, and Norah drew closer to Jim. Presently came Wally, on her other side, and a few moments later a deep voice behind them said, "Not in bed yet, Norah?" — and Wally made room for Mr. Linton.

"I couldn't go to bed, Dad."

"Apparently most of the ship is of your mind — I didn't feel like bed myself," admitted the squatter, letting his hand rest for a moment on his daughter's shoulder. He gave a great sigh of happiness. "Eh, children, it's great to be near home again!"

"My word, isn't it!" said Jim. "Only it's hard to take in. I keep fancying that I'll certainly wake up in a minute and find myself in a trench, just

getting ready to go over the top. What do you
suppose they're doing at Billabong now, Nor?"

"Asleep," said Norah promptly. "Oh, I don't
know — I don't believe Brownie's asleep."

"I know she's not," Wally said. He and the old
nurse-housekeeper of Billabong were sworn allies;
though no one could ever quite come up to Jim
and Norah in Brownie's heart, Wally had been a
close third from the day, long years back, that he
had first come to the station, a lonely, dark-eyed
little Queenslander. "She's made the girls scrub
and polish until there's nothing left for them to
rub, and she's harried Hogg and Lee Wing until
there isn't a leaf looking crooked in all the garden,
and she and Murty have planned all about
meeting you for the hundred and first time."

"And she's planning to make pikelets for you!"
put in Norah.

"Bless her. I wouldn't wonder. She's planning
the very wildest cooking, of course — do you
remember what the table used to be the night we
came home from school? And now she's gone round
all the rooms to make sure she couldn't spend
another sixpence on them, and she's sitting by her
window trying to see us all on the *Nauru* 'specially
you, old Nor."

" 'Tis the gift of second sight you have," said
Jim admiringly. "A few hundred years ago you'd
have got yourself ducked as a witch or something."

"Oh, Wally and Brownie were always twin
souls. No wonder each knows what the other is
thinking of," Norah said, laughing. "It all sounds
exactly true, at any rate. Boys, what a pity you

can't land in uniform — wouldn't they all love to see you!"

"Can't do it," Jim said. "Too long since we were shot out of the army; any enterprising provost-marshal could make himself obnoxious about it."

"I know — but I'm sorry," answered Norah. "Brownie won't be satisfied unless she sees you in all your war paint."

"We'll put it on some night for dinner," Jim promised. He peered suddenly into the darkness. "There's a moving light — it's the pilot steamer coming out for us."

They watched the light pass slowly from the dim region that meant the Heads, until, as the pilot boat swung out through the Rip to where the *Nauru* lay, her other lights grew clear, and presently her whole outline loomed indistinctly, suddenly close to them. She lay to across a little heaving strip of sea, and presently the pilot was being pulled across to them by a couple of men and was coming nimbly up the *Nauru*'s ladder, hand over hand. He nodded cheerily at his welcome — a fusillade of greetings from every "digger" who could find a place at the railings, and a larger number who could not, but contented themselves with shouting sweet nothings from behind their comrades. A lean youngster near Jim Linton looked down enviously at the retreating boat.

"If I could only slide down into her, an' nick off to the old Alvina over there, I'd be home before breakfast," he said. "Me people live at Queenscliff

— don't it seem a fair cow to have to go past 'em, right up to Melbourne?"

The pilot's head appeared above on the bridge, beside the captain's, and presently the *Nauru* gathered way, and, slowly turning, forged through the tossing waters of the Rip. Before her the twin lights of the Heads opened out; soon she was gliding between them, and under the silent guns of the Queenscliff forts, and past the twinkling house lights of the little seaside town. There were long coo-ees from the diggers, with shrill, piercing whistles of greeting for Victoria; from ashore came faint answering echoes. But the four people from Billabong stood silently, glad of each other's nearness, but with no words, and in David Linton's heart and Norah's was a great surge of thankfulness that, out of many perils, they were bringing their boys safely home.

The *Nauru* turned across Port Phillip Bay, and presently they felt the engines cease, and there came the rattle of the chain as the anchor shot into the sea.

"As the captain thought," said Jim. "He fancied they'd anchor us off Portsea for the night and bring us up to Port Melbourne in the morning, after we'd been inspected. Wouldn't it be the limit if someone developed measles now, and they quarantined us!"

"You deserve quarantining, if ever anyone did," said Norah, indignantly. "Why do you have such horrible ideas?"

"I don't know — they just seem to waft themselves to me," said Jim modestly. "Anyhow, the quarantine station is a jolly little place for a holiday, and the sea view is delightful." He broke off, laughing, and suddenly flung his arm round her shoulders in the dusk of the deck. "I think I'm just about insane at getting home," he said. "Don't mind me, old kiddie — and you'd better go to bed, or you'll be a ghost in the morning."

They weighed anchor after breakfast, following a perfunctory medical inspection — so perfunctory that one youth who, having been a medical student, and knowing well that he had a finely developed feverish cold, with a high temperature, and not wishing to embarrass his fellow passengers, placed in his mouth the wrong end of the clinical thermometer handed him by the visiting nurse. He sucked this gravely for the prescribed time, reversing it just as she reappeared, and, being marked normal and given a clean bill of health, returned to his berth to shiver and perspire between huge doses of quinine. More than one such hero evaded the searching eye of regulations, until finally the *Nauru*, free to land her passengers, steamed slowly up the Bay.

One by one the old, familiar landmarks opened out — Mornington, Frankston, Mordialloc, while Melbourne itself lay hidden in a mist cloud ahead. Then, as the sun grew stronger the mist lifted, and domes and spires pierced the dun sky, towering above the jumbled mass of the grey city. They drew closer to Port Melbourne, and lo! St. Kilda and all the foreshore were gay with flags, and all the ships in the harbour were dressed to welcome them; and beyond the pier were long lines

of motors, each beflagged, waiting for the fighting
men whom the *Nauru* was bringing home.

"Us!" said a boy. "Why, it's us! Flags an' motors
— an' a blessed band playin' on the pier! Wot on
earth are they fussin' over us for? Ain't it enough
to get home?"

The band of the *Nauru* was playing "Home,
Sweet Home", very low and tenderly, and there
were lumps in many throats, and many a pipe
went out unheeded. Slowly the great ship drew in
to the pier, where officers in uniform waited, and
messengers of welcome from the Government.
Beyond the barriers that held the general public
back from the pier was a black mass of people;
cheer upon cheer rose, to be wafted back from the
transport, where the "diggers" lined every inch of
the port side, clinging like monkeys to yards and
rigging. Then the *Nauru* came to rest at last, and
the gangways rattled down, and the march off
began, to the quick lilt of the band playing "Oh,
it's a Lovely War". The men took up the words,
singing as they marched back to Victoria —
coming back, as they had gone, with a joke on
their lips. So the waiting motors received them,
and rolled them off in triumphal procession to
Melbourne, between the cheering crowds.

From the top deck the Lintons, with the
Rainhams, watched the men go — disembarkation
was for the troops first, and not till all had gone
could the unattached officers leave the ship. The
captain came to them, at last a normal and
friendly captain — no more the official master of
a troopship, in which capacity, as he ruefully said,

he could make no friends, and could scarcely regard his ship as his own, provided he brought her safely from port to port. He cast a disgusted glance along the stained and littered decks.

"This is her last voyage as a trooper, and I'm not sorry," he said. "After this she'll lie up for three months to be refitted; and then I'll command a ship again and not a barracks. You wouldn't think now, to see her on this voyage, that the time was when I had to know the reason why if there was so much as a stain the size of a sixpence on the deck. Oh yes, it's been all part of the job, and I'm proud of all the old ship has done, and the thousands of men she's carried; and we've had enough narrow squeaks, from mines and submarines, to fill a book. But I'm beginning to hanker mightily to see her clean!"

The Lintons laughed unfeelingly. A little mild grumbling might well be permitted to a man with his record; few merchant captains had done finer service in the war, and the decoration on his breast testified to his cool handling of his ship in the "narrow squeaks" he spoke of lightly.

"Oh yes, I never get any sympathy," said the captain, laughing himself. "And yet I'll wager Miss Linton was 'house-proud' in that 'Home for Tired People' of hers, and she ought to sympathise with a tidy man. You should have seen my wife's face when she came aboard once at Liverpool, and saw the ship; and she's never had the same respect for me since! There — the last man is off the ship, and the gangways are clear; nothing to keep all

your homesick people now." He said goodbye, and
ran up the steps to his cabin under the bridge.

It was a queer home-coming at first, to a vast
pier, empty save for a few officials and policemen
— for no outsiders were allowed within the
barriers. But once clear of customs officials and
other formalities they packed themselves into
cabs, and in a few moments were outside the
railed-off space, turning into a road lined on either
side with people — all peering into the long
procession of cabs, in the hope of finding their own
returning dear ones. It was but a few moments
before a posse of uncles, aunts and cousins
swooped down upon the Lintons, whose cab
prudently turned down a side street to let the
wave of welcome expend itself. In the side street,
too, were motors belonging to the aunts and
uncles; and presently the new arrivals were
distributed among them, and were being rushed
up to Melbourne, along roads still crowded by the
people who had flocked to welcome the "diggers"
home. The Rainhams found themselves adopted by
this new and cheery band of people — at least half
of whose names they never learned; not that this
seemed to matter in the least. It was something
new to them, and very un-English; but there was
no doubt that it made landing in a new country a
very different thing from their half-fearful
anticipations.

"And you really came out all alone — not
knowing anyone!" said an aunt. "Aren't you
English people plucky! And I believe that most of
you think we're all black fellows — or did until

our diggers went home, and proved unexpectedly white!"

"I don't think we're quite so bad as that!" Bob said, laughing. "But certainly we never expected quite so kind a welcome."

"Oh, we're all immensely interested in people who take the trouble to come across the world to see us," said Mrs. Geoffrey Linton. "That is, if they don't put on 'side'; we don't take kindly to being patronised. And you have no idea how many new chums do patronise us. Did you know, by the way, that you're new chums now?"

"It has been carefully drilled into us on the ship," Bob said gravely. "I think we know pretty well all we have to face — the snakes that creep into new chums' boots and sleep under their pillows, the goannas that bite our toes if we aren't watchful, and the mosquitoes that sit on the trees and bark!"

"Also the tarantulas that drop from everywhere, especially into food," added Tommy, dimpling. "And the bush fires every Sunday morning! There is much spare time on a troopship, Mrs. Linton, and all of it was employed by the subalterns in telling us what we might expect!"

"I can quite imagine it," Mrs. Geoffrey laughed. "Oh well, Billabong will be a good breaking-in. Norah tells me you are going up there at once?"

"Well, not quite at once," Bob said. "We think it is only fair to let them get home without encumbrances, and as we have to present other letters of introduction in Melbourne, we'll stay here for a few days, and then follow them."

"Then you must come out to us," said Mrs. Geoffrey firmly. "No use to ask my brother-in-law, of course; he has just one idea, and that is to stay at Scott's, get his luggage through the customs, see his bankers as quickly as possible, and then get back to his beloved Billabong. If we get them out to dinner tonight, it's as much as we can hope for. But you two must come to us — we can run you here and there in the car to see the people you want." She put aside their protests, laughing. "Why, you don't know how much we like capturing brand new English people — and think what you have done for our boys all these four years! From what they tell us, if anyone wants to go anywhere or do anything he likes in England, all he has to do is to wear a digger's slouched hat!"

They stopped in Collins Street, and in a moment the newcomers, slightly bewildered, found themselves in a tea-room; a new thing in tea-rooms to Tommy and Bob, since it was a vision of russet and gold — brown wood, masses of golden wattle and daffodils, and of bronze gum leaves; and even the waitresses flitted about in russet-brown dresses. David Linton hung back at the doorway.

"It isn't a party, Winifred?"

"My dear David, only a few people who want to welcome you back. Really, you're just as bad as ever!" said his sister-in-law, half vexed. "The children's schoolfriends, too — Jim and Wally's mates. You can't expect us to get you all back, after so long — and with all those honours, too! — and not give people a chance of shaking hands with you." At which point Norah said, gently, but firmly, "Dad, you mustn't be naughty," and led him within.

Someone grasped his hand. "Well, Linton, old chap!" And he found himself greeting the head of a big "stock and station" firm. Someone else clapped him on the shoulder, and he turned to meet his banker; behind them towered half a dozen old squatter friends, with fellow clubmen, all trying at once to get hold of his hand. David Linton's constitutional shyness melted in the heartiness of their greeting. Beyond them Norah seemed to be the centre of a mass of girls, one of whom presently detached herself, and came to him. He said in amazement, "Why, it's Jean Yorke — and grown up!" and actually kissed her, to the great delight of Jean, who had been an old mate of Norah's. As for Jim and Wally, they were scarcely to be seen, save for their heads, in a cluster of lads, who were pounding and smiting them wherever space permitted. Altogether, it was a confused and cheerful gathering, and, much to the embarrassment of the russet-brown waitresses, the last thing anybody thought of was tea.

Still, when the buzz of greetings had subsided, and at length "morning tea" — that time-honoured institution of Australia — had a chance to appear, it was of a nature to make the new arrivals gasp. The last four years in England had fairly broken people in to plain living; dainties and luxuries had disappeared so completely from the table that everyone had ceased to think about them.

Therefore, the Linton party blinked in amazement
at the details of what to Melbourne was a very
ordinary tea, and, forgetting its manners, broke
into open comment.

"Cakes!" said Wally faintly. "Jean, you might
catch me if I swoon."

"What's wrong with the cakes?" said Jean
Yorke, bewildered.

"Nothing — except that they are cakes! Jim!"
— he caught at his chum's sleeve — "that
substance in enormous layers in that enormous
slice is called cream. Real cream. When did you
see cream last, my son?"

"I'm hanged if I know," Jim answered, grinning.
"About four years ago, I suppose. I'd forgotten it
existed. And the cakes look as if they didn't fall
to pieces if you touched 'em."

"What, do the English cakes do that?" asked a
pained aunt.

"Rather — when there are any. It's something
they take out of the war flour — what is it, Nor?"

"Gluten, I think it's called," said Norah
doubtfully. "It's something that ordinarily makes
flour stick together, but they took it all out of the
war flour, and put it into munitions. So everything
you made with war flour was apt to be dry and
crumbly. And when you made cakes with it, and
war sugar, which was half full of queer stuff like
plaster of paris, and egg substitute, because eggs
— when you could get them — were eightpence
halfpenny, and butter substitute (and very little
of that) — well, they weren't exactly what you
would call cakes at all."

"Butter substitute!" said the aunt faintly. "I could not live without good butter!"

"Bless you, Norah and Dad hadn't tasted butter for nearly three years before they came on board the *Nauru*," said Jim. "It was affecting to see Nor greeting a pat of butter for the first time!"

"But you had some butter — we read about it."

"Two ounces per head weekly — but they put all their ration into the Tired People's food," said Wally.

"It wasn't only Dad and I," said Norah quickly. "Every soul we employed did that — Irish maids, butler, cook-lady and all. And we hadn't to ask one of them to do it. The Tired People always had butter. They used to think we had a special allowance from Government, but we hadn't."

"Dear me!" said the aunt. "It's too terrible. And meat?"

"Oh, meat was very short," said Norah, laughing. "Of course we were fairly well off for our Tired People, because they had soldiers' rations; but even so, we almost forgot what a joint looked like. Stews and hot pots and made dishes — you call them that because you make them of anything but meat! We became very clever at camouflaging meat dishes. Somehow the Tired People ate them all. But" — she paused, laughing — "you know I never thought I could feel greedy for meat. And I did — I just longed, quite often, for a chop!"

"And could you not have one?"

"Gracious, no!" Norah looked amazed. "Chops were quite the most extravagant thing of all — too much bone. You see, the meat ration included bone and fat, and I can tell you we were pretty badly worried if we got too much of either."

"To think of all she knows," said the aunt, regarding her with a tearful eye. Whereat Norah laughed.

"Oh, I could tell you lots of homely things," she said. "How we always boiled bones for soup at least four times before we looked on them as used up; and how we worked up sheep's heads into the most wonderful chicken galantines; and — but would you mind if I ate some walnut cake instead? It's making me tremble even to look at it."

After which Jean Yorke and the russet-brown waitresses vied in plying the newcomers with the most elaborate cakes, until even Jim and Wally begged for mercy.

"You ought to remember we're not used to these things," Wally protested, waving away a strange erection of cream, icing and wafery pastry. "If I ate that it would go to my head, and I'd have to be removed in an ambulance. And the awful part of it is — I want to eat it. Take it out of my sight, Jean, or I'll yield, and the consequences will be awful."

"But it is too dreadful to think of all you poor souls have gone through," said an aunt soulfully. "How little we in Australia know of what war means!"

"But if it comes to that, how little we knew!" Norah exclaimed. "Why, there we were, only a few miles from the fighting — you could hear the guns on a still day, when a big action was going on; and except for the people who came directly in the way of air raids, England knew little or nothing of war. I mean, war as the people of Belgium and Northern France knew it. The worst we had to admit was that we didn't get everything we liked to eat, and that was a joke compared to what we might have had. Hardly anyone in England went cold or hungry through the war, and so I don't think we knew much about it either." She broke off blushing furiously, to find everyone listening to her. "I didn't mean to make a speech."

"It's quite true, though," said her father, "even if you did make a speech about it. There were privations in some cases, no doubt — invalids sometimes suffered, or men used to a heavy meat diet, whose wives had not knowledge — or fuel — enough to cook substitutes properly. On the other hand, there was no unemployment, and the poor were better fed than they had ever been, since everyone could make good wages at munitions. The death rate among civilians was very much lower than usual. People learned to eat less, and not to waste — and the pre-war waste in England was terrific. And I say — and I think we all say — that anyone who grumbles about 'privations' in England deserves to know what real war means — as the women of Belgium know it."

He stopped, and Norah regarded him with great pride, since his remarks were usually strictly limited to the fewest possible words.

"Well, it's rather refreshing to hear you talk," remarked another squatter. "A good many people have come back telling most pathetic tales of all

they had to endure. I suppose, though, that some
were worse off than you?"

"Oh, certainly," David Linton said. "We knew
one Australian, an officer's wife, who was stranded
in a remote corner of South Wales with two
servants and two babies; it was just at the time
of greatest scarcity before compulsory rationing
began, when most of the food coming in was kept
in the big towns and the Midlands. That woman
could certainly get milk for her youngsters; but for
three months the only foods she and her maids
were sure of getting were war bread, potatoes,
haricot beans and salt herrings. She was a good
way from the nearest town, and there was deep
snow most of the time. There was no carting out
to her place, and by the time she could get into
the town most of the food shops would be empty."

"And if you saw the salt herrings!" said Norah.
"They come down from Scotland, packed
thousands in a barrel. They're about the length
and thickness of a comb, and if you soak them for
a day in warm water and then boil them, you can
begin to think about them as a possible food. But
Mrs. Burton and her maids ate them for three
months. She didn't seem to think she had anything
to grumble about — in fact, she said she still felt
friendly towards potatoes, but she hoped she'd
never see a herring or a bean again!"

"She had her own troubles about coal, too,"
remarked Jim. "The only coal down there is a
horrible brownish stuff that falls into damp slack
if you look at it; it's generally used only for
furnaces, but people had to draw their coal

allowance from the nearest supply, and it was all she could get. The only way to use the beastly stuff was to mix it with wet, salt mud from the river into what the country people call culm — then you cut it into blocks, or make balls of it, and it hardens. She couldn't get a man to do it for her, and she used to mix all her culm herself — and you wouldn't call it woman's work, even in Germany. But she used to tell it as a kind of joke."

"She used to look on herself as one of the really lucky women," said David Linton, "because her husband didn't get killed. And I think she was — herrings and culm and all. And we're even luckier, since we've all come back to Australia, and to such a welcome as you've given us." He stood up, smiling his slow, pleasant smile at them all. "And now I think I've got to go chasing the Customs, if I'm ever to disinter our belongings and get home."

The girls took possession of Norah and Tommy, who left their menfolk to the drear business of clearing luggage, and thankfully spent the afternoon in the Botanical Gardens, glad to have firm ground under their feet after six weeks of sea. Then they all met at dinner at Mrs. Geoffrey Linton's, where they found her son, Cecil, who greeted Norah with something of embarrassment. There was an old score between Norah and Cecil Linton, although they had not seen each other for years; but its memory died out in Norah's heart as she looked at her cousin's military badge and noted that he dragged one foot slightly. Indeed, there was no room in Norah's heart for anything but happiness.

The aunts and uncles tried hard to persuade David Linton to remain a few days in Melbourne, but he shook his head.

"I've been homesick for five years," he told them. "And it feels like fifty. I'll come down again, I promise — yes, and bring the children, of course. But just now I can't wait. I've got to get home."

"That old Billabong!" said Mrs. Geoffrey, half laughing. "Are you going to live and die in the backblocks, David?"

"Why, certainly — at least I hope so," he said. "I suppose there must be lucid intervals, now that Norah is grown up, or imagines she is — not that she seems to me a bit different from the time when her hair was down. Still I suppose I must bring her to town, and let her make her curtsy at Government House, and do all the correct things —"

Someone slipped a hand through his arm.

"But when we've done them, Daddy," said Norah cheerfully, "there will always be Billabong to go home to!"

CHAPTER 10

Billabong

"WILL it be fine, Murty?"

The person addressed made no answer for a moment, continuing to stare at the western horizon with his eyes wrinkled and his face anxious. He turned presently; a tall, grizzled man, with the stooping shoulders and the slightly bowed legs that are the heritage of those who spend nine-tenths of their time in the saddle.

"Sorra a one of me knows," he said. "It's one of thim unchancy days that might be anything. Have you looked at the glass?"

"It's mejum," replied the first speaker. She was a vast woman, with a broad, kindly face, lit by shrewd and twinkling blue eyes, dressed, as was her custom, in a starched blue print, with a snowy apron. "Mejum only. But I don't feel comferable at that there bank of clouds, Murty."

"I'd not say myself it was good," admitted Murty O'Toole, head stockman on the Billabong run. He looked again at the doubtful sky, and then back to Mrs. Brown. "Have you no corns, at all, that 'ud be shootin' on you if rain was coming?"

"Corns I 'ave, indeed," said Mrs. Brown, with the sigh of one who admits that she is but human. "But no — they ain't shootin' worth speakin' about,

Murty. Nor me rheumatic knee ain't givin' tongue, as Master Jim would say."

"Yerra, that's all to the good," said the stockman, much cheered. "I'll not look at the old sky any longer — leastways, not till I have that cup of tea ye were speakin' about."

"Come in then," said Mrs. Brown, leading the way into the kitchen — a huge place so glittering with cleanliness and polish that it almost hurt the eye. "Kettle's boilin' — I'll have it made in a jiffy. No, Murty, you will not sit on that table. Pounds of bath-brick 'ave gone into me tables this last week."

"Ye have them always that white. I do not see how ye'd want them to be whiter," remarked Murty, gazing round him. "But I never see anything to aiqual the shine ye have on them tins an' copper. And the stove is that fine it's a shame to be cookin' with it." He looked with respect at the black satin and silver of the stove, where leaping flames glowed redly. "Well, I'll always say there isn't a heartsomer place to come into than the Billabong kitchen. And isn't it the little mistress that thinks so?"

"Bless her, she was always in and out of it from the time she could toddle," said Mrs. Brown, pausing with the teapot in her hand. "And she wasn't much more than toddlin' before she was at me to teach her to cook. When she was twelve she could cook a dinner as well as anyone twice her age. I never see the beat of her — handy as a man out on the run, too —"

"She was that," said Murty solemnly. "Since she

was a bit of a thing I never see the bullock as
could get away from her. And the ponies she'd
ride! There was nothin' ever looked through a
bridle that could frighten her."

"Poof! Miss Norah didn't know what it was to
be afraid," said Mrs. Brown, filling the huge brown
teapot. "Sometimes I've wished she was, for me
heart's been in me mouth often and often when I
see her go caperin' down the track on some
mad-'eaded pony."

"An' there was never a time when they was late
home but you made sure the whole lot of 'em was
killed," said Murty, grinning. "I'd come in here
an' find you wit' all the funerals planned, so to
speak —"

"Ah, go on! At least, I always stayed at home
when I was nervous," said Mrs. Brown. "Who was
it I've known catch a 'orse in the dark, an' go off
to look for 'em when they were a bit late? Not me,
Mr. O'Toole!" She filled his cup and handed it to
him with a triumphant air.

"Yerra, I misremember doin' any such thing,"
said Murty, slightly confused. " 'Tis the way I was
most likely goin' after a sick bullock, or it might
be 'possum shootin'." He raised his cup and took
a deep draught; then, with a wry face, gazed at
its contents. "I dunno — is this a new brand of
tea you're after usin', now? Sure, it looks pale."

Mrs. Brown cast a glance at the cup he held
out, and gave a gasp of horror.

"Well, not in all me born days 'ave I made tea
an' forgot to put the tea in!" she exclaimed,
snatching it from his hand. "Don't you go an' tell

Dave and Mick, Murty, or I'll never hear the end
of it. Lucky there's plenty of hot water." She
emptied the teapot swiftly, and refilled it, this
time with due regard to the tea caddy.

"Now, Murty, don't you sit there grinnin' at me
like a hyener — it isn't every day I get Miss Norah
home."

"It is not," said Murty, taking his renewed cup
and a large piece of bread and butter. "Sure, I'd
not blame ye if ye fried bacon in the teapot — not
this morning. I dunno, myself, am I on me head
or me heels. All the men is much the same; they've
been fallin' over each other, tryin' to get a little
bit of extra spit-an'-polish on the whole place. I
b'lieve Dave Boone would 'a' set to work an'
whitewashed the paddock fences if I'd encouraged
him at all."

"There's that Sarah," said Mrs. Brown. "Ornery
days it takes me, an alarm clock, an' Mary, to say
nothin' of a wet sponge, to get her out of bed. But
bless you — these last three days she's up before
the pair of us, rubbin' an' polishin' in every corner.
An' she an' 'Ogg at each other's throats over
flowers; she wantin' to pick every one to look
pretty in the 'ouse, an' 'Ogg wantin' every one to
look pretty in the garden."

"Well, Hogg's got enough an' to spare," was
Murty's comment. "No union touch about his work.
I reckon he's put in sixteens hours a day at that
garden since we heard they were comin'."

"But there never was any union touch about
Billabong," said Mrs. Brown.

"Not much! We all know when we're well off,"

said Murty. "I'll bet no union was ever as good a boss as David Linton."

Two other men appeared at the kitchen door — Mick Shanahan and Dave Boone — each wearing, in defiance of regulations, some battered remnant of uniform that marked the "digger", while Mick, in addition, would walk always with a slight limp. He was accustomed to say 'twas a mercy it didn't hinder his profession — which, being that of a horsebreaker, freed him, as a rule, from the necessity of much walking. Other men Billabong had sent to the war, and not all of them had come back; the lonely station had been a place of anxiety and of mourning. But today the memories of the long years of fighting and waiting were blotted out in joy.

"Come in, boys," Mrs. Brown nodded at the men. "Tea's ready. What's it going to be?"

"Fine, I think," said Boone, replying to this somewhat indefinite question with complete certainty as to the questioner's meaning. "I seen you an' Murty pokin' your heads up at them clouds, but there ain't nothin' in them." A smile spread over his good-looking, dark face. "Bless you, it couldn't rain today, with Miss Norah comin' home!"

"I don't believe, myself, that Providence 'ud 'ave the 'eart," said Mrs. Brown. "Picksher them now all flyin' round and gettin' ready to start, and snatchin' a bite of breakfast —"

"If I know Master Jim 'twill be no bite he'll snatch!" put in Mick.

"Well, all I hope is that the hotel don't poison

them," said Mrs. Brown darkly. "I only stopped in a Melb' 'otel once, and then I got po-o'mine poisoning, or whatever they call it. I've heard they never wash their saucepans!"

"No wonder you get rummy flavours in what you eat down there, if that's so," said Dave. "Surprisin' what the digestion of them city people learn to put up with. Well, I suppose you won't be addin' to their risks by puttin' up much of a dinner for them today, Mrs. Brown." He grinned wickedly.

"You go on, imperence!" said the lady. "If I let you look into the larder now (which I won't, along of knowin' you too well), there'd be no gettin' you out to work today. Murty, that turkey weighed five-and-thirty pound!"

"Sure he looked every ounce of it," said Murty. "I never see his aiqual — he was a regular Clydesdale of a bird!"

"I rose him from the aig myself," said Mrs. Brown, "and I don't think I could 'a' brung myself to 'ave 'im killed for anything less than them comin' 'ome. As it was, I feel 'e's died a nobil death. An' 'e'll eat beautiful, you mark my words."

"Well, it'll be something to think of the Boss at the head of his table, investigatin' a Billabong turkey again," said Boone, putting down his empty cup. "And as there's nothing more certain than that they'll all be out at the stables d'reckly after dinner, wantin' to see the 'orses, you an' I'd better go an' shine 'em up a bit more, Mick." They tramped out of the kitchen, while Mrs. Brown waddled to the veranda and cast further anxious glances at the bank of clouds lying westward.

Norah was watching them, too. She was sitting
in the corner of the compartment, as the swift
train bore them northward, with her eyes glued
to the country flying past. Just for once the others
did not matter to her; her father, Jim, and Wally,
each in his own corner, as they had travelled so
many times in the past, coming back from school.
Then she had eyes only for them; today her soul
was hungry for the dear country she had not seen
for so long. It lay bare enough in the early winter
— long stretches of stone-walled paddocks where
the red soil showed through the sparse, native
grass; steep, stony hillsides, with little sheep
grazing on them — pygmies, after the great
English sheep; oases of irrigation, with the deep
green of lucerne growing rank among weed-fringed
water-channels; and so on and on, past little towns
and tiny settlements, and now and then a stop at
some place of more importance. But Norah did not
want the towns; she was homesick for the open
country, for the scent of the gum trees coming
drifting in through the open window, for the long,
lonely plains where grazing cattle raised lazy eyes
to look at the roaring engine, or horses flung up
nervous heads and went racing away across the
grass — more for the fun of it than from fear. The
gum trees called to her, beckoned to her; she forgot
the smooth perfection of the English landscape as
she feasted her eyes on the dear, untidy trees,
whose dangling strips of bark seemed to wave to
her in greeting, telling her she was coming home.
They passed a great team of working bullocks in
a wagon loaded with an enormous tree trunk;

twenty-four monsters, roan and red and speckled, with a great pair of polled Angus in the lead; they plodded along in their own dust, their driver beside them with his immense whip over his shoulder. Norah pointed them out to the others with a quick exclamation, and Jim and Wally came to look out from her window.

"By Jove, what a team!" said Jim. "Well, just at this moment I'd rather see those fellows than the meet of the Coaching Club in Hyde Park — and I had a private idea that that was the finest sight in the world!"

"Aren't you a jungly animal!" quoth Wally.

"Rather — just now," Jim rejoined. "Some day, I suppose, I'll be glad to go back to London, and look at it all again. But just now there doesn't seem to be anything to touch a fellow's own country — and that team of old sloggers there is just a bit of it. Isn't it, old Nor?" She nodded up at him; there was no need of words.

The morning was drawing towards noon when they came in sight of their own little station: Cunjee, looking just as they had left it years ago, its corrugated iron roofs gleaming in the sunlight, its one street green with feathery pepper trees along each side. The train pulled up, and they all tumbled out hastily; presumably the express wasted no more time upon Cunjee than in days gone by, when it was necessary to hustle out of the carriage, and to race along to the van, lest the whistle should sound and your trunks be whisked away somewhere down the line.

There were many people on the platform, and,

wonderful to relate, a band was playing — "Home Sweet Home"; a little band, some of its musicians still in the aprons in which they had rushed from their shop duties; with instruments few and poor, and with not much training, so that the cornet was apt to be half a bar ahead of the euphonium. The Lintons had heard many bands since they had been away, and some had played before the King himself; but no music had ever gripped at their heartstrings like the music of the little backblocks band that stood on the gravelled platform of Cunjee and played to welcome them home.

Suddenly, as they stood bewildered, there seemed people all round them; kindly, homely faces, gripping their hands, shouting greetings. Evans, the manager of Billabong, showed a delighted face for a moment, said, "Luggage in the van. I'll see to it; don't you bother," and was gone. Little Dr. Anderson and his wife, friends of long years, were trying to shake hands with all four at once. They were the centre of an excited little crowd — and found it hard to believe that it was really for them. The train roared away, unnoticed, and the station-master and the porter ran up to add their voices to the chorus. Somehow they were outside the station, gently propelled; and there was a great arch of gum leaves, with a huge WELCOME in red letters, and beneath it were the shire president and his councillors, and other weighty men, all with speeches ready. But the speeches did not come to much, for the shire president had lads himself who had gone to the war, and a lump came in his throat as he looked

at the tall boys from Billabong, whom he had
known as little children; so that half the fine
things he had prepared were never said — which
did not matter, since he had it all written out and
gave it to the reporter of the local paper
afterwards! Something of speech-making there
undoubtedly was, but no one could have told you
much about it — and suddenly it ended in
someone calling for "Three cheers!" which
everyone gave with a will, while the band played
that they were Jolly Good Fellows — and some of
the band cheered while they played, with very
curious results. Then David Linton tried to speak,
and that was a failure also, as far as eloquence
went; but nobody seemed to mind. So, between
hand grips and cheers, they made their way
through the welcome of Cunjee to where the big
double buggy of Billabong stood, with three
fidgeting brown horses, each held by a volunteer.
Beyond that was the carry-all of the bush; an
express wagon, with a grinning Aborigine at the
horses' heads — and Norah went to him with
outstretched hands.

"Why, Billy!" she said.

Billy's grin expanded in a perfectly reckless
fashion.

"Plenty glad!" he stammered — and thereby
doubled his usual output of words.

Willing hands were tossing their luggage into
the wagon — unfamiliar luggage to Cunjee, with
its jumble of ship labels, Continental hotel brands,
and the name of towns all over England, Ireland
and Scotland. There were battered tin uniform

cases of Jim and Wally's, bearing their rank and regiment in half effaced letters: "Major J. Linton", "Captain W. Meadows" — it was hard to realise that they belonged to the two merry-faced boys, who did not seem much changed from the days when Cunjee had seen them arrive light-heartedly from school. Mr. Linton ran his eye over the pile, pronouncing it complete. Then Evans was at his side.

"The motor you sent is ready at the garage in the township if you want it," he said. "But you wired that I was to bring the buggy."

"I did," said David Linton, with a slow smile. "I suppose for convenience sake we'll have to shake down to using the motor. But I drove the old buggy away from Billabong, and I'll drive home now. Jump in, children."

He gathered up the reins, sitting, erect and spare, with one foot on the brake, while the brown horses plunged impatiently, and the volunteers found their work cut out in holding them. Norah was by him, Evans on her other hand; Jim and Wally "tumbled up" into the back seat, as they had done so many times. David Linton looked down at the crowd below.

"Thank you all again," he said. "We'll see you soon — it's not goodbye now, only 'so-long'. Let 'em go, boys."

The volunteers sprang back, thankfully. The browns stood on their hind legs for a moment, endeavouring to tie themselves in knots; then the whip spoke, and they came to earth, straightened themselves out with a flying plunge, and wheeled

out of the station yard and up the street. Behind
them cheers broke out afresh, and the band blared
once more — which acted as a further spur to the
horses; they were pulling double as the high buggy
flashed along the street, where every house and
every shop showed smiling faces, and
handkerchiefs waved in welcome. So they passed
through Cunjee, and wheeled to the right towards
the open country — the country that meant
Billabong.

There were seventeen miles of road ahead, but
the browns made little of them. They had come
into the township the evening before, and had
done nothing since but eat the hotel oats and wish
to be out of a close stable and back in their own
free paddocks. They took the hills at a swift,
effortless trot, and on the down slopes broke into
a hand-gallop; light-hearted, but conscious all the
time of the hand on the reins, that was as steel,
yet light as a feather upon a tender mouth. They
danced merrily to one side when they met a motor
or a hawker's van with flapping cover; when the
buggy rattled over a bridge they plainly regarded
the drumming of their own hoofs as the last
trump, and fled widely for a few hundred yards,
before realising that nothing was really going to
happen to them. But the miles fled under their
swift feet. The trim villas near the township gave
place to scattered farms. These in their turn
became further and further apart, and then they
entered a wide belt of timber, ragged and
wind-swept gums, with dense undergrowth of
dogwood and bracken fern. The metalled road gave

place to a hard, earthen track, on which the spinning tyres made no sound; it curved in and out among the trees, which met overhead and cast upon it a waving pattern of shadows. Grim things had once happened to Norah in this belt of trees, and the past came back to her as she looked at its gloomy recesses again.

They were all silent. There had been few questions to ask of Evans, a few to be answered; then speech fled from them and the old spell of the country held them in its power. Every yard was familiar; every little bridge, every culvert, every quaint old skeleton tree or dead grey log. Here Jim's pony had bolted at sight of an Indian hawker, in days long gone, and had ended by putting his foot into a hole and turning a somersault, shooting Jim into a well-grown clump of nettles. Here Norah had dropped her whip when riding alone, and her fractious young mare had succeeded in pulling away when she dismounted, and had promptly departed post-haste for home; leaving her wrathful owner to follow as she might. A passing bullock-wagon had given her a lift, and the somewhat anxious rescue party, setting out from Billabong, had met its youthful mistress, bruised from much bumping, but otherwise cheerful, progressing in slow majesty towards its gates. Here — but the memories were legions, even to the girl and the two boys. And David Linton's went further back, to the day when he had first driven Norah's mother over the Billabong track; little and dainty and merry, while he had been as always, silent, but unspeakably proud of

her. The little mother's grave had long been green,
and the world had turned topsy-turvey since then,
but the old track was the same, and the memory,
and the pride, were no less clear.

They emerged from the timber at last, and spun
across a wide plain, scattered with clumps of gum
trees. Then another belt of bush, a narrow one
this time; and they came out within view of a great
park-like paddock where Shorthorn bullocks,
knee-deep in grass, scarcely moved aside as the
buggy spun past, with the browns pulling hard.
The track ran near the fence, and turned in at a
big white gate glistening with new paint. It stood
wide open, and beside it was a man on a splendid
bay horse.

"There's Murty, and he's on Garryowen," spoke
Jim quickly. "The old brick!"

"I guess if anyone else had wanted to open the
gate for you today, he'd have had to fight Murty
for the job," said Evans. "And Garryowen's been
groomed till he turns pale at the sight of a brush.
Great horse he's made, Mr. Jim."

"He's all that," said his owner, leaning out to
view him better, with his eyes shining. He raised
his voice in a shout as they swung in through the
gateway. "Good for you, Murty! Hurroo!"

"Hurroo for ye all!" said Murty, and found to
his amazement that his voice was shaky. "Ah,
don't stop, sir, they're all waitin' on ye. I'll be up
as soon as ye."

Norah had tried to speak, and had found that
she had no voice at all. She could only smile at
him, tremulously — and be sure the Irishman did

not fail to catch the smile. Then, as they dashed
up the paddock, her hand sought for her father's
knee under the rug, in the little gesture that had
been hers from babyhood. The track curved round
a grove of great pines, and suddenly they were
within sight of Billabong homestead, red walled
and red roofed, nestled in the deep green of its
trees.

"By Jove!" said Jim, under his breath. "I
thought once I'd never see the old place again."

They flashed through mighty red gums and box
trees, Murty galloping beside them now. There
was a big flag flying proudly on Billabong house
— they found later that the household had
unanimously purchased it on the day they heard
that Jim had got his captaincy. The gate of the
great sanded yard stood open, and near it, on a
wide gravel sweep, were the dear and simple and
faithful people they loved. Mrs. Brown first,
starched and spotless, her hair greyer than it had
been five years before with Sarah and Mary beside
her — they had married during the war, but
nothing had prevented them from coming back to
make Billabong ready. Near them the storekeeper,
Jack Archdale, and his pretty wife, with their
selfish small daughter; and Mick Shanahan and
Dave Boone, with the Scotch gardener, Hogg, and
his Chinese colleague — and sworn enemy — Lee
Wing. They were all there, a little welcoming
group — but Norah could see them only through
a mist of happy tears. The buggy stopped, and
Evans sprang out over the wheel; she followed him

almost as swiftly, running to the old woman who had been all the mother she had known.

"Oh, Brownie — Brownie!"

"My precious lamb!" said Brownie, and held her tightly. She had no hands left for Jim and Wally, and they did not seem to mind; they kissed her, patting her vast shoulders very hard. Then Mrs. Archdale claimed Norah, and Brownie found herself looking mistily up at David Linton and he was gripping her hand tightly, the other hand on her shoulder.

"Why, old Brownie!" he said. "Dear old Brownie!"

They were shaking hands all round, over and over again. Nobody made any speeches of welcome — there were only disjointed words, and once or twice a little sob. Indeed, Brownie only found her tongue when they had drifted across the yard in a confused group, and had reached the wide veranda. Then she looked up at Jim and seemed suddenly to realise his mighty height and breadth.

"Oh!" she said. "Oh! Ain't 'e grown big an' beautiful!" Whereat Wally howled with laughter, and Jim, scarlet, kissed her again, and told her she was a shameful old woman.

No one on Billabong could have told you much of that day, after the first wonderful moment of getting home. It was a day of blurred memories. The newcomers had to wander through the house where every big window stood open to the sunlight, and every room was gay with flowers; and from every window it was necessary to look out at the view across the paddocks and down at the gardens, and to follow the winding course of the creek. The gong summoned them to dinner in the midst of it, and Brownie's dinner deserved to be remembered; the mammoth turnkey flanked by a ham as gigantic, and somewhat alarming to war-trained appetites; followed by every sweet that Brownie could remember as having been a favourite. They drifted naturally to the stables afterwards, to find their special horses, apparently little changed by five years, though some old station favourites were gone, and the men spoke proudly of some new young ones that were going to be "beggars to go", or "a caution to jump". Then they wandered down to the big lagoon, where the old boat yet lay at the edge of the reed-fringed water; and on through the home paddock to look at the little herd of Jerseys that were kept for the use of the house, and some great bullocks almost ready for the Melbourne market. So they came back to the homestead, wandering up from the creek through Lee Wing's rows of vegetables, and came to rest naturally in the kitchen, where they had afternoon tea with Brownie, who beamed from ear to ear at the sight of Jim and Wally again sitting on her table.

"I used to think of you in them 'orrible trenches, an' wonder wot you got to eat, an' if it was anything at all," she said tremulously.

"We got something, but it was apt to be queer," said Jim, laughing. "We used to think of sitting on the table here, Brownie, and eating hot scones — like this. May I have another?"

"My pore dears!" said Brownie, hastily

supplying him with the largest scone in sight.
"Now, Master Wally, my love, ain't you ready for
another? Your appetite's not 'alf wot it used to be.
A pikelet, now?"

"I believe I've had six!" said Wally, defending
himself.

"An' wot used six pikelets to be to you? A mere
fly in the ointment," said Brownie, whose similes
were always apt to be peculiar. "Just another,
then, my dear. An' I've got your fav'rite sponge
cake, Miss Norah — ten aigs in it!"

"Ten!" said Norah faintly. "Hold me, Daddy!
Doesn't it make you feel light-headed to think of
putting ten eggs in one cake again?"

"An' why not?" sniffed Brownie. "Ah, you got
bad treatment in that old England. I never could
see why you should go short, an' you all 'elpin' on
the war as 'ard as you could." Brownie's
indifference to national considerations where her
nurselings were concerned was well known, and
nobody argued with her. "Anyhow, the cake's
there, an' just you try it — it's as light as a
feather, though I do say it."

Once in the kitchen Norah and the boys went
no further. They remained sitting on the tables,
talking, while presently David Linton went away
to his study, and, one by one, Murty and Boone
and Mick Shanahan drifted in. There was so much
to tell, so much to ask about; they talked until the
dusk of the short winter afternoon stole into the
kitchen, making the red flames in the stove leap
more redly. It was time to dress for tea. They went
round the wide verandas and ran upstairs to their

rooms, while old Brownie stood in the kitchen doorway listening to the merry voices.

"Ain't it just 'evinly to 'ear 'em again!" she uttered.

"It is that," said Murty. "We've been quare an' lonesome an' quiet these five years."

CHAPTER 11

Colonial Experiences

CECILIA — otherwise Tommy — and Bob Rainham came up to Billabong three days later, and were met by Jim, who had ridden into Cunjee with Billy, and released the motor from inglorious seclusion in the local garage. Billy jogged off, leading Garryowen, and Jim watched them half wistfully for a minute before turning to the car. Motors had their uses certainly; but no Linton ever dreamed of giving a car the serious and respectful consideration that naturally belonged to a horse.

Nevertheless, it was a good car; a gift to Norah from an Irishman they had known and loved; and Jim drove well, having developed the accomplishment over Flemish roads that were chiefly a succession of shell holes. He took her quietly up to the station, and walked on to the platform as the train thundered in.

Tommy and Bob were looking eagerly from their carriage window, and hailed him with delight; they had been alone, for the first time since leaving England, and had begun to feel that

Australia was a large and slightly populated country, and that they were inconsiderable atoms, suddenly dumped into its vacant spaces. Jim was like a large and friendly rock, and Australia immediately became less wide and desolate in their eyes. He greeted them cheerily and helped Bob to pack their luggage into the car.

"Now, I could get you afternoon tea here," he said, "and I warn you, it will be bad. Or I could have you home in well under an hour, and you wouldn't be too late for tea there. Which is it to be, Tommy?"

"Oh — home," said Tommy. "I don't care a bit about tea; and I want to see this Billabong of yours. Do let's go, Jim."

"I hoped you wouldn't choose tea here," said Jim, striding off to the car. "Bush townships don't run to decent tea places, as a rule; the hotel is the only chance, and though they can give you a fair dinner, tea always seems to be a weak spot." He packed them in, and they moved off down the winding street.

"Do you know," Jim said, "that I never went down this street before except on a horse, or behind one? It seems quite queer and unnatural to be doing it in a car. I suppose I'll get used to it. Had a good trip up?"

"Oh, quite," Tommy told him. "Jim, how few people seem to be living in Australia!"

Jim gave a crack of laughter.

"Well, you saw a good many in Melbourne, didn't you?" he asked.

"Oh, yes. But Melbourne isn't Australia. It's

only away down in a wee little corner." Tommy
flushed a little. "You see, I haven't seen much of
any country except France and the England that's
near London," she said. "And there isn't much
waste space there."

"No, there isn't," Jim agreed. "I suppose we'll
fill up Australia some day. But the people who
come out now seem to have a holy horror of going
into the 'waste spaces', as you call 'em, Tommy.
They want to nestle up to the towns, and go to
picture theatres."

"Well, I want to go and find a nice waste space,"
said Tommy. "Not too waste, of course, only with
room to look all round. And I'd like it to be not
too far from Norah, 'cause she's very cheering to
a lone new-chum. But don't you go planning to
settle in one of those horrid little tin-roofed towns,
Bobby, for I should simply hate it."

"Certainly, ma'am,' said Bob cheerfully. "We'll
get out into the open. I can always run you about
in an aeroplane, if you feel lonesome, provided we
make enough money to buy one, that is. Only
new-chums don't always make heaps of money, do
they, Jim?"

"Not at first, I'm afraid," Jim said. "The days of
picking up fortunes in Australia seem to be over;
anyway, there's no more gold lying about.
Nowadays, you have to put your back into it
extremely hard, if you've no capital to start with;
and even if you have, you can't loaf. How did you
get on in Melbourne? I hope you didn't buy a
station without consulting us."

"Rather not," Bob answered. "We raced round

magnificently in your aunt's car and presented our letters, and had more invitations to sundry meals than we could possibly accept. Everyone was extraordinarily kind to us. I've offers and promises of advice in whatever district we settle; three squatters asked me up to their places, to stay awhile and study the country; and one confiding man — I hadn't a letter to him at all, by the way, only someone introduced us to him in Scott's — actually offered me a job as jackeroo on a Queensland run. But he was a lone old bachelor, and when he heard I had a sister he shied off in terror. I think he's running yet."

Jim shouted with laughter.

"Poor old Tommy!" he said.

"Yes, is it not unfair?" said Tommy. "I told Bob I was a mere encumbrance, but he would bring me."

"You wait until you've settled, and Bob wants someone to run his house, and then see how much of an encumbrance you are," rejoined Jim. "Then you'll suddenly stop being meek and get a swelled head."

"And not be half so nice," interjected Bob.

"But so useful!" said Tommy demurely. "Only sometimes I become afraid — for you seem always to kill a whole sheep or bullock up in the bush, and how I am to deal with it I do not know!"

"It sounds as if you preferred someone to detach an occasional limb from the sheep as it walked about!" said Jim, laughing.

"Much easier for me — if not for the sheep," said Tommy.

"Well, don't you worry — the meat problem will
get settled somehow," Jim told her cheerfully. "All
problems straighten out, if you give 'em time. Now
we're nearly home — that's the fence of our home
paddock. And there are Norah and Wally coming
to meet you."

"Oh — where?" Tommy started up, looking
excitedly round the landscape. "Oh — there she is
— the dear! And isn't that a beautiful horse!"

"That's Norah's special old pony, Bosun," said
Jim. "We're making her very unhappy by telling
her she's grown too big for him, but he really
carries her like a bird. A habit might look too
much on him, but not that astride kit. You got
yours, by the way, Tommy, I hope?"

"Oh yes. I look very strange in it," said Tommy.
"And Bob thinks I might as well have worn out
his old uniforms. But I shall never ride like that
— as Norah does."

She looked at Norah, who was coming across
the paddock with Wally, at a hard canter. Her
pony was impatient, reefing and plunging in his
desire to gallop; and Norah was sitting him easily,
her hands well down, giving to the strain on the
bit, her slight figure, in coat and breeches, swaying
lightly to each bound. The sunlight rippled on
Bosun's glossy, bay coat, and on the big black
horse Wally rode. They pulled up, laughing, at the
gateway, just as the car turned off the road. There
were confused and enthusiastic greetings, and the
car dashed on up the track with an outrider on
each side — both horses strongly resenting this
new and ferocious monster. The years had brought

a good deal of sober sense to Bosun and Monarch, but motors were still unfamiliar objects on Billabong. Indeed, no car of the size of Norah's Rolls-Royce had ever been seen in the district, and the men gaped at it open-mouthed as Jim drove it round to the stable after unloading his passengers.

"Yerra, but that's the fine carry-van," said Murty. "Is that the size they have them in England, now?"

"No, it isn't, Murty — not as a rule," Jim answered. "This was built specially for a man who was half an invalid; he used to go for long tours, and sleep in the car because he hated hotels. So it's a special size. It used to be jolly useful taking out wounded men in England."

"Sure, it would be," Murty said. "Only — somehow, it don't seem to fit into Billabong, Mr. Jim!"

"So big as that! I say, Murty!"

"Yerra, there's room enough for it," grinned the Irishman. "Only, motors and Billabong don't go hand in hand — we've always stuck to horses, haven't we, Mr. Jim?"

"We'll do that still," Jim said. "But it will be useful, all the same, Murty." He laughed at the stockman's lugubrious face. "Oh, I know it's giving you the sort of pain you had when Dad had the telephone put on —"

"Well, 'tis the quare onnatural little machine, an' I never feel anyways at home with it, Mr. Jim," Murty defended himself.

"There's lots like you, Murty. But you'll admit

that when we've got to send a telegram, it's better to telephone it than make a man ride thirty-four miles with it?"

"I suppose it is," said the Irishman doubtfully. Jim chuckled.

"There's no getting round as Irishman when he makes up his mind," he said. "And if you had to catch the eight o'clock train to Melbourne I believe you'd rather wake up at three in the morning and run up the horses to drive in, than leave here comfortably in the car at seven."

"Is it me to drive in it?" demanded Murty, in horror. "Begob, I'd lose my life before I'd get into one of thim quare, sawed-off things. Give me something with shafts, Mr. Jim, and a dacint horse in them. More by token, I would not get up at three in the morning either, but drive in easy an' comfortable the night before." He beamed on Jim with so clear a conviction that he was unanswerable that Jim hadn't the heart to argue further. Instead he ran the car deftly into a buggy-shed whence an ancient double buggy had been deposed to make room for her, and then fell to discussing with Murty the question of building a garage, with a turntable and pit for cleaning and repairs. To which Murty gave the eager interest and attention he would have shown had Jim proposed building anything, even had it been an Eiffel Tower on the front lawn.

Brownie came out through the box-trees to the stables, presently.

"Now, Master Jim, afternoon tea's in these ten minutes."

"Good gracious! I forgot all about tea!" Jim exclaimed. "Thanks awfully, Brownie. Had your own?" He slipped his arm through hers as they turned back to the house.

"Not yet, my dear," said Brownie, beaming up at him. That this huge Major, with four years of war service to his credit, was exactly the same to her as the little boy she had bathed and dressed in years gone by, was a matter of nightly thanksgiving in her prayers. "I was just goin' to settle to it when it come over me that you weren't in — and the visitors there an' all."

"I'd come and have mine with you in the kitchen if they weren't there," Jim told her. "Tea in your kitchen is better than anything else." He patted her shoulders as he left her at the door of her domain, going off with long strides to wash his hands.

"We didn't wait for you," Norah said, as he came into the drawing-room; a big cheery room, with long windows opening out upon the veranda, and a conservatory at one end. A fire of red gum logs made it pleasantly warm; the tea table was drawn near its blaze, and the armchairs made a semicircle round it. "These poor people looked far too hungry to wait — to say nothing of Wally and myself. How did the car go, Jimmy?"

"Splendidly," Jim said, taking his cup, and retiring from the tea-table with a scone. "Never ran better; that man in Cunjee knows his job, which I didn't expect. Are you tired, Tommy?"

"Tired? No," said Tommy. "I was very hungry, but that is getting better. And Norah is going to show me Billabong, so I could not possibly dream of being tired."

"If Norah means to show you all Billabong before dark, she'll have to hurry," said Jim lazily. "Don't you let yourself be persuaded into anything so desperate, Tommy."

"Don't you worry; I'll give her graduated doses," Norah said. "I'll watch the patient carefully, and see if there is any sign of strength failing. When do you begin to teach Bob to run a station?"

"I never saw anyone in such a hurry," said Jim. "Why, the poor beggar hasn't had his tea yet — give him time."

"But we are in a hurry," said Tommy. "We're burning to learn all about it. Norah is to teach me the house side, while you instruct Bob how to tell a merino bullock — is it not? — from an Ayrshire." Everybody ate with suspicious haste, and she looked at them shrewdly. "Now, I have said that all wrong, I feel sure, but it's just as well for you to be prepared for that. Norah will have a busy time correcting my mistakes."

"You aren't supposed to know anything about cattle and things like that," said Norah. "And when it comes to the house side, I don't think you'll find I can teach you much — if anyone brought up to know French cooking and French housekeeping has much to learn from a backblocks Australian, I'll be surprised."

"In fact," said Mr. Linton. "I should think that the lessons will generally end in the students of domestic economy fleeing forth upon horses and

studying how to deal with beef — on the hoof.
Don't you, Wally?"

"Rather," said Wally. "And Brownie will wash
up after them, and say, 'Bless their hearts, why
would they stay in a hot kitchen!' And so poor old
Bob will go down the road to ruin!"

"It's a jolly prospect," said Bob placidly. "I think
we'll knock a good deal of fun out of it!"

They trooped out in a body presently on their
preliminary voyage of discovery; touring the house
itself, with its big rooms and wide corridors, and
the broad balconies that ran round three sides,
from which you looked far across the run — miles
of rolling plains, dotted with trees and clumps of
timber, and merging into a far line of low,
scrub-grown hills. Then outside and to the stables
— a massive red brick pile, creeper-covered, where
Monarch and Garryowen, and Bosun, and the
buggy ponies, looked placidly from their loose
boxes, and asked for — and got — apples from
Jim's pockets. Tommy even made her way up the
steep ladder to the loft that ran the whole length
of the stables — big enough for the men's yearly
dance, but just now crammed with fragrant oaten
hay. She wanted to see everything, and chatted
away in her eager, half-French fashion, like a
happy child.

"It is so lovely to be here," she told Norah later,
when the keen evening wind had driven them
indoors from a tour of the garden. She was
kneeling on the floor of her bedroom, unpacking
her trunk, while Norah perched on the end of the
bed. "You see, I am no longer afraid; and I have

always been afraid since Aunt Margaret died. In Lancaster Gate I was afraid all the time, especially when I was planning to run away. Then, on the ship, though everyone was so kind, the big, unknown country was like a wall of fear ahead; even in Melbourne everything seemed uncertain, doubtful. But now, quite suddenly, it is all right. I just know we shall get along quite well."

"Why, of course you will," Norah said, laughing down at the earnest face. "You're the kind of people who must do well, because you are so keen. And Billabong has adopted you, and we're going to see that you make a success of things. You're our very own immigrants!"

"It's nice to be owned by someone who isn't my step-mother," said Tommy happily. "I began to think I was hers, body and soul — when she appeared on that awful moment in Liverpool I made sure all hope was over. Bob says I shouldn't have panicked, but then Bob had not been a toad under her harrow for two years."

"I'm very glad you panicked, since it sent you straight into our arms," said Norah. "If we had met you in an ordinary, stodgy way — you and Bob presenting your letter of introduction, and we saying 'How do you do?' politely — it would have taken us ages to get to know you properly. And as it was, we jumped into being friends. You did look such a poor, hunted little soul as you came dodging across the street!"

"And you took me on trust, when, for all you know, the police might have been after me," said

Tommy. "Well, we won't forget; not that I suppose Bob and I will ever be able to pay you back."

"Good gracious, we don't want paying back!" exclaimed Norah, wrinkling her nose disgustedly. "Don't talk such utter nonsense, Tommy Rainham. And just hurry up and unpack, because tea will be ready at half-past six."

"My goodness!" exclaimed the English girl, to whom dinner at half-past seven was a custom of life not lightly to be altered. "And I haven't half unpacked, and oh, where is my blue frock? I don't believe I've brought it." She sought despairingly in the trunk.

"Yes, you have — I hung it up for you in the wardrobe ages ago," said Norah. "And it doesn't matter if you don't finish before tea. There's lots of time ahead. However, I certainly won't be dressed if I don't hurry, because I've to see Brownie first, and then sew on a button for Jim. You'll find me next door when you're ready." Tommy heard her go, singing downstairs, and she sighed happily. This, for the first time for two years, was a real home.

The education of the new-chums began next morning, and was carried out thoroughly, since Mr. Linton did not believe in showing their immigrants only the pleasanter side of Australian life. Bob was given a few days of riding round the run, spying out the land, and learning something about cattle and their handling as he rode. Luckily for him, he was a good horseman. The stockmen, always on the alert to "pick holes" in a new-chum, had little fault to find with his easy seat and hands, and approved of the way in which he waited for no one's help in saddling up or letting go his horse; a point which always tells with the man of the bush.

"We've had thim on this run," said Murty, "as wanted their horses led gently up to thim, and then they climb into the saddle like a lady. And when they'd come home, all they'd be lookin' for 'ud be someone to cast their reins to, the way they could stroll off to their tay. Isn't that so, Mick?"

"Yairs," said Mick. He was riding an unbroken three year old, and had no time for conversation.

After a few days of "gentle exercise", Bob found himself put on to work. He learned something of cutting out and mustering, both in cleared country and in scrub; helped bring home young cattle to brand, and studied at first hand the peculiar evilness of a scrub cow when separated from her calf. They gave him jobs for himself, which he accomplished fairly well, aided by a stock horse of superhuman intelligence, which naturally knew far more of the work than its rider could hope to do. Bob confided to Tommy that never had he felt so complete a fool as when he rode forth for the first time to cut out a bullock alone under the eyes of the experts.

"Luckily, the old mare did all the work," he said. "But I knew less about it than I did the first time I went up alone at the flying school!"

His teaching went on all the time. Mr. Linton and Jim were tireless in pointing out the points of cattle, and the variations in the value of feed on the different parts of the run, with all the details of bush lore; and the airman's eyes, trained to observe, and backed by keen desire to learn, picked up and retained knowledge quickly. Billabong was, in the main, a cattle run, but Mr. Linton kept as well a flock of high class sheep, with the usual small mob for killing for station use, and through these a certain amount of sheep knowledge was imparted to the new-chum. To their surprise, for all his instructors were heart and soul for cattle, Bob showed a distinct leaning towards mutton.

"They're easier to understand, I think," he said. "Possibly it's because they're not as intelligent as cattle, and I don't think I am, either!"

"Well, I know something about bullocks, but these woolly objects have always been beyond me," said Jim. "Necessary evils, but I can't stand them. I used to think there was nothing more hopeless than an old merino ewe, until I met a battery mule — he's a shade worse!"

"Wait till you've worked with a camel in a bad temper, Mr. Jim," said Dave Boone darkly; he had put in a weary time in Egypt. "For downright wickedness them snake-headed beggars is the fair limit!"

"Yes, I've heard so," said Jim. "Anyhow, we haven't added mules and camels to our worries in Victoria yet; sheep are bad enough for me. Norah says turkey hens are worse, and she's certainly tried both; there isn't much about the run young Norah doesn't know. But you aren't going to make a living out of turkeys."

"No — Tommy can run them as a side line,"

said Bob. "I fancy sheep will give me all I want in the way of worry."

"And you really think you'll go in for sheep, old man?" asked Jim with pity.

Bob set his lips obstinately.

"I don't think anything yet," he said. "I don't know enough. Wait until I've learned a bit more — if you're not sick of teaching such an idiot."

"Yerra, ye're no ijit," said Murty under his breath.

Education developed as the weeks went on. Wally had gone to Queensland, to visit married brothers who were all the "people" he possessed; and Jim, bereft of his chum, threw himself energetically into the training of the substitute. Bob learned to slaughter a bullock and kill a sheep — being instructed that the job in winter was not a circumstance to what it would be in summer, when flies would abound. He never pretended to like this branch of learning, but stuck to it doggedly, since it was explained to him that the man who could not be his own butcher in the bush was apt to go hungry, and that not one hired hand in twenty could be trusted to kill.

More to Bob's taste were the boundary riding expeditions made with Jim to the furthest corners of the run; taking a pack horse with tucker and blankets, and camping in ancient huts, of which the sole furniture was rough sacking bunks, a big fireplace, and empty kerosene cases for seats and tables. It was unfortunate, from the point of view of Bob's instruction, that the frantic zeal of Murty and the men to have everything in order for "the

Boss" had left no yard of the Billabong boundary unvisited not a month before. Still, winter gales were always apt to bring down a tree or two across the wires, laying a few panels flat; the creeks, too, were all in flood, and where a wire fence crossed one, floating brushwood often damaged the barrier, or a landslip in a water-worn bank might carry away a post. So Jim and his pupil found enough occupation to make their trips worthwhile; and Bob learned to sink post holes, to ram a post home beyond the possibility of moving, and to strain a wire fence scientifically. He was not a novice with an axe, though Jim's mighty chopping made him feel a child; still, when it was necessary to cut away a fallen tree, he could do his share manfully. His hands blistered and grew horny callouses, even as his muscles toughened and his shoulders widened; and all the time the appeal of the wide, free country called to his heart and drew him closer and closer to his new life.

"But he's too comfortable, you know," David Linton said to Jim one night. "He's shaping as well as anyone could expect; but he won't always have Billabong at his back."

Jim nodded wisely.

"I know," he said. "Been thinking of that. If you can spare me for a bit we'll go over and lend ourselves as handy men to old Joe Howard."

His father whistled.

"He'll make you toe the mark," he said, laughing. "He won't have you there as gentlemen boarders, you know."

"Don't want him to," said Jim.

So it came about that early on Monday morning Jim and Bob fixed swags more or less scientifically to their saddles — Jim made his disciple unstrap his three times before he consented to pass it — and rode away from Billabong, amidst derisive good wishes from Norah and Tommy, who kindly promised to feed them up on their return, prophesying that they would certainly need it. They took a westerly direction across country, and after two or three hours' riding came upon a small farm nestling at the foot of a low range of hills.

"That's old Howard's," Jim said. "And there's the old chap himself, fixing up his windmill. You wait a minute, Bob; I'll go over and see him."

He gave Bob his bridle, and went across a small paddock near the house. Howard, a hard-looking old man with a long, grey beard, was wrestling with a home-made windmill — a queer erection, mainly composed of rough spars with sails made from old wheatsacks. He clambered to the ground as Jim approached, and greeted him civilly.

"I thought you'd have forgotten me, Mr. Howard," said Jim.

"Too like your dad — an', anyhow, I know the horses," was the laconic answer. "So you're back. Like Australia better'n fightin'?"

"Rather!" said Jim. "Fighting's a poor game, I think, when you hardly ever see the other fellow. Want any hands, Mr. Howard?"

"No." The old man shook his head. "They want too much money nowadays, an' they're too darned particular about their tucker. Meat three times a day, whether you've killed it or not. An' puddin'.

Cock 'em up with puddin' — a fat lot of it I ever saw where I was raised. An' off to the township on Saturday afternoon, an' lucky if they get back in time for milkin' nex' mornin'. No — the workin' man ain't what 'e was, an' the new kind'll make precious little of Australia!"

"That's about right, I'm afraid," said Jim, listening sympathetically to this oration. "Well, will you take me and my friend as hands for a few weeks, Mr. Howard?"

"You!" The old man stared at him. "Ain't 'ad a quarrel with yer dad, 'ave yer? You take my tip, if yer 'ave — go back and make it up. Not many men in this district like yer dad."

"I know that, jolly well," said Jim, laughing. "No — but my friend's a new-chum, and I want to show him something of work on a place like yours. We've been breaking him in on Billabong, but he'll have to take a small place for himself, if he settles, and he'd better see what it's like."

The old man shook his head doubtfully.

"English officer, I suppose?"

"Yes."

"I dunno," said Howard. "Too much of the fine gent about that sort, Mr. Jim. I dunno 'ow I'd get down to orderin' the pair of yous about. An' I ain't got no 'comodation for yous; an' the tucker's not what yous 'ave bin used ter."

"You needn't let any of that worry you," said Jim cheerfully. "He isn't a bit of a fine gent, really, and we'll tackle any job that's going. As for accommodation, we've brought our blankets, and, in case you were short of tucker, we've a big piece

of corned beef and some bread. I wish you'd try it,
Mr. Howard; we don't want pay, and we'll do no
end of work. Murty reckons you won't be sorry if
you take on Captain Rainham."

"Oh, Murty says that, does 'e?" asked the old
man, visibly cheered. "Well, Murty ain't the man
to barrack for a useless new-chum."

"Great Scott, do you think I am?" demanded
Jim, laughing. "Or my father?"

"Yous cert'nly didn't ought to be," agreed
Howard. "All the same" — he pushed his hat back
from his worried brow — "I dunno as I quite like
it. If I take on a chap I like 'im to step quick an'
lively when I tell him anything I want done; an'
I don't make no guests of 'em either. They got to
do their own cookin', an' keep things clean an' tidy,
too."

"We'll take our share," said Jim. "As for
stepping quick and lively, we've both been trained
to that pretty thoroughly during the last few
years. If you're worse than some of the
Sergeant-Majors I met when I was training, I'll
eat my hat."

"I'm told they're 'ard," said Howard. "Well, I
s'pose I'd better take yous on, though it's a queer
day when the son of Linton of Billabong comes
askin' old Joe Howard for a job. But, I say" — and
anguish again settled on his brow — "wot am I to
call yous? I can't order you about as Mr. Jim. It
wouldn't seem to come natural."

"Oh, call us any old thing," said Jim, laughing.

The old man pondered.

"Well, I'll call yous Major an' Captin," he

declared, at length. "That'll sound like a pair of workin' bullocks, an' I'll feel more at 'ome."

"Right-o," said Jim, choking slightly. "Where shall we put our horses?"

"Put 'em in the little paddock over there, an' stick yer saddles in the shed," said his employer. "An' then bring in yer beef, an' we'll 'ave a bit o' dinner. I ain't killed for a fortnight."

Then began for Bob Rainham one of the most strenuous fortnights of his existence. Once having agreed to employ them, old Joe speedily became reconciled to the prospect of cheap labour, and worked his willing guests with a devouring energy. Before dawn had reddened the eastern sky a shout of "Hi, Captin! Time the cow was in!" drove him from his blankets, to search in the darkness of a scrub-covered paddock for a cow, who apparently loved a game of hide-and-seek, and to drive her in and milk her by the fitful light of a hurricane lantern. Then came the usual round of morning duties; chopping wood, feeding pigs, cleaning out sheds and outhouses, before the one-time airman had time to think of breakfast. By the time he came in Howard and Jim had generally finished and gone out — the old man took a sly delight in keeping "Major" away from "Captin" — and after cooking his meal, it was his job to wash up and to clean out the kitchen, over which old Joe proved unexpectedly critical. Then came a varied choice of tasks to tackle to while away the day. Sometimes he would be sent to scrub cutting, which he liked best, particularly as Jim was kept at it always; sometimes he slashed mightily at a blackberry-infested paddock, where the brambles would have daunted anyone less stout of heart — or less ignorant. Then came lessons in ploughing on a dry hillside; he managed badly at first, and came in for a good deal of the rough side of old Joe's tongue before he learned to keep to anything approaching a straight line. Ploughing, Bob reflected, was clearly an art which needed long apprenticeship before you learned to appreciate it, and he developed a new comprehension and sympathy for the ploughman described by Gray as "homeward plodding his weary way". He also wondered if Gray's ploughman had to milk and get his own tea after he got home.

Other relaxations of the bush were open to him. Old Joe had a paddock, once a swamp, which he had drained; it was free of water, but abounded in tussocks and sword grass which "Captin" was detailed to grub out whenever no duty more pressing awaited him. And sword grass is a fearsome vegetable, clinging of root and so tough of stem that, if handled unwarily, it can cut a finger almost to the bone; wherefore the unfortunate "Captin" hated it with a mighty hatred, and preferred any other branch of his education. There were stones to pick up and pile in cairns; red stones, half buried in grass and tussocks, and weighing anything from a pound to half a hundred-weight. He scarred his hands and broke his fingernails to pieces over them, but, on the whole, considered it not a bad employment, except when old Joe took it into his head to perch on the fence and spur him on to greater efforts by

disparaging remarks about England. Whatever his
work, there was never any certainty that old Joe
would not appear, to sit down, light his short,
black pipe, and make caustic remarks about his
methods or his country — or both. Bob took it all
with grin. He was a cheerful soul.

They used to meet for dinner — dinner
consisting of corned beef and potatoes until the
corned beef ran out; then it became potatoes and
bread and jam for some days, until Joe amazed
them by saddling an ancient grey mare and riding
into Cunjee, returning with more corned beef —
and more jam. He boiled the beef in a kerosene
tin, and Bob thought he had never tasted anything
better. Appetites did not need pampering on
Howard's Farm. Work in the evening went on until
there was barely light enough to get home and
find the cow; it was generally quite dark by the
time milking was finished, and Bob would come
in with his bucket to find Jim just in, and lighting
the fire — "Major", not being the milking hand,
worked in the paddocks a little longer. Tea
required little preparation, since the only menu
that occurred to old Joe seemed to be bread and
jam. Jim, being a masterful soul, occasionally took
the matter into his own hands and, aided by Bob,
made "flap-jacks" in the frying-pan; they might
have been indigestible for delicately constituted
people, but at least they had the merit of being
hot and comforting on a biting winter night. Old
Joe growled under his breath at the "softness" of
people who required "cocking up with fal-lals". But
he ate the flap-jacks.

After tea the "hands" divided the duties of the
evening; taking it in turn, one to wash up, while
the other "set" bread. Joe's only baking implement
was a camp oven, which resembles a large
saucepan on three legs; it could hold just enough
for a day's supply, so that it was necessary to set
bread every night, and bake every morning. This
wounded their employer, who never failed to tell
them, with some bitterness, that when alone he
had to bake only twice a week. However, he knew
all that there was to know about camp oven
baking, and taught them the art thoroughly, as
well as that of making yeast from potatoes. "That's
an extra," he remarked thoughtfully, "but I won't
charge yer for it, yous 'avin' bin soldiers!"

With the bread set, and rising pleasantly before
the fire, under a bit of old blanket, and the kitchen
tidy, a period of rest ensued, when "Major" and
"Captin" were free to draw up chairs — seated
with greenhide with the hair left on, and very
comfortable — and smoke their pipes. This was
the only time of the day when old Joe unbent. At
first silent, he would presently shift his pipe to
the corner of his mouth and spin them yarns of
the early days, told with a queer, dry humour that
kept his hearers in a simmer of laughter. It was
always a matter of regret to poor "Captin" that he
used to be the one to end the telling, since no story
on earth could keep him, after a while, from
nodding off to sleep. He would drag himself away
to his blankets in the next room, hearing, as sleep
fully descended upon him, the droning voice still

entertaining Jim — whose powers of keeping awake seemed more than human!

Saturday brought no slackening of work. Whatever his previous hired men had done, old Joe was evidently determined that his present "parlour-boarders" should not abate their efforts, and even kept them a little later than usual in the paddocks, remarking that, "ter-morrer bein' Sunday, yous might as well cut a bit more scrub". The next morning broke fine and clear, and he looked at them a little doubtfully after breakfast.

"Well, there ain't no work doin' on Sunday, I reckon. I can manage the ol' keow tonight, if yous want to go home."

The guests looked at each other doubtfully.

"What do you say, Bob? Shall we ride over?"

Bob pondered.

"All one to me, o' course," said Joe, getting up and stumping out. He paused at the door. "Only if yous mean ter stick on 'ere a bit you'll find comin' back a bit 'ard, onced yous see Billabong."

"Just what I was thinking," said Bob, as the old man disappeared. "I'm not going, Jim; I know jolly well I'd hate to come back after — er — fleshpotting at your place. But look here, old chap — why don't you go home and stay there? You've done quite enough of this, especially as you've no earthly need to do it at all. You go home, and I'll stay out my fortnight."

"What, leave you here alone?" queried Jim. "Not much, Bobby."

"But why not? I've Joseph, and we'd become

bosom friends. And your father must think it ridiculous for you to be kept over here, slaving —"

"Don't you worry your old head about Dad," said Jim cheerfully. "It's a slack time, and he doesn't need me, and he's perfectly satisfied at my being here. Bless you, it's no harm for me to get a bit of this sort of life."

"You'll never have to do it."

"No one can tell that," said Jim. "The bottom has dropped out of land in other countries, and it may happen here. Besides, if you've got to employ labour it's just as well to know from experience what's a fair thing to expect from a man as a day's work. For which reason, I have desired our friend Joseph to take me off scrub-duty, which I feel I know pretty well, and to detail me for assorted fatigues, like yours, next week. And anyhow, my son, having brought you to this savage place, I'm not going to leave you. Finally, we couldn't go anywhere, because this is the day that we must wash."

"I have washed!" said Bob indignantly.

"I didn't mean your person, Bobby, but your clothes. The laundress doesn't call out here."

"Oh!" said Bob, and grinned. "Then I'd better put on a kettle."

So they washed, very cheerfully, taking turns in the one bucket, which was all Joe could offer as laundry equipment. He had an iron, but after brief consultation, "Major" and "Captin" decided that to iron working shirts would be merely painting the lily. Old Joe watched them with a twinkle, saying nothing. But a spirit of festivity

and magnificence must have entered into him, for
when the washermen went for a walk after
disposing their damp raiment upon bushes, he
entered the kitchen hurriedly and dived for the
flour bag; and later, they found unwonted
additions to the corned beef and potatoes — the
said additions being no less than boiled onions and
a jam tart.

The week that followed was a repetition of the
first, save for a day of such rain that even old Joe
had to admit that work in the paddocks was out
of the question. He consoled himself by making
them whitewash the kitchen. Large masses of soot
fell down into the fireplace throughout the day,
seriously interfering with cooking operations,
which suggested to Joe that "Captin" might
acquire yet another art — that of bush chimney
sweeping — which he accomplished next day,
under direction, by the simple process of tugging
a great bunch of tea-tree up and down the flue.
"Better'n all them brushes they 'ave in towns,"
said Joe, watching his blackened assistant with
satisfaction.

"Well, we're off tomorrow, Mr. Howard," said
Jim on Saturday night. They were seated round
the fire, smoking.

"I s'pose so. Didn't think you'd stick it out as
long," the old man said.

"We've had a very good time," said Bob; and was
astonished to find himself speaking truthfully.
"Jolly good of you to have me; I know a new-chum
isn't much use."

"Well, I wouldn't say as how you weren't," said

old Joe deliberately. "I ain't strong on new-chums, myself — some of them immigrants they send out are a fair cow to handle; but I will say, Captin, you ain't got no frills, nor you don't mind puttin' your back into a job. I worked you pretty 'ard, too." He chuckled deeply.

"Did you?" asked Bob — and chuckled in his turn.

"Well, I didn't see no points in spoon-feedin' you. If a man's going' on the land he may as well know wot 'e's likely to strike. There's lots'll tell you you won't strike anything 'arder than ol' Joe — an' p'raps you won't," he added. "Anyhow, yous asked for work, an' it was up ter me ter see that yous got it. But don't go imaginin' you've learned all there is there know about farmin' yet."

"If there's one thing I'm certain of, it's that," said Bob a trifle grimly.

"That's right. I ain't got much of a farm, an' any'ow, it's winter. I only showed yous a few of the odd jobs — an' wot it is to 'ave to batch fer yerself, not comin' in like a lord to Billabong ter see wot Mrs. Brown's been cookin' for yous. Nothin' like a bit o' batchin' ter teach a cove. An' you mind, Captin — if you start anywhere on yer own, you batch decent; keep things clean an' don't get into the way o' livin' just any'ow. I ain't much, nor the meenoo ain't excitin'; but things is clean."

"Well — I have a sister," said Bob. "So I'm in luck. But I guess I know a bit more about her side of the job now."

"And that's no bad thing for Tommy," said Jim.

"Oo's 'e?" demanded Joe.

"Oh — that's his sister."

"Rum names gals gets nowadays," said Joe, pondering. "Not only gels, neither. 'S a chap on top of the 'ill 'as a new baby, an' 'e's called it 'Aig Wipers Jellicoe. Course, 'e did go to the war, but 'e ain't got no need ter rub it into the poor kid like that." He paused to ram the tobacco into the bowl of his pipe with a horny thumb. "One thing — I'd like to pay you chaps somethin'. Never 'ad blokes workin' fer me fer nothin', an' I don't much care about it."

"No, thanks, Mr. Howard," said Jim. "We came for colonial experience."

"You!" said old Joe, and permitted himself the ghost of a grin. "Well, I ain't goin' ter fight yous about it, an' I'm not worryin' a mighty lot about you, Major, 'cause your little bit o' country's ready made for you. But Captin's different. We won't 'ave no fight about cash, Captin; but that last year's calf of the ol' keow's goin' ter be a pretty decent steer, an' when you gets yer farm 'e's goin' on it as yer first bit o' stock. An' 'e'll get the best o' my grass till 'e goes."

"Rubbish!" said Bob, much embarrassed. "Awfully good of you, Mr. Howard, but that wasn't the agreement. I know I'm not worth wages yet."

"Oh, ain't you?" Joe asked. "Well, there's two opinions about that. Any'ow, 'e's yours, an' I've christened 'im Captin, so there ain't no way out of it." He rose, cutting short further protests. "Too much bloomin' argument about this camp; I'm off ter bed."

CHAPTER 12

On Influenza and Furniture

"SO you think he'll do, Jim?"

"Yes, I certainly do," Jim answered. He was sitting with his father in the smoking-room at Billabong, his long legs outstretched before the fire, and his great form half-concealed in the depths of an enormous leather armchair. "Of course he'll want guidance; you couldn't expect him to know much about stock yet, though he's certainly picked up a good bit."

"Yes — so it seems. His great point is his quick eye and his keenness. I haven't found him forget much."

"No, and he's awfully ashamed if he does. He's a tiger for work, and very quick at picking up the way to tackle any new job. That was one of the things that pleased old Joe about him. I fancy the old chap had suffered at the hands of other new-chums who reckoned they could teach him how to do his work. 'Captin ain't offered me not one bit of advice,' he told me with relief."

Mr. Linton laughed.

"Yes, I've had them here like that," he said.

"Full of sublime enthusiasm for reforming Australia and all her ways. I don't say we don't need it, either, but not from a new-chum in his first five minutes."

"Not much," agreed Jim. "Well, there's nothing of that sort about old Bob. He just hoes in at anything that's going, and doesn't talk about it. Joe says he must have been reared sensible. He's all right, Dad. I've had a lot of men through my hands in the last few years, and you learn to size 'em up pretty quickly."

David Linton nodded, looking at his big son. Sometimes he had a pang of regret for Jim's lost boyhood, swallowed up in war. Then, when he was privileged to behold him rough-and-tumbling with Wally, singing idiotic choruses with Norah and Tommy, or making himself into what little Babs Archdale ecstatically called "my bucking donkey", it was borne in upon him that there still was plenty of the boy left in Jim — and that there always would be. Nevertheless, he had great confidence in his judgment; and in this instance it happened to coincide with his own.

The door opened, and Bob Rainham came in, hesitating as he caught sight of the father and son.

"Come in, Bob," Mr. Linton said. "I was just wishing you would turn up. We've been talking about you. I understand you've made up your mind to get a place of your own."

"If you don't think I'm insane to tackle it, sir," Bob answered. "Of course, I know I'm awfully ignorant. But I thought I could probably get hold of a good man, and if I can find a place anywhere in this district, Jim says he'll keep an eye on me. Between the two, I oughtn't to make very hopeless mistakes. And I might as well have my money invested."

"Quite so. I think you're wise," the squatter answered. "As it happens, I was in Cunjee yesterday, talking to an agent, and I heard of a little place that might suit you very well — just about the price you ought to pay, and the land's not bad. There's a decent cottage on it — you and Tommy could be very comfortable there. It's four miles from here, so we should feel you hadn't got away from us."

"That sounds jolly," said Bob. "I'd be awfully glad to think Tommy was so near to Norah. Is it sheep country, Mr. Linton?"

"So it's to be sheep, is it? Well, I'd advise you to put some young cattle on to some scrub country at the back, but you could certainly run sheep on the cleared paddocks," Mr. Linton answered. "We could drive over and look at it tomorrow, if you like. The terms are easy; you'd have money over to stock it, or nearly so. And there's plenty to be done in improving the place, if you should buy it; you could easily add a good deal to its value."

"That's what I'd like," Bob answered eagerly. "It doesn't take a whole lot of brains to dig drains and cut scrub. I could be doing that while the sheep turn into wool and mutton!"

"So you could; though there's a bit more to be done to sheep than just to watch them turn," said

the squatter, with a twinkle. "I fancy Tommy will
be pleased if you get this place."

"Tommy's mad keen to start," Bob said. "She
says Norah has taught her more than she ever
dreamed that her head could contain, and she
wants to work it all off on me. I think she has
visions of making me kill a bullock, so that she
can demonstrate all she knows about corning and
spicing and salting beef. I mentioned it would take
two of us quite a little while to work through a
whole bullock, but she evidently didn't think much
of the objection."

"I'll see you get none fat enough to kill," grinned
Jim. "Norah says Tommy's a great pupil, dad."

"Oh, they have worked as if they were
possessed," Mr. Linton answered. "I never saw
such painfully busy people. But Norah tells me
she has had very little to teach Tommy — in fact,
I think the teaching has been mutual, and they've
simply swapped French and Australian dodges. At
all events they and Brownie have lived in each
other's pockets, and they all seem very content."

"Are you all taking business, or may we come
in?" demanded a cheery voice; and Norah peeped
in, with Tommy dimly visible in the background.

"Come in — 'twas yourselves we were talking
about," Jim said, rising slowly from the armchair;
a process which, Norah was accustomed to say, he
accomplished yard by yard. "Sit here, Tommy, and
let's hear your views on Australia!"

Tommy shook her head.

"Too soon to ask me — and I've only seen
Billabong," she said, laughing. "Wait until I've

kept house for Bob for a while, and faced life without nice soft buffers like Norah and Mrs. Brown!"

"I'm not a nice soft buffer!" said Norah indignantly. "Do I look like one, Jimmy?"

"Brownie certainly fits the description better," Jim said. "Never mind, old girl, you'll probably grow into one. We'd be awfully proud of you if you got really fat, Norah."

"Then I hope you'll never have cause for pride," retorted his sister. "I couldn't ride Bosun if I did, and that would be too awful to think about. Oh, and Tommy's making a great stock-rider, Bob. She declared she could never ride astride, but she's perceiving the error of her ways."

"I thought I could never stick on without the moral support of the pommels," said Tommy. "When you arrange yourself among pommels and horns and things on a side-saddle, there seems no real reason why you should ever come off, except of your own free will. But a man's saddle doesn't offer any encouragement to a poor scared new-chum. I pictured myself sliding off it whenever the horse side-stepped. However, somehow, it doesn't happen."

"And what happens when your steed slews around after a bullock?" asked Jim.

"Indeed, I hardly know," said Tommy modestly. "I generally shut my eyes, and hold on to the front of the saddle. After a while I open them, and find, to my astonishment, that nothing has occurred, and I'm still there. Then we sail along after Norah, and I hold up my head proudly and look as if that were really the way I have always handled cattle. And she isn't a bit taken in. It's dreadfully difficult to impress Norah."

Everyone laughed, and looked at the new-chum affectionately. This small English girl, so ready to laugh at her own mistakes, had twined herself wonderfully about their hearts. Even Brownie, jealous to the point of prickliness for her adored Norah, and at first inclined to turn up a scornful nose at "Miss Tommy's" pink and white daintiness, had been forced to admit that she "could 'andle things like a workman". And that was high praise from Brownie.

The telephone bell whirred in the hall, and Jim went out to answer it. In a few minutes they heard his voice.

"Norah, just come here a moment."

He came back presently, leaving Norah at the telephone.

"It's Dr. Anderson," he said. "They're in trouble in Cunjee — there's a pretty bad outbreak of influenza. Some returned men came up with it, and now it's spreading everywhere, Anderson says. Mrs. Anderson has been nursing in the hospital, but now two of her own kiddies have got it, so she has had to go home, and they're awfully shorthanded. Nurses seem to be scarce everywhere; they could only get one from Melbourne, and she's badly overworked."

"Norah will go, I suppose," said David Linton, with a half-sigh — the sigh of a man who has looked forward to peace and security, and finds it again slipping from his grasp.

"Oh, yes, I'm sure she will. They have a certain number of volunteers, not nearly enough."

"I'm going," said Tommy, and David Linton nodded at her kindly.

"What about you and me, Jim?" Bob asked.

"Well, Anderson says they have a number of men volunteers. Such a lot of returned fellows about with nothing to do yet. I told him to count on us for anything he wanted, but the need seems chiefly for women."

"Must they go tonight? It's pretty late," said Mr. Linton.

"No, not tonight," Norah answered, entering. "It would be eight o'clock before I could get in, and Dr. Anderson says I'm to get a good sleep and come in early in the morning. Tommy, darling, will you mind if I leave you for a few days?"

"Horribly," said Tommy drily. "It would be unpardonably rude for a hostess. So I'm coming too."

Norah laughed down at her.

"Somehow, I thought you would," she said. "Well, Jimmy, you'll take us in after breakfast, won't you? We'll have it early." She perched on the arm of her father's chair, letting her fingers rest for a moment on his close-cropped grey hair. "And I've never asked you if I could go, Daddy."

"No," said David Linton, "you haven't." He put his arm gently round her.

"But then I knew that you'd kick me out if I didn't. So that simplifies matters. You'll take care of yourself while I'm away, won't you, Dad? No wild rides by yourself into the ranges, or anything of that sort?"

"Certainly not," said her father. "I'll sit quietly at home, and let Brownie give me nourishment at short intervals."

"Nothing she'd like better." Norah laughed. "I don't believe Brownie will really feel that she owns us again until one of us is considerate enough to fall ill and give her a real chance of nursing and feeding us. Then the only thing to do is to forget you ever had a will of your own, and just to open your mouth and be fed like a young magpie, and Brownie's perfectly happy."

"She won't be happy when she hears of this new plan," Mr. Linton said. "Poor old soul, I'm sorry she should have any worry, when she has just got you home."

"Yes, I'm sorry," Norah answered. "But it can't be helped. I'll go and talk to her now, and arrange things — early breakfast among them."

"You might make it a shade earlier than you meant to, while you're at it, Nor," Jim observed. "Then we could turn off the track as we go in to-morrow to let Tommy have a look at the place that has been offered Bob — you know that place of Henderson's, off the main road. Bob can go over the land with us when we're coming back. But once you and Tommy get swallowed up in Cunjee, there's no knowing when we could get you out; and Tommy ought to inspect the house."

"Oh, I'd love to," said Tommy enthusiastically. "No mere man can be trusted to buy a house."

"Don't go to look at it with any large ideas of

up-to-date improvements floating in your mind," Jim warned her. "It's sure to be pretty primitive, and probably there isn't even a bathroom."

"Don't you worry, Tommy; we'll build you one," said Mr. Linton.

"I'm not going to worry about anything; there are always washtubs," spoke Tommy cheerfully. "And thank you, all the same, Mr. Linton. I didn't expect much when I came out to Australia, but I'm getting so much more than I expected that I'm in a state of bewilderment all the time. Someday I feel that I shall come down with a bump, and I shall be thankful if it's only over a bathroom."

"Distressing picture of the valiant pioneer looking for discomforts and failing to find them," said Bob, laughing. "It's so difficult to feel really pioneerish in a place where there are taps, and electric light, and motors, and no one appears to wear a red shirt, like every Australian bushman I ever saw on the stage."

"Did you bring any out with you?" demanded Norah wickedly.

"I didn't. But honest, it was only because I had so many khaki ones, and I thought they'd do. Otherwise I'd certainly have thought that scarlet shirts were part of the ordinary outfit for the Colonies. And if you believed all the things they tell you in outfitting shops, you would bring a gorgeous assortment. We'd have even arrived here with tinware. It was lucky I knew some Australians — they delicately hinted that you really had a shop or two in the principal cities."

"I've often marvelled at the queer collection

people seem to bring out," said Mr. Linton. "It's not so bad of late years, but ten years ago a jackeroo would arrive here with about a lorry-load of stuff, most of which he could have bought much more cheaply in Melbourne or Sydney — and he'd certainly never use the greater part of it. Apparently a London shop will sell you the same kind of outfit for a Melbourne suburb as if you were going into the wilds of West Africa. They haven't any conscience."

"They just never learn geography," said Norah. "And 'the Colonies' to them mean exactly the same thing, no matter in what continent the colony may be. If they can sell pioneers tinware to take out to Melbourne, so much the better for them. Well, I must see Brownie, or there may not be early breakfast for pioneers or anyone else."

Brownie rose to the occasion — there had never been any known occasion to which Brownie did not rise — and the hospital at Cunjee was still grappling with early morning problems next day when the Billabong motor pulled up at the door, after a flying visit to the new home — which Tommy, regarding with the large eye of faith, had declared to be full of boundless possibilities. Dr. Anderson came out to meet the newcomers, Norah and Tommy, neat and workmanlike; Jim, bearing their luggage; and Mr. Linton and Bob sharing a large hamper, into which Brownie had packed everything eatable she could find — and Brownie's capacity for finding things eatable at short notice was one of her most astonishing traits. The little doctor, harassed as he was, greeted them with a twinkle.

"You Lintons generally appear bearing your sheaves with you," he said. "Well, you're very welcome. How many of you do I keep?"

"Tommy and Norah, for certain," said Mr. Linton. "And as many more of us as you please. Want us all, doctor?"

"Well, I really don't; there are a good many men volunteers. But if I might commandeer the car and a driver for a few hours, I should be glad," the doctor went on. "There are some cases to be brought in from Mardale and Clinthorpe. I heard of them only this morning, on the telephone, and I was wondering how to get them in."

"We're at your disposal, and you've only to telephone for us or the car whenever you want it," said Mr. Linton. "How are things this morning?"

"Oh — bad enough. We have several very troublesome cases; people simply won't give in soon enough. My youngsters are very ill, but I'm not really worried about them as long as my wife keeps up. Our biggest trouble is that our cook here went down this morning. She told me she couldn't sleep a wink all night, and when she woke up in the morning her tongue was sticking to the roof of her head! — and certainly she has temperature enough for any strange symptoms. But we feel rather as if the bottom had dropped out of the universe, for none of our volunteers are equal to the job."

"I can cook," said Norah and Tommy together.

"Can you?" said the little doctor, staring at them

as though the heavens had opened and rained down angels on his head. "Are you sure? You don't look like it!"

"I can guarantee them," said Mr. Linton, laughing. "Only you'll have to watch Norah, for the spell of the war is heavy upon her, and she'll boil your soup bones thirteen times, and feed you all on haricot beans and lentils if nobody checks her!"

"Dad, you haven't any manners," said Norah severely. "May I cook, Doctor?"

"You can share the job," said Dr. Anderson thankfully. "I really think it's more than enough for one of you. This place is getting pretty full. Of course, I've wired to town for a cook, but goodness knows if we'll get one; it's unlikely. Come on, now, and I'll introduce you to Sister."

Sister proved to be a tall, capable, quiet woman, with war decorations. She greeted the volunteers thankfully, and unhesitatingly pronounced their place to be cooks, rather than nurses.

"I can get girls who will do well enough in the wards," she said, "where I can direct them. But I can't be in the kitchen too. If you two can carry on without supervision it will be a godsend."

So the kitchen swallowed up Norah and Tommy, and there they worked during the weeks that followed, while the influenza scourge raged round Victoria. The little cottage hospital became full almost to bursting point. Even the rooms for the staff had to be appropriated, and nurses and helpers slept in a cottage close by. Luckily for the cooks, Cunjee now boasted a gas supply and its citizens supplied them with gas stoves, as Norah said, "in clutches", so that they worked in comfort. It was hard work, with little time to spare, but the girls had learned method, and they soon mapped out a routine that prevented their ever being rushed or flurried. And they blessed the cold weather that saved constant watching lest supplies should go bad.

From Billabong came daily hampers that greatly relieved their labours. It was a matter of some amazement to the Lintons that Brownie did not volunteer for the hospital, and indeed, it had been the first thought of Brownie herself. But she repressed it firmly, though by no means feeling comfortable. To Murty she confided her views, and was relieved by his approval.

"I know I did ought to go," she said, almost tearfully. "There's those two blessed lambs in the kitchen, doing wot I'd ought to be doing; and I know Mrs. Archdale 'ud come up an' run things 'ere for me. But wot 'ud 'appen if I did go, I ask you, Murty? Simply they'd take the two blessed lambs out of the kitchen an' put 'em to nursing in the wards, an' next thing you knew they'd both be down with the beastly flu' themselves. They're safer among the pots and pans, Murty. But when the master looks at me I don't feel comfortable."

"Yerra, let him look," said Murty stoutly. " 'Tis the great head ye have on ye; I'd never have thought of it. Don't go worryin', now. Are ye not sendin' them in the height of good livin' every day?"

"That's the least I can do," said Brownie,

brightening a little. "Only I'd like to think Miss Norah and Miss Tommy got some of it, and not just them patients, gathered up from goodness knows where."

"Yerra, Miss Norah wouldn't want to know their addresses before she'd feed 'em," said the bewildered Murty. But there came a suspicious smell from the kitchen, as of something burning, and Mrs. Brown fled with a swiftness that was surprising, considering her circumference.

Jim lived a moving existence in those days, flying between Billabong and Cunjee in the car, bringing supplies, always on hand for a job if wanted, and insisting that on their daily "time off" Norah and Tommy should come out for a spin into the country. Sometimes they managed to take Sister, too, or some of the other helpers. The car never went out with any empty seats. Presently there were recovering patients to be given fresh air or taken home; white-faced mothers, longing to be back to the house and children left in the care of "Dad", and whatever kindly neighbours might drop in; or "dads' themselves, much bewildered at the amazing illness that had left them feeling as if neither their legs nor their heads belonged to them. Occasionally, after dropping one of these convalescents, Jim would find jobs waiting to his hand about the bush homestead; cows to milk, a fence to be mended, wood waiting to be chopped. He used to do them vigorously, while in the house "Mum" fussed over the restored man and tried to keep him from going out to run the farm immediately. There were

generally two or three astonished children to show
him where tools were kept — milk buckets, being
always up-ended on a fence post, needed no
introduction, and the pump, for a sluice
afterwards, was not hard of discovery. The big
Rolls-Royce used to purr gently away through the
bush paddock afterwards, often with a bewildered
"mum" looking amazedly at the tall young man
who drove it.

Meanwhile Bob Rainham, left alone with his
host, set about the business of his new farm in
earnest, since there seemed nothing else for him
to do; and David Linton, possibly glad of the
occupation, threw himself into the work. The farm
was bought on terms that seemed to Bob very easy
— he did not know that Mr. Linton stood security
for his payments — and then began the task of
stocking it and of planning just what was best to
do with each paddock. The house, left bare and
clean by the last owners, was in good repair, save
that the dingy white painting of the exterior, and
the varnished pine walls and ceilings within were
depressing and shabby. Mr. Linton decided that
his house-warming present to Tommy should be a
coat of paint for her mansion, and soon it looked
new — dark red, with a gleaming white roof, while
the rooms were painted in pretty fresh colours.
"Won't Tommy get a shock!" chuckled Bob
gleefully. The dinginess of the house had not
escaped him on the morning that they had made
their first inspection, but Tommy, who loved
freshness and colours, had made no sign. Had you
probed the matter, Tommy would probably have

remarked, with some annoyance, that it was not her job to begin by grumbling.

Wally came hurtling back from Queensland at the first hint of the influenza outbreak, and was considerably depressed at finding his twin souls, Jim and Norah, engaged in jobs that for once he could not share. Therefore he, too, fell back on the new farm, and found Bob knitting his brow one evening over the question of furniture.

"I don't want to buy much," he said. "Tommy doesn't, either; we talked it over. We'd rather do with next to nothing, and buy decent stuff by degrees if we get on well. Tommy says she doesn't want footling little gimcracky tables and whatnots and things, nor dressing-tables full of drawers that won't pull out. But I've been looking at the cheap stuff in Cunjee, and, my word, it's nasty! Still, I can't afford good things now, and Tommy wouldn't like it if I tried to get 'em. Tommy's dead on the simple life."

"How are you on tools?" queried Wally.

"Using tools? Pretty fair," admitted Bob. "I took up carpentering at school; it was always a bit of a hobby of mine. I'm no cabinet-maker, if that's what you mean."

"You don't need to be," Wally answered. "Up where I come from — we were pretty far back in Queensland — we hardly ever saw real furniture, the stuff you buy in shops. It was all made out of packing cases and odd bits of wood. Jolly decent, too; you paint 'em up to match the rooms, or stain 'em dark colours, and the girls put sort of petticoats round some of the things."

"We began that way," said David Linton, with a half-sigh. "There was surprisingly little proper furniture in our first house, and we were very comfortable."

"Couldn't we begin, sir?" asked Wally eagerly. "This wet weather looks like setting in. Bob can't do much on the farm. If we could get out a few odd lengths of timber and some old packing cases from the township —"

"Heavens, you don't need to do that!" exclaimed their host. "The place is full of both; packing cases have been arriving at Billabong since Jim was a baby, and very few of them have gone away again. There's plenty of timber knocking about, too. We'll go over to the farm if you like, Bob, and plan out measurements."

"I think it's a splendid idea, thanks, sir," said Bob slowly. "Only I don't quite see why I should bother you —"

"Oh, don't talk rubbish!" said David Linton, getting up. "I believe I'm glad of the job — the place seems queer without Jim and Norah."

"My word!" said Wally. "Let's all turn carpenters, and give Tommy the surprise of her life!"

They flung themselves at the work with energy. A visit to the new house, and a careful study of each room, revealed unsuspected possibilities to Bob, whose English brain, "brought up", as Wally said, "on a stodgy diet of bedroom suites", had failed to grasp what might be done by handy people with a soul above mere fashion in the matter of furniture. They came back with a notebook bulging with measurements and heads seething with ideas. First, they dealt with the bedrooms, and made for each a set of long shelves and dressing table-cupboard — the latter a noble piece of furniture, which was merely a packing case, smoothed, planed and fitted with shelves; the whole to be completed with seemly petticoat when Tommy should be able to detach her mind from influenza patients. They made her, too, a little work table, which was simply a wide, low shelf, at which she could write or sew — planned to catch a good light from her window, so that as she sat near it, she could see the line of willows that marked the creek and the rolling plains that ended in the ranges behind Billabong. Tommy's room was painted in pale green; and when they had stained all these exciting additions dark green, Bob heaved a great sigh, and yearned audibly for the swift recovery of the influenza patients, so that Tommy could return and behold her new possessions.

"We could make washstands," said Mr. Linton, when they had fitted out the two remaining bedrooms. "But washstands are depressing things, and would take up a good deal of space in these little rooms. You have a good water supply, Bob; why not have built-in basins with taps, and lay on water through the bedrooms?"

Bob whistled.

"My aunt! Is that really possible?"

"Quite, I should say. It wouldn't take elaborate plumbing, and the pipes could discharge into an irrigation drain for your vegetable garden. It would save Tommy ever so much work in carrying water, too. There's a fearsome amount of water carried in and out of bedrooms, and I can't see why pipes shouldn't do the work. It need not cost you much — just a shelf across a corner, with an enamelled basin let in."

"Save you buying jugs and basins," said Wally. "Great money-saving idea!"

"Rather," said Bob. "Is there anyone in Cunjee who can plumb?"

"Oh, yes; there's a handy man who can do the whole thing. We'll get Jim to go and see him to-morrow."

They left this job to the handy man, who proved equal to all demands, and went on themselves to higher flights. Kitchen and pantry were already fitted with shelves, but they built in a dresser, and found a spare corner, where they erected a linen press warranted to bring tears of joy to the eye of any housewife. Round the little dining-room and sitting-room they ran a very narrow shelf, just wide enough to carry flowers and ornaments, and they made wide, low window seats in each room. Then, becoming bold by success, they turned to cabinet making, and built into the dining-room a sideboard, which was only a glorified edition of the kitchen dresser, but looked amazingly like walnut, aided by a little stain; and for both sitting-rooms made low cupboards, with tops wide enough to serve as little tables. Even the verandah was furnished with wide shelf tables and a cupboard, and with low and broad seats.

"And it's all done by kindness — and packing

cases!" said Jim, surveying the result with admiration.

"Indeed, I'm afraid a lot of your father's good timber has gone into it," said Bob half ruefully. "He was awfully good about it, and the supply of just-what-you-want timber on Billabong seemed inexhaustible."

"No, you really used very little good stuff," David Linton said. "It's chiefly packing cases, truly, Jim. But we had plenty of time to plane it up and make it look decent. Bob ran an electric light into the workshop and we worked every night. I believe it's kept us from getting influenza from sheer boredom, with all you people away."

"They'll soon be home," Jim said cheerfully. "Influenza's dying out, I believe. No fresh cases for three days, and all the patients are getting better. The little Andersons are up and about. By the way, Dad, couldn't we bring those kiddies out to Billabong for a change?"

"Why, of course," his father answered. "Tell Mrs. Anderson to come too, or, if she won't leave her husband, Brownie will be delighted at the chance of getting two children to look after again. Are the cooks quite cheery, Jim?"

"As cheery as possible," Jim answered. "They got off early today, and I took them and Sister and the Anderson youngsters out for a run. Did 'em all good. I'm coming home tonight, and they don't want me tomorrow, because they're going to afternoon tea with someone or other. Flighty young things, those cooks! So I can help you carpenters or do any odd jobs."

"We've lots," said Wally, who was putting a finishing coat of dark green enamel to a rod destined as a towel rail for Tommy's room. "Simple jobs, suitable for your understanding. Take care, Jimmy, I've a wet paint brush, and you have a good suit on! I want to put shelves from floor to ceiling of the bathroom, because the walls are rough and unlined, and nothing on earth will make it a beautiful room. So Tommy may as well store there all the things she doesn't want anywhere else. And you can make her a medicine cupboard. I shan't have time to look at any of you unskilled labourers, for I'm going to build her a draining-rack for plates and things over the kitchen sink. And I can tell you, that takes brains!"

"Then it's not your job!" said Jim definitely.

"Isn't it? I'll show you, you old Bond Street fashion plate!" Wally stretched his long form, simply attired in a khaki shirt and dungaree trousers, much besplashed by paint, and looked scornfully at his neatly dressed friend. "You needn't think, because you come here dressed like the lilies of the field and fresh from motoring girls round the country, that —"

"My hat!" said Jim justly incensed. "And I after cleaning out and whitewashing the hospital fowl-houses all the morning! Young Wally, you need someone to sit on your head." He took off his coat slowly.

"Ten to one," said Wally hastily, "if we had time to look into the matter we'd find you'd whitewashed the fowls as well! These Army

Johnnies are so beastly impractical!" He gathered
up his brushes and fled, pursued by his chum.
Sounds of warfare came faintly from the distance.

"It's a good thing some of us are sane," said Mr.
Linton laughing. "Nearly finished, Bob?"

He was painting a shelf-table, screwed to the
wall within a space at the end of the verandah,
which they had completely enclosed with wire
mosquito netting. Bob was hanging the door of this
open-air room in position, a task requiring
judgment, as the floor of the verandah was old
and uneven.

"Nearly, sir," he mumbled, his utterance made
difficult by the fact of having several screws in his
mouth. He worked vigorously for a few moments,
and then stood back to survey his job. "This is
going to be a great little room — though it's hard
just now to imagine that it will ever be warm
enough for it."

"Just you wait a few months until we get a
touch of hot weather, and the mosquitoes come
out!" said David Linton. "Then you and Tommy
will thankfully entrench yourselves in here at
dusk, and listen to the singing hordes dashing
themselves against the netting in the effort to get
at you!"

"That's the kind of thing they used to tell me
on the *Nauru*," Bob said, laughing, "but I didn't
quite expect it from you, Mr. Linton!"

The squatter chuckled.

"Well, indeed, it's no great exaggeration in some
years," he said. "They can be bad enough for
anything, though it isn't always they are. But an

open-air room is never amiss, for if there aren't
mosquitoes a lamp will attract myriads of other
insects on a hot night. That looks all right, Bob;
you've managed that door very well."

"First rate!" said Jim and Wally approvingly,
returning arm in arm.

"You're great judges!" David Linton rejoined,
looking at the pair. "Have you returned to work,
may I ask, or are you still imitating the lilies of
the field?"

"Jim is — he couldn't help it," said Wally. "But
I have been studying that oak tree out in the front,
Mr. Linton. It seems to me that a seat built round
it would be very comforting to weary bones on
warm evenings —"

Bob gathered up his tools with decision in each
movement.

"Wally has come to that state of mind in which
he can't look at anything on the place without
wanting to build something out of a packing case
in it, or round it, or on top of it!" he said. "When
the sheep come I'll have to keep you from them,
or you'll be building shelves round them!"

"Why, you're nearly as bad yourself!" grinned
Wally.

"I know I am, and that's why I've got to stop.
I'm going to leave nice little chisels and
spokeshaves and smoothing planes, and mend up
the pigsty; it needs it badly, and so does the cow
shed. And then I've got to think of ploughing, and
cutting that drain across the flat, and generally
earning my living."

"Don't you worry," said David Linton. "You

couldn't have done much outside in this wet weather, and at least your house is half-furnished. And we'll help you through with the other things."

"You're all just bricks," said Bob, his fair skin flushing. "Only I begin to feel as if I were fed with a spoon. I can't always expect to have my work done for me."

"You haven't shown much wish to leave it for anyone else," Jim said drily. "Neither you nor Tommy strikes this district as a loafer. Just stop talking bosh, old man, and think what Tommy's going to say to her mansion."

"Say?" queried Mr. Linton. "Why, she'll point out to us all the places where she wants shelves!"

"Shelves?" yelled the three as one man.

"Yes, certainly. There was never a woman born who had enough. Don't lose sight of your tools, Bob, for you'll go on putting up shelves as long as you've an inch of wall to put them on. Come along, boys, and we'll go home."

The Home on the Creek

"I THINK it's the loveliest home that ever was!" said Tommy solemnly.

"Well, indeed, it takes some beating," Wally agreed.

"Creek Cottage" — the name was of Tommy's choosing — was ready for occupation, and they had just finished a tour of it. There was nothing in it that was not fresh and bright and dainty — like Tommy herself. The rooms were small, but they had good windows, where the crisp, short curtains were not allowed to obscure the view. There were fresh mattings and linoleums on the floors, and the home-made furniture now boasted, where necessary, curtains of chintz or cretonne, that matched its colouring. Norah and Tommy had spent cheery hours over those draperies. The curtains for Tommy's "suite" had been Norah's gift — of dark-green linen, embroidered in dull blue silks; and in the corner there was a little sofa with cushions of the same. Tommy had purred — was, in fact, still purring — over that home-made furniture, and declared it superior to any that money could buy. She had also suggested new ideas for shelves.

They had not troubled furniture shops much. Save for a few comfortable armchairs, there was nothing solid and heavy in the house; but it was all pleasant and home-like, and the little rooms, bright with books and pictures and flowers, had about them the touch of welcome and restfulness that makes the difference between a home and a mere house. The kitchen was Tommy's especial pride — it was cool and spotless, with fresh-painted walls and ceilings, and shining white tiles round the white sink — over which Wally's draining-rack sat in glory. Dazzling tinware decorated the walls, and the dresser held fresh and pretty china. For weeks it had been a point of honour for no one to visit Cunjee without bringing Tommy a gift for the kitchen — meat fork, a set of skewers, a tin pepper castor; offerings wrapped in many coverings of tissue paper, and presented with a great solemnity, generally at dinner. The last parcel had been from Mr. Linton, and had eclipsed all the others — an alarm clock, warranted to drive the soundest sleeper from her bed. Bob declared it specially designed to ensure his getting fed at something approaching a reasonable hour.

A wide verandah ran round the whole house, and rush lounges and deck chairs stood about invitingly — Tommy had insisted that there should be plenty of seating accommodation on the verandah for all the Linton party, since they filled the little rooms to an alarming extent. Near where they stood the drawing-room opened out by a French window. Something caught Tommy's eye, and she dived into the room — to return, laughing with new treasure trove — a sink brush and saucepan scrubber, tied up with blue ribbon.

"Your doing?" she asked, brandishing them.

"Not mine," Wally shook his head. "I don't do frivolous things like that. But I heard Jim wheedling blue ribbon out of Norah this morning, and I don't fancy he has much use for it ordinarily. You'd better ask him."

"It's like both of you — you nice stupids!" she said.

"What? — the pot scrub! That's not polite of you, Miss Rainham; and so untrue, where I'm concerned." Wally sat down on the arm of a lounge and regarded her with a twinkle. "What's old Bob doing?"

Tommy laughed happily.

"I think whenever we don't know where Bob is, he's safe to be out looking at either the sheep or the pigs," she said. "He just loves them; and he says he can see them growing."

There was a hint of spring in the air, and more than a hint of good grass in the green paddocks stretching away from the house. By the creek the willows were putting out long, tender shoots that would soon be a thick curtain. The lucerne patch that stretched along its bank was dense and high. The Rainhams had been delayed in taking possession of Creek Cottage; a severe cold had smitten Tommy just at the end of her labours in the hospital, and being thoroughly tired out, it had been sometime before she could shake off its effects. Mr. Linton and Norah had put down their feet with joint firmness, declaring that in no circumstances should she begin housekeeping until she was thoroughly fit; so the Rainhams had remained at Billabong. Tommy was petted and nursed in a way she had not known since Aunt Margaret had died, while Bob worked feverishly at his farm, riding over every day from Billabong, with a package of Brownie's sandwiches in his pocket, and returning at dusk, dirty and happy. Bob was responding to Australian conditions delightfully, and was only discontented because he could not make his farm all that he wanted it to be within the first week.

Therein, however, he had unexpected help. The Cunjee district was a friendly one; station owners and farmers alike looked kindly on the young immigrant who turned so readily to work after four years' fighting. Moreover, Tommy's work in the hospital was well known; the general opinion being that "anything might be expected from young Norah Linton, but you wouldn't think a bit of a new-chum kid like Bob Rainham's sister would turn to and cook for a crowd, and she hardly off the ship!" So the district laid its heads together and consulted Mr. Linton; with the result that one morning Bob found himself unexpectedly accompanied to work by his host. It was nothing unusual for Jim or Wally, or both, to go with him. He was cutting a drain, which they declared to be a job for which they had a particular fancy. But today he found Monarch saddled with the other horses, and Mr. Linton not only ready to start, but hurrying them off; and there was no lunch to carry, Norah airily declaring that since she and Tommy were to be deserted they declined to be downtrodden, and would motor over with a hamper and picnic at Creek Cottage. There was a mysterious twinkle in Norah's eye; Bob scented something afoot, and tried — in vain — to pump her on the matter. He rode away, his curiosity unsatisfied.

But when they rode up the homestead paddock at his farm, he gave a long whistle.

"What on earth —?" he began amazedly.

There were men in sight everywhere, and all working. Eight or nine ploughs were moving across the paddocks destined for cultivation; already wide strips of freshly turned earth showed that they had been some time at work. On the flat where Bob had begun his drain was a line of men, and some teams with earth scoops, cutting a deep channel. There were even men digging in the garden; and the sound of axes came faintly from a belt of scrub that Bob was planning to clear — some day. He gaped at them.

"What does it mean?"

"It's a bee," said Wally kindly. "A busy bee, improving each shining hour."

Bob turned a puzzled, half-distressed face to Mr. Linton.

"I say, sir — what is it?"

"It's just that, my boy," said David Linton. "The district had a fancy to help you — Cunjee thinks a heap of soldiers, you see. So a lot of the fellows got together and planned to put in a day on the creek, doing odd jobs."

"I say," said poor Bob, flushing scarlet, "I never heard such a thing — and I hardly know any of them. Whatever am I to say to them, sir?"

"I wouldn't say much at all," said David Linton laughing. "You'll only embarrass them if you do. Just take a hand in any job you like, and carry on — as we're all going to do."

"There's one man you know, anyhow," said Jim, grinning. He pointed out old Joe Howard, the nearest to them among the ploughmen.

"Heavens!" ejaculated Bob. "You don't mean to tell me old Joe has come of his own accord!"

"Couldn't keep him away," Jim said. "He remarked that you were a very decent young feller, and he'd taught you how to work, so he might as well lend an 'and. It's like old Joe's cheek, but he'll claim forever that he made you a worker."

"Oh, let him," said Bob. "It doesn't hurt me, and it may amuse him." His gaze travelled across the busy paddocks. "Well — I'm just staggered," he said. "The least I can do is to get to work quickly."

They turned the horses out and scattered; Bob to cutting scrub — it was the job he liked least, so it seemed to him the decent thing to tackle it — Jim to the drain construction, while Wally joined the band of workers in the garden, since he knew Tommy's plans concerning it; and Mr. Linton attacked a fence that needed repairs. In the middle of the morning came the Billabong motor, driven by Norah, with Brownie and a maid in the tonneau with Tommy, and hampers packed

wherever possible. A cart with other supplies had
been driven over by Evans in the very early
morning, since Billabong had undertaken the
feeding of the workers for the day. The Rolls-Royce
picked its way delicately round the paddocks,
while the girls carried drinks and huge slabs of
cake to the different bands of workers — this being
the time for "smoke-oh". Then they hurried back
to the cottage, where Brownie and Maria were
busy unpacking hampers on the verandah, and
Brownie was preparing to carve great joints of beef
and mutton and pork in readiness for the hungry
horde that would descend on them at dinner time.

It was all ready when the men trooped up from
the paddocks — squatters and stockmen, farmers,
horse breakers, bush workers of every degree; all
dirty and cheery, and filled with a mighty hunger.
Soap and water awaited them at the back; then
they came round to sit on the edge of the long
verandahs, balancing heaped plates on their
knees, and making short work of Brownie's
provisions. Jokes and cheery talk filled the air.
Tommy, carrying plates shyly at first, found
herself the object of much friendly interest. "Little
Miss Immigrant", they called her, and vied with
each other in making her feel that they were all
welcoming her. But they did not waste much time
over dinner — soon one after another got up and
sauntered away, lighting his pipe, and presently
there were straggling lines of figures going back
to work across the paddocks. After which Norah
and Tommy bullied Bob into eating something —
he had been far too anxious to wait on his hungry

"bee" to think of feeding himself, and then the
ladies of the party lunched with the ardour of the
long-delayed, and fell upon the colossal business
of dish-washing.

Afternoon tea came early, by which time nearly
all the ploughing was done, and the brown ribbon
of the new drain stretched, wide and deep, across
the flat. The girls took the meal round the
paddocks, this time with Bob to carry the steaming
billies of tea; it gave him a chance to thank his
helpers, when it was difficult to say whether the
thanker or the thanked were the more
embarrassed. Soon after "cow time" loomed for
some of the workers, and whatever waits in
Australia, it must not be the cow; so that here and
there a man shouldered his tools, and leaving
them at the shed, caught his horse and rode away
— apologising to Bob, if he happened to meet him,
for going so early, with the brief apology of the
dairy farmer, "Gotter get home an' milk." But the
majority worked on until dusk came down and put
an end to their efforts, and then came up for their
horses, singing and laughing.

Bob stood at the gate, bareheaded, as they rode
away. By this time he had no words at all. He
wished from the bottom of his heart that he could
tell them what good fellows he thought them; but
he could only stand, holding the gate for them with
Tommy by his side; and it may be that the look
on each tired young face moved "the bee" more
than eloquence would have done. They shouted
cheery goodbyes as they went. "Good luck, Miss
Immigrant! Good luck, Captain!" And the dusk

swallowed them up, leaving only the sound of the cantering hoofs.

Thanks to "the bee", the little farm on the creek looked very flourishing on the great day when the lady of the house came down in state to take possession of her domain. Bob had worked hard in the garden, where already rows of vegetables showed well; Jim and Wally had aided Norah and Tommy in the making of a flower garden, laying heavy toll on Hogg's stores for the purpose; today it was golden and white with daffodils and narcissi and snowdrops. The cultivation paddocks, no longer brown, rippled with green oats; and cattle were grazing on the rough grass of the flats, once a swamp, but already showing the influence of the big drain. Bob had great plans for ploughing all his flats next year. Dairy cows pastured in the creek paddock near the house; beyond, Bob's beloved sheep were steadily engrossed in the fascinating pursuit of "turning into wool and mutton". He never grew tired of watching the process.

The ever-present problem of labour, too, had solved itself pleasantly enough. Sarah, for many years housemaid at Billabong, had married a man on a farm near Cunjee, whose first attempt at renting a place for himself had been brought to an untimely end by the drought; and Sarah had returned to Billabong, to help in preparing for the homecoming of the long-absent family, while her husband secured a temporary job in Cunjee and looked about for another chance. There Jim had found him, while helping at the hospital; the end

of the matter being that Sarah and Bill and their
baby were installed at Creek Cottage, Bill to be
general utility man on the farm, and to have a
share of profits, while Sarah helped Tommy in the
house. Everyone was satisfied, and already there
were indications that Tommy would be daft over
the baby.

Sarah came out now to say that tea was ready
— she had insisted on being responsible for
everything on this first day. Not that there was
much to do, for Brownie had sent over a colossal
hamper, declaring that Miss Tommy shouldn't be
bothered with thinking about food when she
wasn't 'ardly settled. So they packed into the little
dining-room; where, indeed, it took no small
ingenuity to stow so large a party, when three of
the six happened to be of the size of David Linton
and Jim and Wally; and Tommy did the honours
of her own table for the first time.

"And to think," she said presently, "that six
months ago there was only Lancaster Gate! Of
course, there was always Bob" — she flashed him
a quick smile — "but Bob was —"

"In the air," put in Norah.

"Very much so. And it didn't seem a bit certain
that I could ever get him out of it; or, if I did, that
I could ever escape from Lancaster Gate."

"And you wouldn't, if the she-dragon had had
her way," Bob said.

"No. There was nothing to do but run. But even
when I dreamed of running, I never thought of
more than a workman's cottage, with you earning
wages and me trying to make both ends meet. And

now — look at us! Bloated capitalists and station owners."

"Well, you were a cook not so long ago. I wouldn't be too proud," Wally gibed.

"All the more reason for me to be proud — I've risen in the world," declared Tommy. "Left my situation to better myself — isn't that the right way to put it? And we've got the jolliest home in Australia — thanks to all of you. Do have some more cake, Mr. Linton; I'd love to say I made it myself, but Brownie did — still, all the same, it's mine."

"Don't you worry," he told her. "I'm coming here plenty of times for cake of your own baking."

"That's what I want." She beamed at him. "All of you. Bob and I will feel lost and lonesome if we don't see you all — oh, often."

"But you're going to," Norah said. "We'll be over goodness knows how many times a week, and you two are always coming to dinner on Sunday, and ever so many other days as well."

"Was it in your plans that any work should be done on this estate?" queried Bob solemnly.

"Why, yes, in your spare time," Wally answered. "Any time you're not on the road between here and Billabong, or catching a horse to go there, or letting one go after coming back, or minding the Billabong horde when it comes over, you can do a little towards improving the creek. I say, Bob, it sounds the sort of life I'd love. Can't you give me a job, old man?"

"Seeing that you've done little but work on this place since you came back from Queensland, I

shouldn't think you'd need to ask for a job,"
retorted Bob. "However, I'll take you on as milker
if you like — it's about the only thing you haven't
sampled."

"No," said Wally, "you won't. Whatever beast I
finally take to by way of earning my living, it won't
be the cow — if I can help it. I'd sooner graze
giraffes!"

"Oh, do try!" Norah begged. "I'd love to see you
trying to put a bridle on one in a hurry!"

"Wonder what would happen if one rode a
giraffe and he reared?" pondered Jim.

"You'd have to swarm up his neck and hang on
to his little horns," Wally said. "But they're nice,
silent beasts, giraffes, and I think they'd be very
restful to deal with."

Everyone laughed unsympathetically.
Restfulness was the last quality to be associated
with Wally, who had been remarkable throughout
his life for total inability to keep still.

"It's always the way," said Wally, in tones of
melancholy. "Every fortune teller I ever saw told
me that no one understood me."

"All fortune tellers say that, and that's why
people think them so clever," said Tommy. "It's so
soothing to think one is misunderstood. My
stepmother always thought so. Did Bob tell you,
Mr. Linton, that we had had letters from home?"

"No — from your people?"

"From Papa. The she-dragon didn't write. I
think her words would have been too burning to
put on paper. But Papa wrote a pretty decent
letter — for him. He didn't speak of our letters

from Liverpool — the notes we wrote from the hotel, saying we were leaving for Australia. But he acknowledged Bob's letter from Melbourne, saying we were going up country under your wing, and actually wished us luck! Amazing, from Papa!"

"I think he's jolly glad we got away," Bob said.

"I think that's highly probable," said David Linton. "You'll write to him occasionally, won't you?"

"Oh, yes, I suppose so," Bob answered. "Sometimes I'm a bit sorry for him; it must be pretty awful to be always under the heel of a she-dragon. Oh, and there was a really fatherly sort of letter from old Mr. M'Clinton. He's an old brick; and he's quite pleased about our finding you — or you finding us. He was always a bit worried lest Tommy should feel lonesome in Australia."

"And not you?" Norah asked laughing.

"No, he didn't worry a bit about me; he merely hoped I'd be working too hard to notice lonesomeness. I think the old chap always was a bit doubtful that any fellow would get down to solid work after flying; he used to say the two things wouldn't agree. But you sent him a decent report of me, didn't you, sir?"

"Oh, yes — I wrote when you asked me, just after you bought this place," David Linton said. "Told him you were working like a cart horse, which was no more than the truth, and that Tommy was serving her adopted country as a cook; and that I considered your prospects good. He'll have had that letter before now — and I suppose others from you."

"We wrote a few weeks ago — sent him a photograph of the house, and of Tommy on a horse, and Tommy told him all about our furniture," Bob chuckled. "I don't quite know how a staid old London lawyer will regard the furniture; he won't understand its beauty a bit. But he ought to be impressed with our stern regard for economy."

"He should," said Mr. Linton with a twinkle. "And I presume you mentioned the sheep?"

"As a matter of fact," said Tommy confidentially, "his letter was little but mutton. He described all his ewes in detail —"

"Colour of their eyes?" queried Wally.

"And their hair," nodded Tommy. "I never read anything so poetical. And any enthusiasm he had over went to the pigs and the Kelpie pup!"

"But what about the cows?" laughed Norah. "And the young bullocks?"

"Oh, he mentioned them. But cattle are just four-legged animals to Bob; they don't stir his soul like sheep and pigs. He couldn't write beautiful things about them. But when it comes to sheep, he just naturally turns into a poet!"

The object of these remarks helped himself serenely to cake.

"Go on," he nodded at his sister cheerfully. "Wait until my wool cheque comes in, and you want a new frock — then you'll speak respectfully of my little merinos. And if you don't, you won't get the frock!"

"Why, I wouldn't disrespect them for anything," Tommy said. "I think they're lovely beasts. So graceful and agile. Will any of them come yet when you whistle, Bobby?"

"Are you going to put up with this sort of thing, Bob?" demanded Jim.

Bob smiled sweetly.

"I'm letting her have her head," he said confidently. "It's badly swelled just now, because she's got a house of her own — but you wait until she wants a new set of shelves, or a horse caught in a hurry so that she can tear over and find out from Norah how to cook something — then she'll come to heel. It's something in your climate, I think, because she was never so cheeky at home — meek was more the word to describe her."

"Meek!" said his sister indignantly. "Indeed, I never was meek in my life!"

"Indeed you were, and it was very becoming," Bob assured her. "Now you're more like a suffragette —" He stopped, staring. "Why, that's it! It must be in the air! She knows she'll have the vote pretty soon!" He broke into laughter. "Glory! Fancy little Tommy with a vote!"

Tommy joined in the general mirth.

"I hadn't realised it," she said, "and I needn't bother for over eighteen months, anyhow. And I don't believe that any of you have ever voted, even if you are twenty-one — except Mr. Linton, of course; and you don't know a bit more about it than I do."

"Hear, hear!" said Wally. "I certainly don't, and neither does Jim. But when we do vote, it's going to be for the chap who'll let us go and dig our own coal out if there's a strike. That's sense; and it seems to me the only sensible thing I've ever heard of in politics!" A speech which manifested so unusual an amount of reflection in Wally that everyone was spellbound, and professed inability to eat any more.

Bob and Tommy stood on the verandah to watch their visitors go; Mr. Linton and Norah in the motor, while Jim and Wally rode. The merry shouts of farewell echoed through the gathering dusk.

"Bless them," said Tommy, "the dears. I don't believe we'd have a home now but for them, Bob."

"We certainly wouldn't," Bob answered. "And sometimes I feel as if they'd spoon-fed us. Look at all they've done for us — these months at Billabong and all they've taught us, and all the things that they've showered on us. We couldn't pay them back in twenty years."

"And they talk as if the favour were on their side," his sister said. "There's the buggy they've lent us — Mr. Linton spent quite a long time in pointing out to me how desirable it was for them that we should use it, now that they have the car and don't need it. And the horses that apparently would have gone to rack and ruin from idleness if we hadn't come."

"And the cows that don't seem to have had any reason for existence except to supply us with milk," Bob said laughing; "and the farm machinery that never was really appreciated until immigrants came along — at least, you'd think so to hear Jim talk, only its condition belies him. Oh, they're bricks, all right. Only I don't seem as if I were standing squarely on my own feet."

"I don't think we could expect to, just yet," said Tommy pondering. "And if they have helped us, Bobby, you can see they have loved doing it. It would be ungracious for us not to take such help — given as it has been."

"Yes, of course," Bob answered and squared his shoulders. "Well, I'm going to work like fury. The only thing I can do now is not to disappoint them. I feel an awful new-chum, Tommy, but I've got to make good."

"Why, of course you're going to," she said, slipping a hand through his arm. "Jim wouldn't let you make mistakes; and the land is good, and even if we strike a bad season, there's always the creek — we'll never be without water, Jim says. And we're going to have the jolliest home — it's that now, and we're going to make it better."

"It's certainly that now," Bob said. "I just can't believe it's ours. Come and prowl round, old girl."

They prowled round in the dusk; up and down the garden paths by the nodding daffodils, out round the sheds and the pigsties, and so down to where the creek rippled and murmured in the gloom, flowing through paddocks that, on either side, were their own. Memories of war and of gloomy London fell away from them; only the bright present and a future yet more bright filled them; and there was no loneliness, since all the big new country had smiled to them and stretched out hands of friendliness. They came back slowly to their house, arm in arm; two young things, like shadows in the gloom, but certain in their own minds that they could conquer Australia.

Bob lit the hanging lamp in the little sitting-room, and looked round him proudly. A photograph caught his eye; a large group at his Surrey Aerodrome, young officers clustered round a bi-plane that had just landed.

"Poor chaps," he said, and stared at them. "Most of 'em don't know yet that there's anything better in the world than flying."

"But they've never met merino sheep," said Tommy solemnly.

CHAPTER 14

The Cunjee Races

"WHO'S going to the races?" demanded Jim. He had ridden over to the creek alone, and Tommy had come to the garden gate to greet him, since the young horse he was riding firmly declined to be tied up. It was a very hot morning in Christmas week. Tommy was in a blue print overall, and her face was flushed, her hair lying in little damp rings on her forehead. Jim, provokingly cool in riding breeches and white silk shirt, smiled down at her across the gate.

"Races!" said Tommy. "But what frivolity. Why, I'm bottling apricots."

"No wonder you look warm, you poor little soul," said Jim. "You oughtn't to choose a scorcher like this for bottling. Anyhow, the races aren't today, but New Year's Day — Cunjee Picnic meeting. We're all going, so you and Bob have got to come. Orders from Norah."

"Oh, New Year's Day. I'd love to come," Tommy said. "I've never seen races."

"Never seen races!" ejaculated young Australia

in sheer amazement. "Where were you dragged up?" They laughed at each other.

"Aunt Margaret wasn't what you'd call a racing woman," Tommy said. "I don't fancy Bob has seen any, either. Bill and Sarah, to say nothing of the baby, are going. I offered to mind the baby, but Sarah didn't seem to think the picnic would be complete without her."

"People have queer tastes," Jim said. "I wouldn't choose a long day at races as the ideal things for a baby; but Sarah seems to think differently. Wonder what Bill thinks? Still, I'm glad she didn't take you at your word, because we'd have had to dispose of the baby somewhere if she had. I suppose we could put it under the seat of the car!"

"Oh, do you?" Tommy regarded him with a glint in her eye. "No; we'd have made you nurse her — she isn't 'it'. She's the nicest baby ever, and I won't have her insulted."

"Bless you, I wouldn't insult the baby for worlds," grinned Jim. "I'll look forward to meeting her at the races — especially as you won't be minding her. Then it's settled, is it, Tommy? We thought of riding; will it be too far for you?"

"Not a bit," Tommy said. "Bob and I rode in and out of Cunjee the other day, and I wasn't tired — and it was dreadfully hot."

"Then you'll be all right on New Year's Day, because the racecourse is two miles this side of the township," Jim said. "But Norah said I was to tell you some of us could easily go in the car if you'd rather drive."

"Oh, no, thanks; I know you always ride, and I

should love it," Tommy answered. "Is Mr. Linton going?"

"Oh, yes. Indeed, as far as I can tell, the whole station's going," Jim said. "All except Brownie, of course; she scorns races. She says she can't imagine why anyone should make anything run fast in the 'eat if they don't want to."

"Does Brownie ever leave Billabong?"

"Hardly ever," Jim answered, laughing, "and it's getting more and more difficult to make her. I think in a year or two it will need a charge of dynamite. Oh, but, Tommy, we got her out in the car the other evening — had to do it almost by main force. It was a hot evening, and we took her for a spin along the road. She trembled like a jelly when we started, and all the time she gripped the side with one hand and Norah's knee with the other — quite unconsciously."

"Do you think she enjoyed it at all?" Tommy smiled.

"No, I'm jolly well sure she didn't," Jim responded. "Brownie's much too well mannered to criticise anyone else's property, but when she got out she merely said, 'You have great courage, my dear.' And wild horses wouldn't get her into it again, unless we promised to 'make it walk', like we did the day we brought her over to help at your working bee. The funny part of it is that Norah believes she was just as frightened that morning, only she had a job on, and so was too busy to think of it. But as for going in a car for mere pleasure — not for Brownie!"

"Brownie's a dear," said Tommy irrelevantly.

"Jim, can't you put that fierce animal in the stable or the horse paddock, or somewhere, and come in for some tea? I simply must get back to my apricots."

"And I've certainly no business to be keeping you standing here in the heat," Jim said. "No, I can't stay, thanks, Tommy — I promised Dad I'd meet him at the Far Plain gate at eleven o'clock, and it's nearly that now. You run in to your apricots, and don't kill your little self over them; it's no day for cooking if you can avoid it."

"Oh, but I couldn't," Tommy answered. "They were just right for bottling; the sun today would have made them a bit too soft. And it's better to get them done; tomorrow may be just as hot, or hotter."

"That's true enough," Jim said. "Feeling the heat much, little Miss Immigrant?"

"Oh, not enough to grumble at," she answered, smiling. "And the bathing hole in the creek is a joy; it's almost worth a hot day to get a swim at the end of it. Bob has built me a bathing box out of a tree, and it's a huge success; he's very pleased with himself as an architect."

"That's good business," approved Jim. "You two never grumble, no matter what comes along."

"Well, but nothing has come along but good luck," Tommy said. "What have we had to grumble at, I should like to know?"

"Oh, some people find cause for grousing, no matter how good their luck is," Jim answered. "I believe you and old Bob would decline to recognise bad luck even if it did come your way."

"It's not coming," Tommy said, laughing. "So don't talk about it — I don't believe it exists." She stood watching him for a moment as he tried to mount; his big young thoroughbred resented the idea of anyone on his back, and Jim had to hop beside him, with one foot in the stirrup, while he danced round in a circle, trying to get away. Jim seized an opportunity, and was in the saddle with a lithe swing; whereupon the horse tried to get his head down to buck, and being checked in that ambition, progressed down the paddock in a succession of short, staccato bounds.

"I think I should have to recognise bad luck coming if I had to ride him instead of Jim," remarked Tommy quaintly. She turned and ran in to her neglected apricots.

New Year's Day broke clear and hot, like all the week before it. Norah, arriving at the Creek about ten o'clock, looked a little anxiously at her friend.

"We're used to riding in the heat, Tommy, dear," she said. "But you're not — are you sure you feel up to it?"

"Why, I'm going to love it," Tommy said. She looked cool and workman-like in a linen habit and white pith helmet — Norah's Christmas present. "I hadn't these nice things to wear when Bob and I brought the sheep out from Cunjee three weeks ago; and it was just as hot, and so dusty. And that didn't kill me. I liked it, only I never got so dirty in my life."

"Well, we shall only have a hot ride one way," said Norah philosophically. "There's a concert in Cunjee, and the boys want to stay for it. The concert won't be much, but the ride home in the moonlight will be lovely. You and Bob can stay, of course?"

"Oh, yes. Bill must bring Sarah and the baby home in good time, so he will milk the cows," Tommy answered. "He wanted them to stay for the concert, but Sarah had an amazing attack of common sense, and said it was no place for a baby. I didn't think she considered any place unfit for a baby, and certainly Bill doesn't."

"Bush people don't," said Norah, laughing. "If they did, they would never go anywhere, because the babies must go too, no matter what happens. And the babies get accustomed to it, and don't cry nearly as much as pampered ones that are always in the nursery."

"Bush kiddies grow a stock of common sense quite early," said Wally's voice from the door. "It leaves them in later life, and they stay gossiping with immigrants in new riding kit, leaving their unfortunate fathers grilling in the sun. Which he says —" But at this point Norah and Tommy brushed the orator from their path, and hastened out to the horses — finding all the men comfortably smoking under a huge pepper tree, and apparently in no hurry to start.

Bob bewailed his yellow paddocks as they rode down to the gate.

"They were so beautifully green a few weeks ago," he said. "Now look at them — why, they're like a crop. The sun has burnt every bit of moisture out of them."

"Don't let that worry you, my boy," David Linton

said. "The stock are doing all right; as long as they have plenty of good water at this time of the year they won't ask you for green grass." He gave a low chuckle. "You wouldn't think this was bad feed if you had seen the country in the drought years — why, the paddocks were as bare as the palm of your hand. Now you've grass, as you say yourself, like a crop." He looked at it critically. "I could wish you hadn't as much; fires will be a bit of an anxiety later on."

"Grass fires?" queried Bob.

"Yes. There's not enough timber here to have a real bush fire. But this grass is dry enough now, and by February it will go like tinder if any fool swagman drops a match carelessly. However, you'll just have to keep your eyes open. Luckily, your creek can't burn — you'll always have so much safeguard, because your stock could take to it; and that row of willows along the bank would check any grass fire."

"My word, wouldn't a fire race across the Billabong plains this year!" said Wally.

"Yes, it would certainly travel," agreed Mr. Linton. "Well, we've ploughed fire-breaks, and burned round the house, and we can only hope for good luck. You'd better burn a break round your house soon, Bob."

"Bill was saying so only this morning," Bob answered. "I nearly chucked the races and stayed at home to do it — only I was afraid it might get away from me single-handed, and I couldn't very well keep Bill at home."

"Oh, time enough," the squatter said lightly.

"You're not so dry as we are, and we only burned last week."

"We'll come over and help you tomorrow, if you like," Jim said. "Wally wants work; he's getting too fat. A little gentle exercise with a racing fire on a hot day would be the very thing for him. We'll come and burn off with you, and then have a bathing party in the creek, and then you and Tommy must come back to tea with us." Which was a sample of the way much of the work was done on the Creek Farm. It had never occurred to the two Rainhams that life in Australia was lonely.

The road to Cunjee was usually bare of much traffic, but on the one race day of the year an amazing number of vehicles were dotted along it, light buggies, farm wagonettes, spring carts and the universal two-wheeled jinker, all crammed with farmers and settlers and their families. Wives, a little red-faced and anxious, resplendent in their Sunday finery, kept a watchful eye on small boys and girls; the boys in thick suits, the girls with white frocks, their well-crimped hair bearing evidence of intense plaiting overnight. Hampers peeped from under the seats, and in most cases a baby completed the outfit. Now and then a motor whizzed by, leaving a long trail of dust cloud in its wake, and earning hearty remarks from every slower wayfarer. There were riders everywhere, men and women — most of the latter with riding-skirts slipped on over light dresses that would do duty that night at the concert and the dance that was to follow.

Sometimes a motor-cycle chugged along, always with a girl perched on the carrier at the back, clinging affectionately to her escort. As Cunjee drew nearer and the farms closer together the crowd on the road increased, and the dust mounted in a solid cloud.

The Billabong people drew to one side, as close as possible to the fence, cantering over the short, dusty grass. It was with a sigh of relief that Jim at last pointed out a paddock across which buggies and horsemen were making their way.

"There's the racecourse," he said.

"Racecourse!" Tommy ejaculated. "But it just looks like an ordinary paddock."

"That's all it is," said Jim, laughing. "You didn't expect a grandstand and a lawn, did you? Cunjee is very proud of itself for having a turf club at all, and nobody minds anything as long as they get an occasional glimpse of the horses."

"But where do they run?"

"Oh, the track goes in and out among the trees. There's some talk of clearing it before the next meeting by means of a working bee. But they won't worry if it doesn't get done — everyone will come and have a picnic just the same. You see, there are only two days in the year when a bush place can really let itself go — Show Day and Race Day. Show Day is more serious and business-like, but Race Day is a really light-hearted affair, and the horses don't matter to most of the people."

They turned into a gate where two men were busily collecting shillings and keeping a wary eye lest foot passengers should dodge in through the fence without paying. There were no buildings at all in the bush paddock in which they found themselves. It lay before them, flat, save for a rise towards the southern boundary, where already the crowd was thickening, and sparsely timbered. As they cantered across it they came to a rough track, marked out more or less effectively by pink calico flags nailed to the trees.

"That's the racing track," Wally said. "Let's ride round it, and we'll have a faint idea of what the horses are doing later on."

They turned along the track, where the grass had been worn by horses training for the races during the few weeks preceding the great day. The trees had been cleared from it, so that it was good going. In shape it was roughly circular, with an occasional dint or bulge where a big red gum had been too tough a proposition to clear, and the track had had to swing aside to avoid it — a practice which must, as Jim remarked, make interesting moments in riding a race, if the field were larger than usual and the pace at all hot. Presently they emerged from the timber and came into the straight run that marked the finish — running along the foot of the southern rise, so that, whatever happened in the mysterious moments in the earlier parts of a race, the end was within full view of the crowd. The winning post was a sawed-off sapling, painted half-black and half-white; opposite to it was the judge's box, a huge log which made a natural grandstand, capable of accommodating the racing committee as well. Behind, a rough wire fence enclosed a small

space known as the saddling paddock. The crowd
picked out its own accommodation — it was
necessary to come early if you wanted a good place
on the rise. Already it was dotted with picnic
parties, preparing luncheon, and a procession of
men and boys, bearing teapots and billies, came
and went about a huge copper, steaming over a
fire, where the racing club dispensed hot water
free of charge, a generosity chiefly intended to
prevent the casual lighting of fires by the
picnickers. All over the paddock people were
hastening through the business of the midday
meal; the men anxious to get it over before the
real excitement of the day began with the racing,
the women equally keen to feed their hungry
belongings and then settle down to a comfortable
gossip with friends perhaps only seen once or twice
in the twelve months. Children tore about wildly,
got in the way of buggies and motors, climbed
trees and clustered thickly round any horse
suspected of taking part in the racing. More than
one candidate for a race appeared on the course
drawing a jinker; and, being released from the
shafts, was being vigorously groomed by his
shirt-sleeved owner.

"There's an awful lot to see!" ejaculated Tommy,
gazing about her.

"That is if you've eyes," Jim said. "But most of
it can be seen on foot, so I vote Wally and Bob
and I take the horses and tie them up while there's
still a decent patch of shade left for them to stand
in — every tree in the paddock will have horses

tied to it before long. Do you know where Evans
was to leave the buggy, Dad?"

"Yes — it's under a tree over there," said his
father, nodding towards a bushy clump of wattles.
"I told him to pick out a good shady place for
lunch. We'll go on and get ready, boys. I'll take
the teapot for hot water."

"Not you!" said Jim. "We'll be back in a few
minutes, and can easily get it. Just help the girls
with the things, Dad, and we'll get lunch over; I'm
as hungry as a hawk."

"I'm not hungry," said Norah. "But I want, oh!
gallons of tea."

Tea seemed the main requirement of everybody.
It was almost too hot to eat, even in the deep
shade of the wattles. The boys, taught by the war
to feed wherever and whenever possible, did some
justice to Brownie's hamper; but Mr. Linton soon
drew aside and lit his pipe at a little distance,
while Tommy and Norah nibbled tomato and
lettuce sandwiches, kept fresh and cool by being
packed in huge nasturtium leaves, and drank
many cups of tea. Then they lay under the trees
until a bell, ringing from the saddling paddock,
hinted that the first race was at hand. There was
a surge of people towards the rise.

"Come on," Jim said, jumping up. "Help me to
stow these things in the buggy, Wally — we'll
want most of them for afternoon tea later on. Then
we might as well go and see the fun. You girls
rested?"

They were, they declared; and presently they
set off towards the rise. Already the horses were

appearing on the track, most of the jockeys
wearing silk jackets and caps, although a few were
content with doffing coat and waistcoat, and riding
in blue and pink shirts — occasionally, but not
always, complete with collar and tie. The horses
were a mixed lot; some bore traces of birth and
breeding but the majority were just grassfed
horses from the neighbouring farms and stations,
groomed and polished in a way that only happened
to them once a year. The well-bred performers
were handicapped with heavy weights, while the
others had been let off lightly, so that all had a
chance.

"Billabong has a horse running today — did you
know?" Jim inquired.

"No!" Tommy looked up, dimpling with interest.
"But how exciting, Jim. Is it yours?"

"No," Jim shook his head. "I won't enter a horse
if I can't ride him myself, and of course I'm too
heavy. He belongs to the station, but he's always
looked upon as Murty's, and Billy's going to ride
him. He's in the hurdle race."

"Do you think he has any chance?"

"Well, he can gallop and jump all right," Jim
said. "But he hasn't had much training, and
whether he'll jump in company is open to doubt.
But I don't think he'll disgrace us. You've seen
Murty riding him — a big chestnut with a white
blaze."

"Oh, yes — he calls him Shannon, doesn't he?"
said Tommy. "I saw him jump three fences on him
last time we were out mustering with your people.
He's a beauty, Jim."

"Yes, he's pretty good. Murty thinks he's better than Garryowen, but I don't," Jim observed.

"If the Archangel Gabriel turned into a horse you wouldn't think he was up to Garryowen!" said Wally.

"No, and he probably wouldn't be," said Jim, laughing. "If you begin life as an archangel, how would you settle down to being a horse after?"

"I suppose it needs practice," Wally admitted. "Look out — here they come!"

The horses were coming down the straight in their preliminary canter, and the crowd abandoned the business of picnicking and turned its attention to the first race. The riders, mostly local boys, looked desperately serious, and, as they pulled up after their canter, and turning, trotted slowly back past the rise, shouts of warning and encouragement and instruction came to them — from the owners of their mounts — which had the effect of making the boys look yet more unhappy. A bookmaker, the sole representative of his profession, yelled steadily from under a lightwood tree; those who were venturesome enough to do business with him were warned solemnly by more experienced men to keep a sharp look-out that he did not get away with their money before the end of the day.

"That happened in Cunjee some years ago," said Mr. Linton. "A bookmaker appeared from goodness knows where, and struck a very solid patch of bad luck. All the district seemed to know how to pick winners that day, and he lost solidly on every race. He plunged a bit on the fourth race, hoping to get his money back; but that was worse still, and when he saw the favourite winning, he knew he had no hope of settling up. So he quietly collected his horse, which he had tied up in a convenient place, in case it was wanted in a hurry, and made tracks before the race finished."

"What happened to him?" asked Bob.

Mr. Linton chuckled.

"Well, he added considerably to the excitement of the day. Someone saw him going, and passed the word round, and every man to whom he owed money — and they were many — ran for his horse and went after him. He had a good start, and no one knew what road he would take, so it was quite a cheery hunt. I think it was Dave Boone who tracked him at last, and he paused at a cross-roads, and coo-eed steadily until he had a number of followers. Then they set sail after the poor bookie, and caught him about seven or eight miles away. They found he had practically no money — not nearly enough to divide up; so they took what he had and presented it to the Cunjee Hospital, and finished up the day happily by tarring and feathering the bookie, and riding him on a fence rail round Cunjee that night!"

"What do your police do in a case like that?" Bob asked.

"Well, there's only one policeman in Cunjee, and, being a wise man, he went to the concert, and probably enjoyed himself very much," said Mr. Linton, laughing.

"And what happened to the bookie?"

"Just what you might expect — the boys got

sorry for him, made a collection for him, bought him some cheap clothes — I believe they didn't err on the side of beauty! — and shipped him off to Melbourne by the first train in the morning. I don't think he'll try his artful dodges on this section of the bush again; and it has made all the boys very watchful about betting, so it wasn't a bad thing, on the whole. They think they know all about the ways of the world now. Look, Tommy — the horses are off! Watch through the trees, and you'll get a glimpse presently."

The gay jackets flashed into view in a gap in the timber, and then were lost again. Soon they came in sight once more and rounded the last curve into the straight, amid shouts from the crowd. They came up the straight, most of the jockeys flogging desperately, while everyone rushed to get as near the winning post as possible. Hats were flung in the air and yells rose joyfully, as a Cunjee boy, riding a desperate finish, got his horse's nose in front in the last couple of lengths and won cleverly.

"She's excited!" said Wally, looking down at Tommy's flushed face.

"I should think so," said Tommy. "Why, it was dreadfully exciting. I'd love to have been riding myself." At which everyone laughed extremely, and a tall young stockman from a neighbouring station, overhearing, was so impressed that he hovered as near as possible to Tommy for the rest of the day.

The next event was the hurdle race, and interest for the Linton party centred in the candidate described on the race card as Mr. M. O'Toole's Shannon. Nothing further could be done for Shannon — he was groomed until the last hair on his tail gleamed; but black Billy, resplendent in a bright green jacket and cap, the latter bearing an embroidered white shamrock, became the object of advice and warning from every man from Billabong, until anyone except Billy would probably have turned in wrath upon the multitude of his counsellors. Billy, however, had one refuge denied to most of his white brothers. He hardly ever spoke; and if some reply was absolutely forced upon him, he merely murmured "Plenty!" in a vague way, which, as Wally said, left you guessing as to his meaning.

"Yerra, lave off badgerin' the boy," said Murty at last, brushing aside Dave Boone and Mick Shanahan, and the other Billabong enthusiasts. "If he listens to the lot of ye any longer he won't know whether he's ridin' a horse or an aeroplane. There's only one instruction to be keepin' in your head, Billy — get to the front an' stay there. Ridin' a waitin' race is all very well on the flat, but whin it comes to jumpin', anything that's in front of ye is apt to turn a somersault an' bring ye down in a heap."

"Plenty!" agreed Billy; and lit a cigarette.

"Shannon don't like any other horse in front of him at all," went on Murty. "He's that full of pride he never tuk kindly to bein' behind, not since he was bruk in. He'll gallop like a machine an' lep like a deer if he gets his head."

"I don't b'lieve you've much show, anyhow,"

Dave Boone said. "There's that horse from the hotel at Mulgoa — Blazer, they call him. He's done no end of racin', and won, too."

"Well, an' if he has, hasn't he the great weight itself to be carryin'?" demanded Murty.

"Why, he's top weight, of course; but you're carryin' ever so much over weight," responded Mr. Boone. "If you'd put up a boy instead of Billy, you could be pounds lighter."

"Ah, git away with your advisin'," replied Murty. "Billy knows the horse — an' where'd a shilip of a boy be if Shannon cleared out with him? I'd rather carry too much weight, an' know I'd put a man up as could hold the horse." His anxious eye fell on the girls. "Miss Norah and Miss Tommy! — come here an' wish him luck without offerin' me any advice, or I'll lose me life over the old race! They have destroyed me with all the things they're after tellin' me to do."

"We won't tell you a thing, Murty — except that he's looking splendid," Norah said, stroking Shannon's nose, to which the horse responded by nuzzling round her pocket in search of an apple. "No, I can't give you one, old man — I wouldn't dare. But you shall have one after the race, whether you win or not, can't he, Murty?"

"He can so," said Murty. "Wance he's gone round that track he can live on the fat of the land — an' Billy, too. It's a dale easier to get the condition off a horse than off Billy. No man on this earth 'ud make a black fellow see why he shouldn't have a good blow-out whenever it came his way. Only that Providence made him skinny by nature, he'd be fat as a porpoise this day. I've been watchin' over his meals like a mother with a delicate baby these three weeks back; but what hope 'ud I have with Christmas comin' in the way? He got away on me at Christmas dinner, an' what he didn't ate in the way of turkey an puddin' wouldn't be worth mentioning — an' him booked to ride today! 'Plenty' always did be his motter, an' he lives up to it. So he's pounds overweight, an' no help for it."

"Never mind, Murty," Jim said. "He knows the horse, and Shannon's able to stand a few pounds extra. He'll give us a good run."

"I believe ye, Masther Jim," said Murty, beaming. "He'll not disgrace us, an' if he don't win itself, then he'll not be far behind. There you are, Billy — that's the bell for weighin'. Hurry up now, and get over to the scales."

The black boy's lean figure, saddle and bridle on arm, threaded its way through the crowd round the weighing enclosure — a little space fenced off by barbed wire. Presently they saw him coming back grinning.

"That feller sayin' I plenty too much pounds," he said in an unusual burst of eloquence.

"Ah, don't be rubbin' it in — don't I know it?" quoth Murty, taking the saddle and slipping it deftly on Shannon's back. "I dunno, did he think he was givin' me a pleasant surprise with the information by way of a New Year's gift. Does he think we've never a scales on Billabong, did ye ask him? There now, he's ready. Get on him, Billy, an' shove out into the track for a canter. I'll get

nothing but chat from everyone as long as you're
here. Take him for a look at some of the hurdles,
that way he'll know all about them when he comes
to jump." He stood with a frown on his
good-humoured face as Shannon and his rider
made off.

Norah laid a hand on his arm.

"There's not a horse on the course better turned
out, Murty," she said. "No one can say the
Billabong representative doesn't look fit."

Murty turned on her, beaming again.

"Well, indeed, he'll not be doin' the station any
discredit, Miss Norah," he said happily, "an' if he
don't win, well, we can't all be winnin', can we?
Only we did win a race last year, whin non of ye
were here to be watching' us an' make it
worthwhile. I'd like to score today, now that ye're
all here to see — an' Miss Tommy too, that's never
seen racin'." He smiled down at the English girl's
pink face.

"I'm going to see you win today, Murty — I feel
it in my bones," said Tommy promptly. "I've
always loved Shannon, ever since I saw you jump
those big fences with him when we put up the
hare out mustering."

"Yerra, that one'd make a steeplechaser if he
got the trainin'," declared Murty, all his troubles
forgotten. "Come a little higher up, won't ye, Miss
Norah; we can see every jump from the top of the
rise, barrin' the wan that's in the timber."

They followed him up the little hill until he
declared himself satisfied with his position; and
he spent the time until the flag fell in pointing out

to Tommy the exact places where the hurdles were erected — pausing only for a proud look when Shannon thundered past below them in his preliminary canter, the green jacket bright in the sun, and every muscle in the horse's gleaming body rippling as he moved. He was reefing and plunging in his gallop, trying to get his head; but Billy soon steadied him, and presently brought him up the straight again at a quiet trot. The other horses went out, one by one, until at length a field of eight faced the starter; and presently they were off, and over the first jump in a body. They came down the straight on the first time round, packed closely, a glittering mass of shining horses and bright colours. One dropped at the jump near the judge's box, and as the other horses raced away round the turn the riderless horse followed, while his jockey lay still for a moment, a little scarlet blur upon the turf. Eager helpers ran forward to pick him up, but he was on this feet before they could reach him, and came limping up the hill, a little bruised and infinitely disgusted.

"He's all right," Murty said. "Yerra, Mr. Jim, did ye see the old horse jump! He went ahead at his fences like a deer!"

The horses were in the timber; they peered anxiously at the bright patch of colour that showed from time to time, trying to see the familiar green jacket. Then, as the field came into view Murty uttered an irrepressible yell, for his horse shot ahead at the next jump and came into the straight in the lead. Murty gripped at the nearest object, which happened to be Norah's shoulder, and clenched it tightly, muttering, in his excitement, words in his native Irish. They thundered up the straight, Billy crouching on Shannon's neck, very still. Then behind him the Mulgoa horse drew out from the ruck and came in chase. Nearer and nearer he came, while the shouts from the crowd grew louder. Up, up, till his nose was at Shannon's quarter — at his girth — at his shoulder, and the winning post was very near. Then suddenly Billy lifted his whip and brought it down once, and Shannon shot forward with a last wild bound. Murty's hat went up in the air — and Wally's with it.

"He's done it!" Murty babbled. "Yerra, what about Billabong now?" He suddenly found himself gripping Norah's shoulder wildly, and would have apologised but that Norah herself was dancing with delight, and looking for his hand to grasp. And the crowd was shouting "Shannon! Shannon! Billabong!" — since all of these Cunjee folk loved Billabong and were steadily jealous of Mulgoa. Jim and Wally were thumping Murty on the back. Bob and Mr. Linton stood beaming at him. Below them Billy came trotting back on his victorious steed, sitting with a grave face, as expressionless as if he had not just accomplished his heart's desire. But his dark mysterious eyes scanned the crowd as he turned from weighing in, and only grew satisfied when he saw the Billabong party hurrying to greet him. They shook his hand, and smote him on the back, Dave Boone and Mick Shanahan prancing with joy. And Shannon, his

glossy coat dark with sweat, nuzzled again at
Norah's pocket for an apple — and this time got
it.

This glorious event over, interest became
focused on a trotting race, which brought out a
queer assortment of competitors, ranging from
King of Lightfoot, a horse well known in
Melbourne, to Poddy, an animal apparently more
fitted to draw a hearse than to trot in a race —
a lean, raw-boned horse of a sad countenance and
a long nose, with a shaggy black coat which rather
resembled that of a long-haired Irish goat. There
were other candidates, all fancied by their owners,
but the public support was only for King Lightfoot,
who ran in elaborate leather and rubber harness,
and was clearly regarded by his rider as of infinite
condescension to be taking part in such a very
mixed company.

It proved, however, not to be King Lightfoot's
lucky day. The horses started at intervals,
according to their performances or merit, Poddy
being the first to move, the Melbourne horse the
last. King Lightfoot, however, obstinately refused
to trot, whereas Poddy revealed unexpected
powers, flinging his long legs abroad in a
whirlwind fashion, and pounding along doggedly,
with his long nose outstretched as if hoping to get
it past the winning post as soon as possible. No
other horse came near him; his initial lead was
never lessened, and he plugged doggedly to
victory, while the crowd roared with laughter, and
out in the timber King Lightfoot's rider wrestled
with his steed in vain. Later, his prejudice against

trotting in the bush removed by stern measures, King Lightfoot flashed up the track like a meteor, with his furious rider determined to show something of what his steed could do. By that time Poddy was once more unsaddled, and was standing under a tree with his weary nose drooping earthwards, so that the crowd merely yelled with laughter anew, while the stewards unfeelingly requested the Melbourne man to get off the track.

"Oh, isn't it hot!" Norah fanned herself with a bunch of gum leaves, and cast an anxious look at Tommy.

It was breathlessly hot. Not a hint of air stirred among the trees or moved the long dry grass that covered the paddock — now showing many depressions, where tired people or horses had lain down to rest. The horses stood about, drooping their heads, and swishing their tails ceaselessly at the tormenting flies; men and women sought every available patch of shade, while dogs stretched themselves under the buggies, panting, with lolling tongues. Children alone ran about, as though nothing could mar their enjoyment; but babies fretted wearily in their mothers' arms. Overhead the sun blazed fiercely in a sky of brass. Now and then came a low growl of thunder, giving hope of a change at night; but it was very far distant, although a dull bank of cloud lay to the west. David Linton watched the cloud a little uneasily.

"I don't quite like the look of it," he muttered

to himself. "I'll go and ask Murty what he thinks of it."

But Murty had been swallowed up in a crowd anxious to congratulate him on Shannon's success, and his employer failed to find him at the moment. He came upon Sarah, however — sitting under a tree, with her baby wailing dismally.

"Too hot for her, Sarah," David Linton said kindly.

"That's right, sir — it's too hot for anyone, let alone a little tiny kid," Sarah said wearily. "I'd get Bill to go home if I could, but I can't get on his tracks — and it's too hot to take baby out in the sun looking for him. If you come across him, sir, you might tell him I want him."

"All right," said the squatter. "But you wouldn't take that long drive home yet, Sarah — better wait until the sun goes down."

"Well, I'd go into Cunjee, to me sister-in-law's," said Sarah. "She'd let me take baby's things off an' sponge her — an' I'd give a dollar to do it. No more races with kids for me in weather like this!" She crooned to the fretting baby as Mr. Linton went off.

He found Tommy and Norah together under a tree near the track — hot, but interested.

"Where are the boys?"

"They're all holding ponies," Norah said. "I don't quite know why, but a very hot and worried man collected them to help start the race. What is it for, Dad, do you know?"

"Oh, I see!" David Linton laughed. "It's a distance handicap — the ponies all start at the same moment, but from different points along the track."

"Yes, that must be it," Norah said. "Jim's away over near the timber with a little rat of a pony, and Bob is shepherding another fifty yards behind him, while Wally is quite near here with that big pony of the blacksmith's that has won ever so many races. She'll have a lot of ground to make up. But why must each one be shepherded, Dad?"

"Human nature," said David Linton, smiling. "These youngsters who are riding would sneak a yard or two if they weren't closely watched, and they would never start fair; the only way is to put each in charge of a responsible man with a good watch, and let him start them. What time is the race? Oh, four o'clock. Well, I never yet saw a pony race that started on time; neither the ponies nor the boys are easy to handle, and I see there are ten of them. Watch them; it's after four, and they must be nearly ready to start."

The ponies were strung out round the course, each with a "shepherd" standing to attention near its bridle, watch in hand. They could see Jim's great form standing sentinel over a tiny animal, whose diminutive rider was far too afraid of the huge Major to try to snatch even a yard of ground; nearer, Wally kept a wary eye on the experienced jockey on the blacksmith's racing mare, who was afraid of nothing, but nevertheless had a certain wholesome respect for the tall fellow who lounged easily against a tree near him, but never for an instant shifted his gaze. The shepherds were waiting for a signal from the official starter.

It came presently, a long shrill whistle, and simultaneously each guardian stepped back, and the released ponies went off like flash — all save Bob's charge, who insisted on swinging round and bolting in the wrong direction, while his jockey sawed at his mouth in vain. Yawing across the track the rebel encountered the blacksmith's pony, who swerved violently in her swift course to avoid him, and lost so much ground that any chance she had in the race was hopelessly lost, whereat the blacksmith, who was standing on the hill, raved and tore his hair unavailingly. A smart little bay pony fought out the finish with Jim's tiny charge, and was beaten by a short head, just as Wally, walking quickly, came back to his party.

"That was a great race," said Norah. "Wally, you shouldn't walk so fast on such a day. It makes one warm only to look at you."

Wally answered with an absent air that was unlike his usual alertness. The girls, watching the ponies come in, noticed nothing, and presently he drew Mr. Linton aside.

"Did you notice that cloud, sir?" he asked, in a low voice. "I didn't until I was down on the track with the pony, looking in that direction. But it's twice the size it was when I went down."

"I've been looking at it, and I don't like it," said Mr. Linton. "It's smoke, I'm positive, and too near Billabong and the Creek to be comfortable. I think we'll make tracks for home, Wally. Have you seen Murty anywhere?"

As if in answer, Mr. O'Toole came running down the hill.

"I've been huntin' ye's everywhere," he panted. "There's a man just came out from Cunjee lookin' for you, sir — someone's telephoned in that there's a big grass fire comin' down on the Creek, an' 'twill be a miracle if it misses Billabong! I've told the men — they're off to get the horses."

Norah and Tommy had turned, with dismayed eyes.

"Will it be at our place, Murty?" Tommy asked.

"I dunno will it, Miss Tommy," the Irishman answered. "But as like as not 'twill miss it — or anyhow, we'll get there first, an' stop it doing much damage. Don't you worry your little head, now."

She looked up at him gratefully. Norah's hand was thrust through her arm.

"It may not be near the Creek at all, Tommy dear," she said.

"Oh, I hope it isn't — my poor old Bob!" Tommy said, under her breath. "Can we hurry, Norah?"

"They're bringing the horses," Norah answered. "We'll be off in a minute — see, Dad has gone to meet Bob."

Wally had turned to Murty.

"Murty, do you mind if I ride Shannon and take him across country? I'm on Marshal today, you know, and he can't jump for nuts. But Shannon can take every fence between here and the Creek, and I can cut the distance in half if I go across. I'm about the lightest of us, I think."

"So ye are — an' the horse'll take ye like a bird," said Murty. "Don't spare him, Mr. Wally, if ye think ye can do any good. He's over there under the big wattle."

"Right-o!" said Wally. "Tell Mr Jim, will you, Murty?" He turned and ran down the hill with long strides.

CHAPTER 15

How Wally Rode a Race

ALREADY the cloud was growing in the western sky — so high that it threatened to obscure the sun that still blazed fiercely down. At first a dull brown, there was a curious light behind it; at the edges it trailed away into ragged wisps like floating mist. There was something mysteriously threatening in its dense heaviness.

There were other men running for their horses, as Wally raced towards Shannon. The news of a grass fire had spread quickly, and every man wanted to be on his own property, for the whole countryside was covered with long, dry grass, and no one could say where a fire might or might not end. Boone and Shanahan passed Wally, leading several horses — his own amongst them. They hailed him quickly.

"We've got Marshal, Mr. Wally."

"Give him to Murty," Wally answered as he ran. "I'm riding Shannon." He raced on.

"That means he's going across country," said Dave Boone. "For two pins I'd go too."

"Don't you — you'd never get your horse over

them fences," Shanahan said. "An' it'll take Mr.
Wally all his time to get across them wired
paddocks of Maclennan's. Hope he don't break
Shannon's legs."

"Not he. Mr. Wally's no fool," said Boone. "Git
up, y' ol' sardine!" He kicked the horse he was
leading, and they trotted up to Norah and Tommy.

Shannon, standing with drooping head, showed
little interest as Wally flung the saddle on his
back. He had won his race handsomely, and it was
a scorching day; possibly the big chestnut felt that
no more should be required of him; in which case
he was soon to be rudely awakened. Wally swung
into the saddle with a quick movement, and
turned him, not towards the gate, but in the
opposite direction, which further puzzled
Shannon. But he was a stock horse first and a
hurdle racer as an afterthought; and a good stock
horse knows his rider's mind, if that rider is a
good man. He made one tentative movement
towards his paddock mates, now moving away
towards the gate; then, feeling the touch of Wally's
hand on the bit, and the light pressure of his knee,
he decided that some new game was on foot, and
cantered easily away.

They crossed the racing track, going westward
over the big paddock, away from the buggies and
the crowd. A belt of timber checked their swift
progress a moment; then they came out into clear
ground in sight of the boundary fence, a stiff
three-railer. Wally peered at it anxiously, unable,
for an instant, to see if there were a wire on top;
but it was clear, and he shook up his horse,

putting him straight at the middle of a panel. Shannon pricked his ears and flew it daintily — this was work he loved, and hot though the day might be, he was ready for any amount of it. Also Wally was lighter than Murty, his usual rider; and although he loved Murty, and respected him greatly, this new man had a seat like a feather and a hand gentle as silk upon his tender mouth. Shannon broke into the gallop that he felt sure his rider wanted.

They were in a wide paddock, bare, save for a few clumps of timber, in the shade of which sheep were thickly clustered. It was good, sound going, with a few little rises; and, knowing that he would have to slacken speed presently, Wally let the chestnut have his head across the clear grass. They took the next fence and the next before he drew rein. He was in country he did not know — all big farms, with many stubble fields with newly erected stacks, and with good homesteads, where now and then a woman peered curiously from a veranda at him. There were no men in sight; every man in the neighbourhood was at the races on New Year's day.

He found himself in a paddock where rough ground, thickly strewn with fallen timber, sloped down abruptly to a creek. Checking Shannon, he rode more steadily down to the water, and trotted along the bank for a hundred yards, looking for a good place to ford — the banks shelved abruptly down, and the water was unusually deep. But the only promising fords were too thickly snagged to be tempting; and presently, with a shrug, Wally

gave up the quest, and choosing a place where the
fall of the bank was a shade less abrupt, he put
the horse at it.

Shannon hesitated, drawing back. Water was
the one thing to which he had not been schooled
on Billabong, and this place was mysterious and
deep. But Wally's hand was firm, and he spoke
sharply — so that the chestnut repented of the
error of his ways, and plunged obediently
downwards. The bank gave under them, and they
slithered down among its remnants and landed in
the water with a profound splash, almost hidden
for a moment by the spray that drenched Wally's
thin silk coat and shirt. Shannon floundered
violently, and nearly lost his footing — and then,
deciding that this was an excellent entertainment
on a hot day, he thrust his thirsty nose into the
water. Wally checked him after one mouthful.

"I'm sorry, old chap," he said regretfully. "I'd
like it as much as you. But I can't let you have a
drink just now."

He pressed him on across the muddy stream,
floundering over sunken logs, slipping into holes,
dodging half-concealed snags; and so they came to
a bank which scarcely seemed a possible place, so
steep was it. But Wally looked at the smoke cloud,
and grew desperate, and for the first time touched
Shannon with the spur; and the chestnut
answered gamely, springing at the bank and
climbing almost like a cat. Twice it broke under
him; the third time he made some footing, and
Wally suddenly flung himself from his back,
scrambling up ahead of him, and hauling at the

bridle. Shannon followed, floundering and snorting; desperately relieved to find himself on firm ground again. Wally swung into the saddle and they galloped forward.

The next two fences were log ones, and the chestnut took them almost in his stride. Then Wally's lips tightened, for he saw a homestead that he knew most be Maclennan's, the most prosperous farmer about; and Maclennan had strong views on the subject of inflammable fences in a country so liable to grass fires, and all his property was wire-fenced. The first fence stretched before him, taut and well strung; he looked up and down its length in search of a gate, but there was none in sight.

"I could put my coat on the top wire for you to jump if it was a thick one, old chap," he told Shannon. "But a scrap of wet silk wouldn't be much good to you. We'll have to chance a post."

He drew rein, trotting up to the fence, where he let the horse put his nose over a post — and set his lips again when he saw that the top wire was barbed.

"Just you remember to pick up all your toes well, old man," he said.

He trotted back a little way, and, turning, came hard at the fence, putting Shannon directly at the post. This also was new to the chestnut; but once, when a foal, he had been badly pricked on barbed wire, and, ever since, one glance at its hideous spikes had been enough for him. Refusing was out of the question — Wally was leaning forward, keeping him absolutely straight, lifting him at the post with a little shout of encouragement. He flew over it as if it had been a hurdle. Wally patted his neck with a big sigh of relief.

"Eh, but I was scared for your legs, old man!" he said.

They galloped across a wide stubble field, while Wally's keen eyes searched the fence for a gate. He caught sight of one presently, a stiff, four-railed gate, considerably higher than the fence. High as it was, Wally preferred it to barbed wire; and by this time he had a queer feeling that no jump would prove too much for the big, honest chestnut, who was doing so gamely everything that he was asked. Nor did Shannon disappoint him; he rose at the gate cheerfully, and barely tipped it with one hind foot as he cleared it. Wally fancied there was something of apology in the little shake of his head as he galloped on.

"If I'd time to take you back over that you wouldn't lay a toe on it again, I believe. Never mind, there's sure to be another."

There was, and the chestnut flew over it with never a touch. Maclennan's paddocks were wide and well cleared — such galloping ground as Wally dared not waste — and he took full advantage of them, leaving one after another behind swiftly, to the beat of Shannon's sweeping stride. Fence after fence the chestnut cleared, taking them cleanly, with his keen ears pricked; never faltering or flagging as he galloped. Wally sat him lightly, leaning forward to ease him, cheering him on with voice and touch. Before him the cloud grew dense and yet more dense; he could feel its hot breath now, although a bush-covered paddock ahead blocked the fire itself from his immediate view. He had to choose between picking his way through the trees or galloping round them; and chose the latter, since Shannon showed no sign of fatigue. He put the last wire fence behind him with a sigh of relief. A small farm with easy enough fences remained to be crossed, and then he swung round the timber at top speed. Once round it, he should come within view of the Rainhams' house.

He came into the open country, and pulled up with a shout of dismay. Before him was the long line of timber marking the creek, but between lay nothing but a rolling cloud of smoke, lit with flashes of flame. A hot gust of wind blew it aside for a moment, and through it he caught a glimpse of Creek Cottage, burning fiercely. Wally uttered a smothered groan, and thrust Shannon forward, over the last fence, and up a little lane that led near the Rainhams' back gate.

The paddock was nearly all on fire. It had started somewhere back in the bush country, and had swept across like a wall, burning everything before it. As Wally reached the gate, it was rolling away across the paddocks, a sheet of flame, licking up the dry grass; leaving behind it bare and blackened ground, with here and there a fence post, or a tree burning, and, in the midst of its track, Creek Cottage wrapped in flames.

The boy slipped from his saddle and flung Shannon's bridle over the gate post. Then, as a thought struck him, he turned back and released him, buckling the reins into one stirrup.

"I don't dare to tie you up, old man," he said. "The beastly fire might swing round. Go home, if you like. I can't take you across that hot ground." He gave the chestnut's neck a hasty pat; then, putting one hand on the gate, he vaulted it cleanly and ran across the burnt ground.

The grass was yet smouldering; it broke away under his feet, crackling and falling into black powder. He ran desperately, not feeling the burning breath of the fire, in blind hope of being able to save something. The house itself, he knew, was doomed; no fire brigade could have checked the flames which had laid hold of the flimsy weatherboard. The fire had divided round it, checked a little by Tommy's flower garden, which was almost uninjured yet, and by Bob's rows of green vegetables which lay singed and ruined; then, unable to wait, it had swept on its way through the long dry grass, which carried it swiftly forward, leaving the burning cottage and the green garden in the midst of a blackened waste.

The front veranda, and one side, were yet untouched, nor had the front rooms caught. Wally raced through the garden and tried the front door. It was locked. He sprang to the nearest window and smashed it with quick blows from a hoe standing near; then, flinging up the sash, dived in. The room was full of smoke, the heat stifling. It was Tommy's room. He gathered up her little personal belongings from the dressing-table and flung them on the quilt, following them with armfuls of clothes hastily swept from shelves. A trunk, covered with a bright Navajo blanket, stood

near the window. He thrust it through to the
veranda, and scrambled out after it with the quilt
and blankets bundled round the things he had
saved. Dragging them across the lawn, he thrust
them under some green bushes, and returned for
the trunk.

"I don't believe you'll catch there," he said,
choking. "Wonder if I can try another room?"

He had opened the door from Tommy's room
into the hall, but the rush of flame and smoke
were so appalling that he had to shut it again
quickly, realising that the draught only helped the
fire. To break in by another window was the only
way. He smashed his way in to the other front
room, and hurriedly gathered up all he could.
There was no time to save anything heavy. His
quick mind guided him to the things he knew Bob
and Tommy valued most — things that had been
Aunt Margaret's in the past, that spoke of their
old happy life in France. He spread an
embroidered cloth on the floor and pitched his
treasure trove into it — working feverishly,
choking and gasping, until the flames began to
crackle through the wall, and the ceiling above
him split across. Then he plunged through the
window, and staggered across the lawn with his
burden — falling beside it at last, spent and
breathless, his throat parched with smoke, and his
eyes almost sightless. But he picked himself up
presently and went back. All the rooms were
blazing now. The side verandah had not yet
caught, and on it he saw an old oaken chest that
did double duty as a seat and as a wardrobe for

Bob's spare clothes. The sight brought fresh energy back to Wally.

"by Jove, there's old Bob's box!" he uttered. "I'll have to get that."

He dragged it across the veranda and on to the path. It was cruelly heavy. He had to stop and rest again and again; but still he struggled on, a few yards at a time, until it, too, was in comparative safety. Then there was nothing else that he could do but sit on the grass and watch the gay little home that they had all loved as it fell into ruins. The flames made mercifully short work of it; they roared and crackled and spat wreathing fiery tongues round the chimneys and up and down the veranda posts; shooting out of the broken windows and turning the white-painted iron of the roof into a twisted and blackened mass. It fell in presently with a deafening roar, bringing one chimney with it; and soon all that Wally had to look at was a smouldering heap of coals, in the midst of which one chimney stood, tottering and solitary, with the kitchen stove a glowing mass of red-hot iron, and strangely contorted masses of metal that once were beds. The boy uttered a groan.

"And they were so proud of it," he said. "Poor souls — how are they going to stick it?"

He got up presently and made his way round to the back. All the sheds and buildings were burned; he turned with a shudder from where Bob's beloved Kelpie had died at his post chained in helplessness. The metal parts of the buggy, writhed into knots and tangles, lay in the ashes of the big shed; beyond, the pigsty smouldered.

"They've gone, too, I suppose," Wally said. "By George, where are all his stock? They can't all be burned, surely."

There was nothing visible in the bare, black paddocks. He cast a wild look round, and then made for the creek at a staggering run. The fire had died away for lack of material as it neared the banks, for great willows overhung them, a camping ground for the stock all through the summer heat, and the ground was always beaten hard and bare. Wally uttered a shout of relief as he came to the trees. Below in the wide, shallow pools, all the stock had taken refuge — cart horses and cows, sheep and pigs, all huddled together, wild-eyed and panting, but safe. They stared up at Wally, dumbly bewildered.

"Poor brutes," said Wally. "Well, you chose a good spot, anyhow. I say, what a jolly good thing Bob let his pigs out. Poor old chap — he's not broke yet." He leaned against the gnarled trunk of a willow for a moment. "Well, I suppose I'd better get up to the gate and tell them — it won't do for Tommy to come on the ruins all of a sudden."

But he realised, as he made his slow way up from the creek, that he was too late. There was a little knot of horses beside the garden gate. His eye caught the light linen habit coats that Tommy and Norah wore. They were looking silently at the blackened heap of ashes, with the tottering chimney standing gaunt in its midst, Bob's face grey under its coating of smoky dust. Norah was holding Tommy's hand tightly. They did not hear Wally as he came slowly across the black powder that had been grass.

"I suppose the stock have gone, too," Bob said heavily.

"No, they haven't, old man," Wally said. "I believe every head is safe; they're in the creek."

They turned sharply, and cried out at the sight of him — blackened and ragged, his eyes red-rimmed in his grimy face, his hands, cut by the broken window glass, smeared with dried blood. His coat and shirt, burnt in a score of places, hung in singed fragments round him. There were great holes burnt in his panama hat, even in his riding breeches. Jim flung himself from his horse, and ran to him.

"Wal, old man! Are you hurt?"

"Not me," said Wally briefly. "Only a bit singed. I say, you two, you don't know how sorry I am. Tommy, I wish I could have got here in time."

"You seem to have got here in time to try, anyhow," said Tommy, and her lip trembled. "Are you sure you're not hurt, Wally?" She slipped from her saddle, and came to him. "Were you in the fire?"

"No, I'm truly all right," Wally assured her. He suddenly realised that he had not known how tired he was; something in his head began to whirl round, and a darkness came before his aching eyes. He felt Jim catch him; and there he was sitting on the ground, propped against the fence, and blinking up at them all, while indignantly assuring them that he had never been better.

"Did you meet the fire? It was away from here before I got here."

"It crossed the road in front of us," Mr. Linton said, "There were a good many men about by that time — we got it stopped before it reached Elston's." His pitying eyes went back to the brother and sister. Anxiety for Wally had drawn them from their own disaster for a moment; now they had moved away together, and stood looking at the ashes of their home, where so many hopes were ashes, too. David Linton went over to them, and put a hand on a shoulder of each.

"You're not to be down-hearted," he said firmly. "It's bad enough, and bitter enough — but it might be worse. The stock are safe, and the land is there — one good shower will turn the paddocks green again. Why, there's even most of your garden left, Tommy. And we'll build the house and sheds better than before."

"You're jolly good, Mr. Linton," Bob said, with dry lips. "But we owe you enough already."

"If you talk that sort of nonsense, I'll be really annoyed," David Linton said. "Why, hard luck comes to all of us — we got burned out ourselves once, didn't we, Norah?"

"Rather — and had to live in tents," said Norah. "No, you'll have to come back to us at Billabong until we build up the cottage again — oh, and, Tommy darling, I've been lonesome for you!" She put a hand on Bob's arm. "You won't worry, Bob? One bit of bad luck isn't going to beat you!"

"I suppose it won't," Bob said slowly. "There's the insurance money, anyhow. But it was the jolliest little home — and our very own. And I was so jolly proud of being independent."

"Well, you're that still," Jim said. "This is a country where everybody helps everybody else — because you and Tommy come to stay with us, and run your stock for a while on Billabong until your own grass grows, that isn't going to make you less independent. Wouldn't you do the same for us, if we were in the same box?"

"That goes without saying — and I'm as grateful as I can be," Bob said. "But the cases are different. I'm deep enough in your debt, as it is. I —" His lip quivered, and he turned away, staring at the ruins.

"I don't see any good arguing about it, at all events," said Norah, practically. "We're all hot and tired, and I vote we just get home and have tea. We'll all feel better after a tub, and then we can begin to make plans. Come on, Tommy dear, it's just lovely to think we're going to have you."

Bob stood with one hand on the scorched gate.

"I wish I could have got here in time to get out a few things," he muttered.

"Oh, I did that," said Wally, brightening. "I forgot, in the shock of finding all Noah's Ark turned out in the creek. Come along, Tommy, and see my little lot of salvage!"

He dragged himself up from the ground and seized Tommy's hand. They trooped across the lawn.

"I saved the cuckoo clock and that set of Swiss

bears," said Wally. "And lots of oddments from goodness knows where — the sort of thing you can't buy in Cunjee. I expect I've hauled out all the things you wouldn't have saved, Tommy, but you'll just have to let me down lightly — I'd have made a shot for the beloved cake tins, only I hadn't time."

"Oh, Wally, you dear old idiot," said Tommy. "And that's how you nearly killed yourself." They came in sight of Wally's heap of loot, and she stopped in amazement.

"Bob — just look!"

"By Jupiter!" said Bob. "You saved my old box! You old brick. How did you manage it? Why, it weighs a ton!"

Tommy was on her knees by the bundles.

"Look!" she said. "Look, Bobby! My silver things — and all Aunt Margaret's, and my little jewel box. And my clothes! How did you do it, Wally?" Suddenly her voice broke. She put her head down on the bundle in a passion of sobs.

"That's the best thing she could do," said David Linton gently. He turned to Norah. "Let her cry — and bring her along presently, and we'll take her home. Come along, boys, we'll get the horses and go and see Wally's Noah's Ark."

CHAPTER 16

Building Up Again

IT was three months later, and Billabong lay in the peace of an exquisite autumn evening. The orchard showed yellow and bronze against the green of the pine trees; here and there oak and elm leaves fluttered down lazily upon the lawn. The garden flamed with dahlias and asters, amidst which Hogg worked contentedly. And there was utter content upon the face of David Linton, as he stood on the broad stone steps of his home, and looked towards the setting sun. Beyond the garden gleamed the reed-fringed waters of the lagoon; further yet, the broad paddocks stretched away, dotted with feeding Shorthorns. It was the view, of all others, that he loved — his soul had longed for it during weary years of exile and war. Now, it seemed that he could never tire of looking at it.

Brownie came up from the garden, a basket on her arm laden with splendid mauve and pink asters. David Linton strolled across the gravel sweep to meet her.

"What, Brownie — taking Miss Norah's job, are you?"

"Well, it ain't 'ardly that, sir," Brownie answered. "Miss Norah — she done the vases this morning, same as usual, an' Miss Tommy 'elpin' her. Only she wouldn't pick these 'ere astors, 'cause they're 'ogg's best, an' she didn't like to 'urt 'im; you see she always remembers that onst they go into the 'ouse, 'ogg, 'e don't see 'em no more. An' she do love 'em in the vases. So I just put the matter sensible like to 'ogg, an', of course, 'e saw reason and give me 'alf; an' I'll 'ave 'em on the table tonight. Only they've filled every vase in the house already. I believe I'll be drove to puttin' 'em in Mason jars!"

"Miss Norah will love them, no matter what they're in," said Mr. Linton. "There's no sign of them yet, Brownie — it's nearly time they were home."

"Well, they meant to 'ave a long day's work fixin' the 'ouse," said Brownie comfortably. "Mrs. Archdale drove me over to see them, an' Sarah gave us all afternoon tea — she an' Bill are real toffs in their little new cottage there. Sarah ain' indulgin' in any regrets over that fire! And they were all busy as bees. Miss Tommy's room's fixed, an' her little sleep-out place off it, and so's Mr. Bob's, an' they were workin' at the drorin'-room; 'omelike it looked with all their nice old things in it again."

"I'm sure it will," David Linton agreed. "How do you like the new house, Brownie?"

"Why, it's lovely," said Brownie. "An' a fair treat to work, with all them new improvements — no corners to the rooms, an' no silly skirtin' boards that'll catch dust, an' the water laid on everywhere, an' the air gas, an' all them other patent fixings. An' so comferable; better than the old one, any way you look at it. Miss Tommy's the lucky young lady to be comin' in for such a place."

"Well, she deserves it, Brownie."

"She do," said Brownie heartily. "Ain't it lovely to see Miss Norah an' 'er so 'appy together? Our blessed lamb never 'ad a friend like that before, and she needed one — every girl do."

"Long may it last, that's all I say," agreed the squatter. "Norah needed her badly, although she didn't know it. And she and her brother are the best type of immigrants, aren't they?"

"They are that," said Brownie. "Always cheery, an' workin' 'ard, an' takin' the ups and downs sensibly. Now, it was a real nasty knock to find their nice little 'ome burnt down on New Year's day, but after the first shock they never 'ung their lip at all — just bucked in to make good again."

She went on her way with her asters, and David Linton walked slowly across the lawn and stood looking over the gate, along the track where his children would come riding home. Somehow, he found it difficult not to think of them all as his children. Wally had made an attempt to go away and set up a place for himself, but the idea had been received with such amazed horror by the whole household that it had been temporarily shelved. After all, Wally had more money than was good for him, the result of having always been an orphan. He could establish himself in a place at any time if he wished. And meanwhile, he was

never idle. David Linton had handed over most of
the outside management of the big run to Jim and
his mate. They worked together as happily as they
had played together as boys. There was time for
play now, as well; Mr. Linton saw to that. The
years that they had left on Flanders fields were
not to rob them of their boyhood.

There had also been time to help the Rainhams
— and there again the district had taken a hand.
It was not to be imagined that the people who had
helped in the first working bee would sit calmly
by when so stupendous a piece of bad luck as the
New Year fire overtook the just established young
immigrants; and so there had been several other
bees, to replace Bob's burnt fencing, to clear away
the ruins of the house and sheds, and finally, to
rebuild for him. There had been long discussion
at Billabong over plans — the first Creek Cottage
had taught them much of what was desirable in
the way of a house; so that the second Creek
Cottage, which rose from the ashes of the old one
when kindly rains had drawn a green mantle over
all the blackened farm, was a very decided
improvement upon the old house, and contained
so many modern ideas and "dodges" that the wives
and sisters of all the working bees, who helped to
build it, came miles to see it, and went home, in
most cases, audibly wishing that they could have
a fire. It was illuminating, too, to the working
bees, to see how Bob and the Billabong men
planned for the comfort of the women who were
to run the house, and for its easy working; so that
presently a wave of labour-saving devices swept

through the Cunjee district in imitation, and wives who had always carried buckets of water found taps conveniently placed where they were needed, and sinks and draining racks built to ease the dreary round of dish-washing, and air-gas plants established to supersede the old kerosene lamps. After which the district was very much astonished that it had not done it before.

The cottage was finished now, and nearly ready for its occupants; Bill, Sarah and the baby had been installed for some time in a neat little two-roomed place with a side veranda, a short distance from the main building. Home-made furniture, even more ambitious than the first built, had been erected, and a fresh supply of household goods bought during an exciting week in Melbourne, where Mr. Linton had taken them all — all, that is, but Bob, who had steadfastly declined to go away and play when other people were helping him. So Bob had remained at his post, giving Tommy a free hand as to shopping; a freedom cautiously used by Tommy, but supplemented by the others with many gifts, both useful and idiotic. Tommy had an abiding affection for the idiotic efforts.

She had spent so much time in the saddle that she now rode like an old hand; the brown-faced girl who came up the paddock presently with the cheery band of workers was very different to the pink and white "little Miss Immigrant" of eight months before. She rode Jim's big favourite, Garry-owen, who, although years had added wisdom to him, was always impatient when nearly home; he was reefing and pulling as they swept up at a hand gallop, but Tommy held him easily, and pulled up near Mr. Linton, laughing. He looked at them with grave content.

"I began to think you meant me to have tea alone," he said. "Have they been doing any work, Bob, or couldn't you keep them in hand at all?"

"Oh, they've been working," Bob answered. "I told Sarah not to give them any afternoon tea if they didn't, and it acted like a charm."

"You to talk!" said Norah, with tilted nose. "They said they'd sample the new deck chairs, Dad, and it took them about an hour to make sure if they liked them — they just smoked while Tommy and I toiled."

"Well, you'd only have been annoyed with us if we hadn't done the sampling properly, and had grumbled afterwards," said Wally. "I'm always trying to teach you to be thorough, Norah. Of course, they say they work all the time, sir — but when they disappear into Tommy's room there's an awful lot of talking."

"There would be something wrong with them if there weren't," said the squatter sagely. "And I have no doubt there yet remains much awaiting their expert supervision in Tommy's room." Whereat Tommy and Norah beamed at him, and commended him as a person of understanding, while Wally remarked feelingly to Bob that there was no chance of justice where those two females were concerned. At this point Jim observed that the conversation showed signs of degenerating into a brawl, and that, in any case, it was time the horses were let go. They trotted off to the stables, a light-hearted body.

Tommy slipped her arm into Bob's as they went upstairs to dress.

"Come into my room and talk for a moment."

He came in and sat down in a low chair by the window.

"Your quarters at the new place won't be as big as this, old girl."

"They'll be bigger, for it will all be ours," rejoined Tommy promptly. "Who wants a big room, anyway? I don't. Bobby, I'd be hard to please if I wanted more than I've got."

"You're always satisfied," he said. "There never was anything easier than pleasing you, old Tommy."

"Life's all so good, now," she said. "No hideous anxiety about you — no Lancaster Gate — no she-dragon. Only peace, and independence, and the work we like. Aren't you satisfied, Bob?"

"I'd like to be really independent," he said slowly. "Our amount of debt isn't heavy, of course, and it doesn't cause real anxiety, with Mr. Linton guaranteeing us to the bank —"

"And as we had to build again, it was worthwhile to improve the house and make it just what we wanted," Tommy added. "We'll pay the debt off, Bob. Mr. Linton assures me that with ordinary seasons we should easily do it."

"I know, and I'm not anxious," Bob said. "Only I'll be glad when it's done; debt, even such an easy debt as this, gives me the creeps. And I want to feel we stand on our own feet."

"And not on the Lintons'!" said Tommy, laughing. "I quite agree — though it's amazing to see how little they seem to mind our weight. Was there ever such luck as meeting them, Bob?"

"Never," he agreed. "We'd have been wage earners still, or struggling little cocky farmers at the best, but for that letter of General Harran's — though I think more was due to the way you butted into their taxi!"

"I believe it was," laughed Tommy. "It was the sort of thing to appeal to the Lintons — it wouldn't to everybody. But the letter was behind it, saying what a worthy young man you were!"

"Well, when you start calling me such a thing as 'worthy', it's time I left and got dressed for tea," said her brother, rising slowly. "English mail ought to be in, by the way; I'm wondering what old Mr. M'Clinton will say when he hears we were burned out in our first season."

"He'll wish he'd sent us to the snows of Canada, where such things don't happen on New Year's Day," Tommy said. "Still, he ought not to be anxious about us — Mr. Linton wrote and told him our position was quite sound."

"Oh, I don't think he'll worry greatly," said Bob. "I must hurry, old girl, or I'll be late — and I want a tub before tea."

The boys came down in flannels, ready for a game of tennis after tea; and Bob and Wally were just leaving the court after a stoutly contested set when Billy brought the mail bag across the lawn to Mr. Linton. The squatter unlocked it and sorted out the letters quickly.

"Nothing for you, Tommy; two for Norah; three for Bob, and bundles for Wally and Jim. Papers beyond counting, and parcels you girls can deal with." He gathered up a package of his own letters. "Chiefly stock and station documents — though, I see, there's a letter from your aunt, Norah; I expect she's anxious to know when I'm going to cease bringing you up like a boy, and send you to Melbourne to be a perfect lady."

"Tell her never," said Norah lazily. "I don't see any spare time ahead — not enough to make me into a lady after Aunt Winifred's pattern. Cecil is much more lady-like than I am."

"He always was," Jim said. "Years ago we used to wonder that he didn't take to wool work, and I expect he'll do it yet. Even serving in the war didn't keep Cecil from manicuring his nails — he gets a polish on them that beats anything I ever saw."

"Never mind — he's got a limp," said Norah, in whose eyes that legacy of the war covered a multitude of sins.

"Well, he has. But he even limps in a lady-like way," grinned Jim. "And he has no time for Wal and me. He told me that he was surprised that five years of France and England hadn't made us less Australian."

"It's a matter of regret to us all," said Norah placidly. "We hoped for great things when you came out — more attention to polite conversation, and a passion for top hats, and —" At which point further eloquence was checked by a cushion placed gently, but firmly, by a brotherly hand on her face, and so she subsided, with gurgle of laughter, into the cool depths of the buffalo grass where they were all lying.

"Oh, by Jove!" said Bob suddenly. He looked at them, and finally at Tommy, his eyes dancing.

"What's u, old man?" Jim asked. "Not your stepmother coming out?"

"England couldn't spare her," Bob said. "But the sky has fallen, for all that. Just listen to old M'Clinton.

" '. . . It was with deep regret that I learned from you and from Mr. Linton of the calamity which had befallen you on New Year's Day. Such disasters seem common in Australia, like blizzards in Canada, and I presume every settler is liable to them. In your case your loss, being partly covered by insurance, will not, Mr. Linton assures me, be crushing, although it seems to me very severe. To have your initial endeavours, too, handicapped by so calamitous an occurrence would have excused despondency, but —"

"Hasn't he a lovely style?" chuckled Wally, as the reader paused to turn over.

" 'But Mr. Linton assures me that you and your sister are facing the situation with calmness and courage.' Did you know you were calmly courageous, Tommy?"

"I am not," said Tommy. "I am courageously calm. Go on, Bobby — my calmness will waver if you don't get to the point. Where does the sky fall?"

"Half a second. 'Further, I am immensely interested to learn from Mr. Linton, who appears

to be the kindest of benefactors' — that's you, sir —
'that the people of the district, who have already
helped you so remarkably by a working bee, are so
much in sympathy with you both that they intend
again lending you their assistance over rebuilding
your house. This shows me, even without Mr.
Linton's letter, that you have earned their esteem
and regard. Nevertheless, I estimate that you
cannot fail to be at some monetary embarrassment,
and this I am luckily able to ease for you. Certain
rubber investments of your late aunt's have
recently risen in value, after the long period of
depression due to the war; and I deemed it prudent
to sell them while their price in the market was
high. The terms of your aunt's will enable me to
reinvest this money, amounting to a little over nine
hundred pounds, for you, or, at my discretion, to
hand it over to you; and such is the confidence I
repose in you, after Mr. Linton's letter, that I feel
justified in remitting you the money, to use as you
think best. I presume that will be in the reduction
of your liabilities. I should like to think you had the
benefit of Mr. Linton's advice in the matter.' Shall
I, sir?"

"I never listened to such language," returned
the squatter. "I should like it read three times a
day, before meals. But if it's my advice you want,
Bob, you can have it. Meanwhile, I'm very glad for
you to have such a windfall, my boy."

Tommy and Norah had collapsed on each other's
shoulders, speechless.

"Joy never kills, they say," said Wally,
regarding them anxiously. "But it's been known to

turn the brain, when the brain doesn't happen to be strong. Will we turn the hose on them, Jim?"

"Sit on him, Bob," came faintly from Norah.

"I will — with the weight of nine hundred pounds!" said Bob — and did so.

"Get off, you bloated capitalist," said Wally, struggling. He succeeded in dislodging him, with a mighty effort. "You're just purse proud, that's what's the matter with you. What'll you do with it, Bobby — go racing? Or buy an aeroplane?"

"Get out of debt," said Bob, sitting up with rumpled hair and a face like a happy child's. "And there'll be a bit over to play with. What shall we put it into, Tommy? Want any pretty things?"

"Just merino sheep," said Tommy.

Afterword

Back to Billabong was first published in 1921. The story is set in 1919, the year following the Armistice which ended the First World War, when thousands of Australians who had fought for the Empire overseas were demobilised and repatriated. The return of the Lintons and Wally Meadows to Australia echoes Mary Grant Bruce's own experience: she and her soldier husband returned from England to Victoria in 1919. They appear in the story as "Colonel and Mrs Burton", with their two small sons.

The Armistice was concluded on 11 November. In January, the Peace Conference began at Versailles. The Labor Prime Minister, W.M. Hughes, and Sir Joseph Cook were Australia's delegates. The Peace Treaty was signed in June. The final Australian engagements of the war were the triumphant entry of the Australian Light Horsemen into Damascus on 1 October, and the capture of Montbrehain, on the Western Front, on 5 October. The total number of troops raised in Australia was 416,809; 331,781 were sent overseas, of which 59,342 were killed and 166,809 wounded, representing an enormous effort for Australia — and a tragic loss. All were volunteers; there was no conscription in Australia. The war was over, but everyone was still very conscious of it. There were returned soldiers everywhere — Norah notices that her cousin Cecil, who behaved so badly in *Mates at Billabong*, drags one foot as a result of his war service. The Returned Sailors' and Soldiers' Imperial League, now called the Returned Services League (RSL), was founded in 1916. Very many war widows were left to bring up their children as "single parents", as we say today. The first Legacy Club for war orphans (first known as the Remembrance Club) was founded in 1922. On a lighter note, another memento of the war was the horse "Artilleryman", which won the 1919 Melbourne Cup.

Australia's population was now approximately 5,303,574. There was widespread conviction that the country needed to attract immigrants; General Harran tells Bob Rainham that Australia badly needs the "right type of settlers" and, later, David Linton refers to the Rainhams as "the best type of immigrants". Immigration still held to the "White Australia" policy; the most desirable settlers were considered those of British stock.

On top of the huge war casualties, the Australia-wide influenza epidemic of 1919 carried off some 12,000 victims. In New South Wales, schools, libraries, churches and theatres were closed to help prevent the spread of disease, and it was compulsory to wear face masks out of doors. The year 1919 was also a year of severe drought, a factor that probably helped the spread of influenza.

Although "Brownie", Murty O'Toole and the rest of the Billabong staff remain happy in their work and loyal to "the master", David Linton, 1919 was a year of discontent and unrest throughout the nation, with strikes on the waterfront and among industrial workers. The social order was changing, largely as a result of the war. The gigantic cost of the war in material terms had brought economic hardship in its wake.

The place of women in society was changing, too; "Tommy" Rainham represents a new type of independently minded girl determined to live her own life and not succumb to family pressure. Her brother Bob has the ingrained notion that he should provide a living for both of them — "Aunt Margaret didn't bring you up to work," he tells her — whereupon Tommy tells him that "the world has turned upside-down". Later, Bob jokingly says that Tommy has become "more like a suffragette" and reminds her that now she's in Australia, she will have the vote once she turns 21. South Australia was the first state to give women the vote, in 1894; by 1909 they were able to vote in all states. But it was not until 1923 that women were able to stand as candidates in all state elections. They achieved both these rights in 1902 so far as the then newly created Federal parliament was concerned.

A telephone is now installed at Billabong and the Lintons make good use of the Rolls Royce which Norah inherited from Sir John O'Neill as a result of an heroic exploit in *Jim and Wally*.

Bob Rainham has flown planes during the war; in Chapter 5 he predicts that soon civil aviation will be well established. In 1919, the Commonwealth Government offered a huge prize of £10,000 to the first Australians to fly a British-made aircraft from Britain to Australia in 30 days, before the end of the year. This was won by Ross and Keith Smith, with Sergeants J.M. Bennett and W.H. Shiers as crew. Flying a Vickers Vimy aircraft, they left England on 12 November and landed in Darwin on 10 December, carrying the first airmail between the two countries. This year also saw the first transcontinental flight, from Point Cook, Victoria to Darwin, and the first crossing of Bass Strait by air. In Sydney, Mascot was chosen as the site of Australia's first airport.

Where entertainment was concerned, Australian children were enjoying May Gibbs' first story, *Snugglepot and Cuddlepie*, and Norman Lindsay's *The Magic Pudding*, two bestsellers published by Angus & Robertson in 1918. The most popular (silent) movie of the year was *The Sentimental Bloke*, based on C.J. Dennis' popular story in verse about a bloke and his girl.

BARBARA KER WILSON

OTHER TITLES AVAILABLE
BY MARY GRANT BRUCE